The *Seduction*
OF MOXIE

By the Author

The Sublime and Spirited Voyage of Original Sin

Visit us at www.boldstrokesbooks.com

The Seduction
OF MOXIE

by

Colette Moody

2009

THE SEDUCTION OF MOXIE

© 2009 By Colette Moody. All Rights Reserved.

ISBN 10: 1-60282-114-3
ISBN 13: 978-1-60282-114-9

This Trade Paperback Original Is Published By
Bold Strokes Books, Inc.
P.O. Box 249
Valley Falls, NY 12185

First Bold Strokes Printing: September 2009

THIS IS A WORK OF FICTION. NAMES, CHARACTERS, PLACES, AND INCIDENTS ARE THE PRODUCT OF THE AUTHOR'S IMAGINATION OR ARE USED FICTITIOUSLY. ANY RESEMBLANCE TO ACTUAL PERSONS, LIVING OR DEAD, BUSINESS ESTABLISHMENTS, EVENTS, OR LOCALES IS ENTIRELY COINCIDENTAL.

THIS BOOK, OR PARTS THEREOF, MAY NOT BE REPRODUCED IN ANY FORM WITHOUT PERMISSION.

CREDITS
Editors: Shelley Thrasher and Stacia Seaman
Production Design: Stacia Seaman
Cover Design By Sheri (graphicartist2020@hotmail.com)

Acknowledgments

As always, thank you, Laura, for your unflagging support and feedback. I have a sneaking suspicion that without your input and encouragement, my novels would be an endless string of boob jokes and limericks.

Also, this book would not exist in its current state without the spellbinding tales of debauchery provided by Cat, Jen, and John that ultimately helped to form the framework of my characters' own carousing—much like the grain of sand that evolves into a pearl. Thank you for shoving your filthy particles into my oyster (you know, in a purely academic way).

Thank you, Bold Strokes Books staff. I'm astounded by the freedom that you give me to blaze my own peculiar trail—usually through the dense brush of farce (though obviously at times stopping in the perilous thicket of preposterous metaphor).

Dedication

For those who sparked my fascination and admiration with their amazing work and the even more spectacular way that they lived their lives: Tallulah Bankhead, Katharine Hepburn, Alla Nazimova, Greta Garbo, Marlene Dietrich, Dorothy Parker, Robert Benchley, Rosalind Russell, Cary Grant, Ginger Rogers, Lauren Bacall, Louise Brooks, and Howard Hawks. You continue to inspire me daily.

PROLOGUE

The night that 1930 fizzled out and 1931 roared in, Moxie Valette stood singing in a chintzy speakeasy in Fayetteville, Nebraska, with a faraway look in her eyes that made her appear as if she was dreaming of something more. The room was thick with the haze of stale cigarette smoke as she sang "Bootlegger's Rag" with more vim than most of the drunken spectators would have anticipated.

A glass of ice and jorum of skee,
Drag your heeler to the speakeasy!
Bring your scratch, shake a leg.
Gold digger, sugar daddy, vamp, and yegg.
There's no time to lollygag.
Everybody wants to do the bootlegger's rag!

Sitting in the back of this somewhat dilapidated, unmarked establishment known to locals as Fat Philly Red's, Cotton McCann watched the performer with considerable interest. He rested his chin in the palm of his left hand while he chewed on his cigar and contemplated her level of talent.

She was blond, though not in an artificial way. Show business had far too many peroxide blondes already, he thought. No, this one had a more natural look. Like Garbo, but without that exotic quality. Like a corn-fed, fresh-faced Constance Bennett. This girl was attractive, but somehow unusual. Sexy, yet wholesome and approachable. He inhaled deeply from his cigar and motioned to the waitress with his other hand.

"You need a refill, mister?" the curvy matron called to him over the music and the din of the crowd.

"I'd rather talk to that singer," he answered, straining to be heard. "What's her name again?"

"Moxie. But she don't usually spend her time bumpin' gums with the customers."

"And would a little jack maybe get me an introduction?" He held up two folded dollar bills between his index and middle fingers.

The waitress's eyes flashed, and she quickly snatched the money and slipped it into her ample cleavage. "I'll see what I can do. I can't guarantee you too much more than that. That kid's a straight arrow. But I'll make sure she stops by after her last number." She winked and disappeared back into the crowd.

Luckily for Cotton, very little about Fat Philly Red's homemade gin compelled him to actually finish the one he had ordered nearly an hour earlier. He had patronized more than his share of these clip joints in the last eight months, and in that time he had never tasted liquor quite this lousy. He held the glass to his nose and sniffed it again, to remind himself exactly how noxious it was. The smell suggested that its distillers had somehow managed to blend sulphur, animal feces, and kerosene. "Holy cats," he muttered, setting it back down on the table and pushing the glass away. He made a mental note to neither smell nor swallow the foul venom again, no matter how thirsty he became.

"Leave it if you're fond of your liver." The singer stood by his table, her left hand propped defiantly on her hip. She looked amused. "I hear that you got something to say." The timbre of her voice was melodic, but the tone was feisty. This girl obviously was no shrinking violet.

"You must be Moxie," he said, her name now an epiphany to him. He politely stood and gestured for her to sit, scrutinizing her again, this time from much closer. She was a striking combination of light hair and dark, smoky eyes. Her lips were full, what the flappers would call bee-stung, and her cheeks were round and pink. He reevaluated his earlier assessment. This girl didn't look like anyone he could think of, and she was mesmeric.

She eyed him appraisingly. He was clearly an out-of-towner. He absolutely radiated the city with his fancy brown suit and dark mustache. She guessed him to be around forty, and he carried the paunch that only a life of leisure could afford. Curious, she decided to see what he had to say and pulled up a chair. "But I don't know your name."

"Cotton McCann. Can I assume from your comment that you're not interested in me buying you a drink?" He nodded to the glass in front of him.

"You can. You can also assume that I'm not a five-cent whore, if that was going to be your next question." She spoke nonchalantly, intent on setting the boundaries clearly and early in the conversation.

He frowned and took another puff of his cigar. "You've got me all wrong. I'm looking for talent. I'm an impresario of sorts."

"Then what the hell are you doing in this jerkwater town, in this crummy speako?"

"I'm on my way from Los Angeles to New York City." He stroked his mustache with his thumb and index finger. "My last act cut out on me just as she was on the verge of her big break."

"Cut out on you how?"

"She married some mook and settled down." He tried unsuccessfully to keep the anger out of his voice. "She could have been the next Jeanette MacDonald."

"Is that so?"

The buxom waitress reappeared and set an open bottle of Dr. Pepper in front of Moxie. "Here you go, sweetie."

"Thanks, Ruby." She eagerly took a sip and motioned for Cotton to continue as Ruby slipped back into the raucous crowd.

"How old are you?"

She brushed her wavy bangs out of her eyes with the back of her hand. "Twenty-two."

Cotton reached into his jacket pocket and removed a business card. "Look, I know you have no reason to trust me."

She picked up the card, printed on stiff, cream-colored stock. It read:

COTTON G. MCCANN

PROFESSIONAL ENTERTAINMENT AGENT

TWELVE YEARS EXPERIENCE

"You reprint these every year?" She took another sip of Dr. Pepper.

He smiled. "This is the first year I've had them. I didn't think about that when I placed the order." He cleared his throat. "Anyway, I'm sure you're skeptical, not knowing me from Adam. But I'm telling you that you've got something special, kid. Something I haven't seen in months. And believe me, I've been looking."

"What exactly are you proposing?"

"Tomorrow I'm taking the Burlington to Chicago, and from there, the Twentieth Century Limited the rest of the way to New York City. I've been hoping to find a talented singer or dancer who'd make the rest of the trip with me."

Moxie's mind reeled at the mention of what was probably the most plush and renowned passenger train in the world, but she remained dubious. After all, men tended to lie. "Make the trip with you…and then what?"

"I need a new talent to sell, and New York's the place to make it happen. Surely you want to play bigger and better clubs than this one."

She looked around at the congested dive she'd been working in for the past four months. It was dirty and smelled, as did most of the clientele. Cotton was right about the fact that Fat Philly Red's was a horrible job to settle for. The prospect of performing for high society—hell, for people who didn't have dirt under their fingernails—tempted her.

"You probably have a father or husband to consult first. I understand that."

"Actually, I don't have either."

His brow furrowed. "Well, you have some family, don't you?"

"No, it's just me these days. The decision's all mine."

Cotton's face took on a serious expression. "Then what do you have to lose?"

CHAPTER ONE

New York City
June 6, 1931, 10:00 p.m.

The portly emcee nimbly slicked back his thinning hair and grabbed the large microphone before him. "And now, ladies and gentlemen, a sweet little Midwestern dish who's been bringing the house down here at the Luna Lounge for the last few weeks—Miss Moxie Valette."

The crowd cheered as Moxie appeared on the stage and the pianist began to play the introduction to Cole Porter's "What Is This Thing Called Love?"

"Hot damn!" Violet sputtered as she focused on the singer before her. "Get a load of that tomato."

Her companion Wil looked toward the stage at the front of the club as she slipped another Chesterfield into her cigarette holder. "My goodness," she remarked wryly, looking for matches. "She *is* a tasty muffin. Are you falling in love for, what, the ninth time today?"

"Don't exaggerate," Violet said. "This is only the fourth time since breakfast."

Moxie began to sing the lyrics slowly, her sultry tones quickening Violet's pulse. While Wil's ribbing was well deserved, Violet had to admit this blonde was affecting her more than the occasional waitress or cigarette girl that she might find attractive and flirt with. She was spellbound.

"Hey, sister," Wil said, poking her with her elbow. "You got apoplexy? Have you swallowed your tongue?"

"No. I was imagining her swallowing my tongue." She grinned.

"And I have to say it was working for me." The gorgeous blonde in the shimmering, deep blue gown seemed contradictory—while her young face conveyed purity and virtue, her deep voice exuded a carnal sensuality that made Violet's temperature rise.

"Well, as they say, the fifth time's the charm. We'll just have to get her over here to meet you. After all, it is your night."

"It's your night too," Violet countered, taking a piece of bread from the wicker basket on the table and tearing off a bite-sized piece that she offered to the small, russet-colored terrier in her lap. He sniffed it warily before devouring it.

Wil laughed. "Don't worry, I plan to get mine tonight too, doll." She called the waiter over, flailing her arm eagerly. "Darling," she said with a broad, insincere smile. "We need a bottle of whatever you have that's sparkling."

"I'm sure something can be arranged," the young man replied.

The Luna Lounge was, after all, one of the most successful speakeasies in the city of New York. It catered to those with money, and for a healthy percentage of the earnings, revenuers happily looked the other way. In fact, the Luna hadn't been raided once in the seven years it had been in business, thanks to the dependable and irrefutable efficacy of the bribery of public officials.

"What's your name, handsome?" Wil asked the waiter, her hand brushing the top of his in a way that was too casual to be inadvertent.

"Fred." He blushed slightly.

"Fred, darling," she said. "Do you think you could send the canary over our way when her set is done? We'd like to extend our compliments."

He seemed petrified of her advances, but nodded rapidly.

"And bring a shot of whatever she drinks too," Violet added. "Let her know it's on us."

Again the waiter nodded, then slipped away into the crowd.

"Look at you," Wil joked, "buying the lady a drink. Very smooth, Vi."

She wiggled her eyebrows. "Well, if I'm going to become a big star, I need to learn how to make time with all the hot numbers, right?"

"Stick with me, kid. I'll show you everything I know."

"I'll settle just for what you can remember," Violet said. "Got your eyes on the waiter, do you?"

Wil took a drag on the delicate tip of her cigarette holder. "Fred? Oh, we're old friends. He understands me in ways no other man can."

"You know he's queer, right?"

Wil exhaled in frustration. "Fuck, another one?"

"Afraid so, sister."

"And how exactly do you know this? You've seen him at your local chapter meetings, have you?"

Violet nodded. "Yup, he usually brings the crullers."

"Damn, it! The tight pants should have tipped me off."

"That, and maybe the way he sashayed to and from our table." Violet turned to direct her attention back to Moxie. She was now performing an upbeat jazzy number that Violet hadn't heard before, and Moxie's hips swayed seductively as she sang about not being able to get enough of her man. Both the tune, as well as the way Moxie sang it, captivated Violet.

"Julian!" Wil called merrily.

Violet turned to see Wil's friend arriving at their table. He was a large, rather effeminate man, wearing a brown suit about a half size too small. The buttons of his jacket seemed to strain in anguish to stay secured. His dark hair was combed straight back, and his mustache was razor thin. Cordially, he kissed Wil on the cheek, then stretched over the table to offer Violet the same salutation.

"How are you, Violet?" he asked, sitting across from her. "I hear congratulations are in order."

"Thanks, Julian. It's good to see you." She smiled brightly.

"Are you ready for a night of nonstop sin and depravity?" Wil asked him.

"Why else would I have agreed to meet you, darling?" He took a piece of stale bread from the basket.

Fred appeared with a bottle of champagne, two glasses, and a stainless-steel bucket for it to chill in. "Here you are, ladies." He set the bucket down and began to open the bottle. "Will you be needing a third glass?"

"Fred," Wil said, "you're always so considerate. That's why I love you so." She turned to Julian magnanimously. "What did you want to drink, darling?"

"I'll take a gin rickey, Fred."

"Very good, sir." The waiter pushed the cork out of the bottle with his thumbs, and it finally burst out with a jubilant pop.

"Music to my ears," Wil remarked happily as Fred began to pour the champagne.

"Does it remind you of your cherry?" Violet raised her newly filled glass.

"I think you overestimate Wil's memory," Julian added. "Wasn't that back during the Trojan War?"

Fred accidentally dropped the open bottle into the bucket, nervously verified that no harm was done, and then darted away again.

"Fred and I are in love," Wil explained to Julian. "We're going to be married."

Julian casually pulled a pack of Lucky Strikes from his jacket pocket. "You don't mind that he's queer?"

"I told you," Violet said, pointing her index finger decisively.

"We plan to have one of those open marriages," Wil said. "Provided that he never stops bringing me whatever I ask for, I can look past his preference for men."

"How progressive," Violet commented.

❖

After Moxie's set ended, Fred approached her backstage and touched her shoulder lightly. "Swell show."

She smiled at the compliment as she dabbed her face with a handkerchief. "Thanks. That's always nice to hear."

"Well, then you might like to hear this as well. Table nine would like you to stop by. They told me to bring whatever you wanted to drink too."

Moxie's gratification quickly evaporated. "Hmm. Did the offer seem seedy?"

He laughed. "It's probably a lot of things. But I don't think any of them are seedy."

At one time, Moxie tried to be gracious when strange men fawned over her, and certainly since she had been in New York, that type of attention had only increased. But she had recently made up her mind that she couldn't bear such social contrivances anymore. She had been hit on by old geezers, married men, and even one fellow so inebriated that he had actually pissed himself and failed to notice it. Fortuitously for him, Moxie had been there to bring his condition to his attention.

While she supposed these advances were all intended to be complimentary, it was hard to feel gratitude under the circumstances. Perhaps this admirer would signal her turning luck. After all, Cotton had been telling her that was due to happen any day.

"All right, Fred. You've piqued my curiosity. Table nine, you said?"

He nodded.

"Just bring my usual drink."

"You got it." He headed back over to the bar.

Checking her face in the mirror, she ran her hands through her wavy blond hair and tossed the damp handkerchief down with the rest of her things.

As she approached table nine, she was suddenly uncertain. Two glamorous-looking women, a plump man, and a small dog sat there—certainly not what she had expected. As she got closer, she observed that the woman with the dog was watching her intently. The woman's straight black hair was cut in a bob, a bit like Louise Brooks's, but her eyes were incredibly light, almost gray. The combination was striking. Her elegant evening gown was sea green, and her features were soft and lovely.

The other woman at the table was pretty in a different way—red-haired and animated—and though Moxie could not make out what she was saying, her voice carried as if she were either a drunk or a madwoman. She was dressed like a member of high society, but clearly not born into it. Her boisterous and gregarious manners gave her away. The gentleman at the table seemed more reserved, and he had noticed her approach by now as well.

Moxie stopped at the table and cleared her throat as the loud redheaded woman was in the middle of a sentence.

"…and I told him, 'Darling, you need to get that away from my vagina'—oh, hello there," she said, suddenly noticing her.

Moxie was stunned, wondering what the beginning of that story could possibly have entailed. "Um, hello. I may have been given the wrong table number."

The other woman at the table smiled, her smoky eyes alight with something. Perhaps amusement? Despite Moxie's natural suspicions, the brunette's expression and demeanor put her slightly at ease. "No, this is the right table. We asked Fred to have you stop by so we could tell you how very much we enjoyed your singing."

Moxie remained wary, as she always did. For her, guarded and vigilant were a way of life. "That's nice of you to say."

"Do have a seat. I'm Violet London, and these are my friends Wilhelmina Skoog and Julian French."

Moxie pulled up a chair and sat, feeling self-conscious around these rather stylish and wealthy people. Why had they asked to see her? They seemed so much more sophisticated than she was. Her eyes were drawn to the small, yawning reddish-brown dog sitting in Violet's lap. "And who is this?"

"Ah, this is Clitty." Violet held up the dog's paw to simulate a friendly wave.

"That's an unusual name." Moxie assured herself that she had either misheard the woman or was simply the victim of her own filthy mind. The dog could not possibly be named that.

Violet took a drink of champagne and nodded as she swallowed. "Yes, it's short for Clitoris."

Apparently Moxie was not the only one with a filthy mind. "Uh... Why would you name your dog that?"

"Well, it seemed appropriate," Violet replied, scratching Clitty's head between the ears. "I mean, he has a beard." She playfully tugged the animal's protracted chin hair. "And he wants to be rubbed all day long."

"But does he want to be licked?" Wil asked.

"Lord, Wil," Julian interjected, exhaling smoke from his nostrils. "I hope you're not offering."

"Hardly, darling. It's far too early in the evening for me to have lowered my standards that much." She looked at her watch. "I won't settle for less than a human for another three hours."

Fred reappeared and set a bottle of Dr. Pepper in front of Moxie. "Here you go."

"That's what you ordered?" Violet asked.

"I'm not much of a drinker."

"Well, you should have some champagne with us," Violet said. "We're celebrating tonight."

"Oh? What for?"

"Well," Violet said, "I've been cast in a movie. And I leave tomorrow on the next train to Hollywood."

Moxie was awestruck. This woman was a film star? "That's wonderful!"

Wil waved at Fred to get his attention. "Fred, please bring your lovely singer a champagne glass." He looked surprised but nodded dutifully.

Violet continued. "And that leaves my understudy here ready to step into the leading role of *Scandals and Lies* on Broadway."

"Ah, that's why your name sounded familiar. You're Violet London, the Broadway actress." Moxie was thrilled not only to meet a successful actress, but one she had actually heard of. It was easy to see why Violet's career was flourishing. She had an easy charisma about her—an affability that drew in others.

"For the rest of tonight I am, at least."

"Wil, you really should do something about your name," Julian said. "Wilhelmina Skoog neither rolls lightly off the tongue nor looks attractive on a marquee."

"Yes," Violet said. "You should choose something sexy."

Wil snorted, apparently indignant that her friends would make such a suggestion. "Well, tragically, your Clitoris is taken."

"I only wish it were," Violet replied as Fred arrived with the champagne glass. He set it in front of Moxie and filled it for her.

"Thank you, darling," Wil cooed. "You poured that like only a real man could."

Fred blushed again, replaced the bottle in the bucket, and sped away.

"So, Moxie." Violet eyed her appreciatively, filling Moxie with a combination of discomfort and warmth. "Perhaps you can convince Wil that she may not be Fred's type."

Moxie picked up her champagne glass and took a sip. It tasted far better than she thought it would. She had tried to steer clear of indulging in anything that might impair her ever-present prudence. "Well, Fred is—"

"You can go ahead and say it, dear," Julian said with obvious sympathy.

"Fred is what?" Wil asked. "A snappy dresser? A mean cribbage player? A large potato bug?"

Violet laughed and patted Moxie's hand. "You don't have to expose him as a potato bug if you don't want to, sweetie. After all, that's nobody's business but his and the farmer whose crops he destroys." She took another sip of champagne.

"But does he have an affinity for penises?" Julian blurted out. "Because crop damage or not, I think that might be a deal breaker."

Moxie gasped as she inhaled a small amount of champagne into her lungs, and she began to cough violently. Violet patted her on the back helpfully, and before Moxie knew it, Violet was rubbing it in soft circles. She was surprised both by how nice it felt and the inexplicable absence of her natural aversion to physical contact with others.

"Now why did you have to go and use that word, Julian? You startled the poor girl," Violet said.

He polished off his gin rickey and set the glass on the table forcefully. "You act as though she's some fawn in the woods. Just because 'penis' is your least favorite word, darling, doesn't mean that everyone else can't stomach it."

"Sorry." Violet had a wry expression on her face. "When you say 'stomach it,' what exactly do you mean?"

Wil laughed loudly, then polished off her champagne and grabbed the bottle aggressively by the neck. "Damn, doll face. I'm going to miss you," she said as she refilled her glass. She looked up from her drink. "Oh, I suppose I'll miss you too, Violet."

Julian gestured to Fred to bring him another round.

Moxie's coughing had abated, but she still sat agog, wondering what these people would say next. They seemed not only candid to the point of mental illness, but they were all decidedly oversexed, and therefore potentially a menace to others. She had never known anyone who bandied about genitalia as they did. Wait, that sounded much worse in her mind than she had intended.

"So, what kind of a name is Moxie?" Violet propped her chin on her fist and adopted an expression that implied she was actually interested in what Moxie had to say.

Thank God, Moxie thought, a normal question. "Apparently I was a rather strong-willed child."

"Your mother has a sense of humor."

"She did, yes. She passed on about ten years ago."

"I'm so sorry. She must have been a beautiful woman, because you are terribly striking."

Moxie dropped her gaze. "Thank you." While she was used to that kind of comment from men and could readily brush it aside as so much phony flattery, coming from a woman, a famous one to boot, it somehow seemed more sincere.

"Raised by your father?" Violet asked.

Moxie shrugged. "Mostly raised by myself."

Violet's eyebrows arched. "You don't say."

"Pop passed away just two years after Mom, so then it was just me."

"Brothers or sisters? Grandparents or aunts?"

Moxie shook her head, feeling ill at ease talking about her past. She took another drink of champagne.

Violet's eyes warmed. "I'm guessing your childhood wasn't all nosegays and lollipops."

Moxie smiled in tacit agreement. "Well, I managed to stay out of the orphanage, and I learned how to fend for myself, so I really can't complain. I had it better than a lot of others."

"Okay, I'll bite." Violet was clearly interested in what Moxie was telling her. "How'd you avoid the orphanage?"

"I took jobs cooking, cleaning, singing—whatever I could get. I lied about my age until I didn't need to anymore and just generally kept to myself."

Violet whistled descending notes of astonishment. "That sounds like an invitation for every bindle stiff and grifter in town to take you for a ride."

Moxie's finger traced the rim of her glass. "I'm not saying they didn't *try*, just that they didn't succeed."

"Clearly you're not from New York."

"How can you tell?"

"Because your soul hasn't been consumed yet." Violet's tone was lighthearted.

"Well, it's nice to know that I still have that to look forward to," she joked, taking another sip of her drink. "You know, this is really quite good."

"I take it you haven't seen much of the nightlife in New York unless you've been the entertainment?"

"No, I try not to participate too much in it. I figure if the cops bust in and raid the place, they'll let the sober people go."

Wil smiled. "Well, aren't you just adorable? Thinking that cops let people who aren't political officials go."

"Adorable is a very good assessment," Violet said softly, looking into Moxie's eyes for what felt like a prolonged period of time.

Moxie panicked. Was this woman—a celebrity, no less—making advances toward her? If so, this was certainly a first. But New York seemed full of firsts for her. "My husband uses that word to describe me sometimes too," she lied.

Violet's gaze narrowed, as though she was scrutinizing Moxie. "Well, your husband's correct. You're just as cute as a box of kittens."

As Fred returned to the table with another gin rickey for Julian, Violet raised her glass. "Let's toast, everyone." They all held their glass to the center of the table. "To continued success." Glasses clinked together and everyone drank.

"I hope you don't have to sing any more tonight," Wil said.

"Oh, no. I only have two sets a night, so far. And that was my second."

"So you might get more?" Julian poured more champagne for all of them.

Moxie was too polite to refuse. "If I start really packing them in, yes. And of course the more sets I play a night, the more money I make."

"How long have you been in New York?" Violet fed another piece of bread to Clitty.

"Only six months." She took a longer sip of bubbly.

"What of the city have you really seen?" Wil asked.

Feeling suddenly embarrassed, Moxie gazed at the ceiling. "Um…I've seen the Statue of Liberty and the Chrysler Building. And I went down to Fifth Avenue to see that brand-new skyscraper that's even taller, the Empire State Building. It's massive."

Violet looked disappointed. "But those are things for tourists. You *live* here now."

"I know. I just don't get out much. By the time I get off work, I don't want to do anything but crawl home and sleep."

"Wil here can give you a tour of the underside of every table in every gin joint in town," Julian said in mock helpfulness.

Wil cleared her throat indignantly. "Excuse me," she said, "but I believe you mean the underside of only the *finest* tables in every gin joint in town."

He laughed. "You're right, darling. How stupid of me."

Moxie chuckled at their teasing and enjoyed the bubbles in the champagne a little more.

"Then you should see the city with us tonight," Violet said. "Visit the places only the locals can take you."

She was hesitant. "I don't know—" All the mental alarms in Moxie's head were still clanging away, but somehow she was becoming increasingly acclimated to their tones of danger. Whether it was the booze or the easy laughter, what had started out as sirens now sounded more like a jazzman on the vibraphone.

"Vi is right," Wil announced. "You absolutely should come out with us. One night with us and you can stay in for the rest of the year and still feel like you've sowed your oats."

"I'd like to hang on to my oats, if that's all right."

Violet looked amused. "Fair enough, doll. You keep a tight hold on your oats and just try to look the other way when Wil starts pelting strangers with hers."

Everyone howled, including Moxie. She didn't feel threatened by this trio, she supposed, and she couldn't remember the last time she'd enjoyed herself so much. She really had been meaning to see the rest of New York, though she internally vowed to keep her wits about her at all times and leave at the first sign of trouble. "Well, I guess I could join you for a bit."

"Excellent. I'll wager you'll see a thing or two you've never seen before the night is over."

❖

12:15 a.m.

Moxie decided—after several glasses of champagne—that not only were these folks not a bad sort, but that they were absolutely hysterical. Though they were, without question, easily the oddest people she had ever met, they were also, at least to some degree, well connected in show business, not to mention astoundingly clever. Moxie personally challenged herself to keep up with all their quips and asides, though she discovered the task was particularly taxing now that she was not completely clearheaded.

At midnight, the group determined that they wanted to head to Swing Street, though she had never heard of such a place, and they all gleefully jammed their bodies into a single taxi. Moxie almost couldn't wait to get back to her apartment and tell her roommate Irene how she had spent her evening. She doubted Irene would even believe her.

"Um, are you from New York originally?" Moxie asked Violet in a thinly veiled attempt to use pleasantries to mask the awkwardness of sitting on Violet's lap. She silently marveled at how Violet seemed to so coolly take everything in stride. She didn't appear to find the arrangement in the cab uncomfortable in the least.

"Baltimore," Violet replied, shaking her head.

"How long have you lived here?"

Violet's eyes took on a wistful glint. "Six years. I came to town on my twenty-first birthday, determined to show everyone else that I really could live my life as a woman of independent mcans."

Wil chortled. "Darling, don't sell yourself short. Anyone who jacks people off in back alleys can be a woman of independent means."

Julian cleared his throat. "Let us not malign back-alley jack-offs. Those have been some of my fondest times. It's a dying art."

"You're such a purist, Julian," Violet said.

"Well, you know the old wives' tale," he replied, picking up Clitty and moving him slightly to the right of his lap. "Why can't this dog's pointy elbows stop gouging my scrotum?"

Violet scoffed. "That is a very obscure old wives' tale. So what does it mean? A scrotum gouge means good luck is coming your way?"

Julian sniffed. "It means if it continues, I will openly weep."

"Those old wives were all dirty whores," Wil said gravely.

"So it's really an old whores' tale," Violet said.

Wil checked her makeup in her compact. "I would think those would be slightly less reliable, darling."

"Here we are," the taxi driver droned, pulling the car to an abrupt stop on Fifty-second Street. As Moxie was catapulted toward the front seat, Violet agilely grabbed her around the waist and stopped her forward progress.

"Whew! You okay, tomato?" Violet didn't move her hands from Moxie's hips.

Moxie, who had entered the cab somewhat disoriented, was certainly no better off now, feeling as though she had nearly been launched like a cannonball. She stared dumbly into Violet's gray eyes.

The door opened and they all spilled out into the balmy evening as Julian paid the driver.

"And where are we again?" Moxie asked, surveying her surroundings for some sign or landmark.

"The Twenty-one Club," Violet answered. "Ever been before?"

Moxie shook her head as they walked through the large cast-iron gates and down the steps to the front door. "I'm starting to think I haven't ever been anywhere."

Violet laughed as Julian and Wil began to sweet-talk the doorman. Moxie felt rather eager when he finally ushered them inside.

"Well, now you're in New York, doll," Violet assured her. "So hang on to your bloomers." She tugged Moxie by the elbow while still carrying her terrier protectively.

The inside of the 21 Club was something that Moxie could never have imagined. The glimpses she got through the haze of smoke were of leather, brass, and dark, deeply stained wood. The place was a lot bigger inside than the outside implied, and people were everywhere—seated at tables, standing at the bar, and milling back and forth between the two.

They were led straight back to a table for four, though Violet stopped when she saw a woman seated a few tables away on the left. "Well, I'll be damned," she muttered, setting Clitty down on her chair.

"Who's that?" Moxie whispered to Julian, sensing that this was not a happy reunion.

Julian eyed the petite brunette across from them. "Oh, that's Dorothy Parker, critic for *The New Yorker*. Vi's probably a little upset at the review she gave both *Scandals and Lies* and Vi personally. It was not flattering. I think she used the word *puke*."

"Well." Violet approached the critic's table. Dorothy Parker was drinking alone and looked as though she wanted to remain that way. "Mrs. Parker, as I live and breathe."

Mrs. Parker looked up from what she was busily writing on a pad of paper. "Ordinarily, I'm not one to be a spoiler. But rumor has it, if you stop doing either one of those things, you tend to end badly." She took another sip of her martini.

Wil looked angry as she began to peel off her gloves. "It's a pity you aren't speaking from experience."

Mrs. Parker appeared both tipsy and indifferent. "I am. I learned it from most of your audience at your last matinee. Luckily, it consisted of only me, two hobos, and a party of cockroaches. So no real damage was done."

Violet raised an eyebrow. "No wonder I didn't see you there. I must have assumed you were part of the cockroach party. Next time just tell us you're coming beforehand, darling, and avoid the confusion. I'd hate for someone to callously step on you."

Wil jumped in to help her friend. "Yes, had we known you were there we would have had you seated more appropriately—in a urine puddle in the alley outside, maybe."

The critic rolled her eyes. "If only your play had been this witty. No, wait. Your play was supposed to be a drama, wasn't it? I suppose your repartee wouldn't have helped much then. Never mind."

"I hear the play's better when you're sober," Violet suggested. "You should try it some time."

Mrs. Parker scoffed. "Sobriety is overrated. Much as your play is. Is the rumor that you're walking away from the abysmal thing and heading to Hollywood true?"

"It is," Violet said.

"Well, I suppose they can always use another shit-peddler out there." The critic signaled for the waiter to bring her another drink by waving her lit cigarette at him.

Violet crossed her arms defiantly. "You know, Mrs. Parker, it's statistically impossible for you to hate everything in the world except gin. Are you saying that there isn't the tiniest part of you, albeit deeply repressed, that might want a job in Hollywood?"

"I'd rather pass a hairbrush through my colon, actually."

During the ensuing moment of silence everyone no doubt pictured the haunting image.

"Well," Wil said flatly, "as always, it's been lovely." She put her arm around Violet's shoulders and led her back to their table, where they took their seats.

"Damn her," Violet whispered angrily as she moved Clitty onto her lap.

"Don't let her ruin your celebration." Moxie felt a pang of sympathy for her. This had been the first moment since she met Violet that she was not composed and sharp-witted. "You *are* celebrating a role in a Hollywood film, while she's here alone. So who really comes out on top?"

"I suppose you're right. Though it's hard to shake the sting of someone who completely eviscerates you for sport."

The waiter arrived at the table to collect everyone's drink order.

"A gin rickey," Julian said.

"I'm ready to move on from champagne," Wil said. "Bring me a Bronx, darling."

"What are you having?" Violet asked Moxie. "It's on me."

"I'm actually a little tipsy. I probably shouldn't have anything else."

"Do you like licorice?"

"I suppose." Moxie wasn't sure what that question had to do with cocktails.

"If you're still feeling adventurous, I have an idea. You're under no obligation other than to taste it." Violet motioned to the waiter. "A bottle of absinthe and three glasses."

"Very good," the waiter said, heading back to the bar.

"Absinthe?" Moxie asked.

Wil smiled as she lit a cigarette. "Ah, absinthe—the green fairy. I have a love-hate relationship with her."

"Which makes it just like every other relationship in your life," Julian said.

"Darling, be kind," Wil chided. "I'm still trying to get over Fred. He broke my heart."

"What color fairy was Fred?" Violet asked.

Moxie laughed loudly, covering her mouth with her hand.

Wil looked amused. "Well, look at that. Mary Pickford over there is finally coming around."

Julian smirked. "You must be rubbing off on her, Violet."

"With any hope at all," Wil muttered under her breath as she brought her cigarette holder to her lips.

"You know," Moxie said, "before I came to New York, I thought I had been around the block."

Violet's eyes softened. "We have longer blocks here."

For a moment, Moxie sensed that something was hanging unspoken in the air. But before she could ponder that thought further, the waiter arrived with the drinks. When he set the bottle of bright green liquor in front of her, she had second thoughts. It definitely did not look safe to drink. "What the hell is that?"

"Mother's milk," Wil answered.

"If your mother happens to be a leprechaun," Moxie said with a snicker.

The waiter uncorked the bottle and set down three glasses, three ornate metal utensils, a pitcher of what looked to be water, and a bowl of sugar cubes before he disappeared back into the crowd.

Violet filled one of the oddly shaped glasses with liquor, to the point where the round bottom part of the glass met the straight upper section. She picked up one of the silver utensils in one hand and a sugar cube in the other. "Watch this."

"You need a special tool to drink this? Please tell me this stuff goes in the mouth."

Violet laughed as she balanced the flat slotted spoon on top of the absinthe glass. "Well, since you're a beginner, I guess we can make an exception this time." She then set the sugar cube on the spoon and poured the water over the top of it until the glass was about two-thirds full. The clear, emerald liquor turned a light milky green as the water, sugar, and absinthe mysteriously coalesced. "This is called the louche." She removed the spoon and took a sip.

"Louche?" Moxie asked. "What does that mean?"

Violet offered her the glass so she could assess her mixing skills. "The louche is kind of like taking something already remarkable and, by adding some other unrelated exceptional ingredient, making it beautiful in a whole new way."

The poetry of Violet's words impressed Moxie, and she wondered if other things in life combined to create a louche—perhaps people. Regardless, Moxie decided to try the drink without reservation. She took a sip and closed her eyes as she swallowed. "Damn! That's not bad."

"In all the time I've known you, when have I ever steered you wrong?"

"You're right. It's been a very pleasant few hours." She watched Violet fill another glass with only water and offer it to the dog in her lap, which drank happily, but sent water flying all around him. Amused, Moxie couldn't pass up the opportunity to comment. "Your Clitoris is making a wet mess."

Violet smiled seductively. "Thanks for noticing."

"Er…Do you take him everywhere you go?"

"Yes, for the most part. I found him one night as I was coming out of the theater." The dog stopped drinking, then lay back down in her lap contentedly and closed his eyes. "He was a sad, bedraggled little mess. And once I took him home, washed and fed him, he never wanted to leave my side."

"I've had dates like that, darling," Wil said, taking a long sip of her Bronx cocktail. "One time I had to pretend I was dead to get the son of a bitch to leave."

Julian laughed. "Was that before or after the sex?"

"During, actually. You know men in bed." She looked at Violet and paused. "Oh, well…" She turned to Julian. "*You* know men in bed. They're happy if you participate, but it's not really necessary for them. It's like the difference between a four-course meal and a five-course meal. They're happy to get dessert, but if need be, they'll just double up on dinner rolls."

Violet began to mix a glass of absinthe for herself. "Well, hopefully the poor man didn't think his lovemaking had killed you."

"I was more likely to perish from the boredom than from anything else."

Julian traced the path of his mustache with his index finger. "Well, if he ever buys tickets to *Scandals and Lies*, he'll get the shock of his life. Our deceased Miss Skoog will be there illuminated by the footlights."

"I thought I was changing my name," Wil reminded them, taking a long drag of her Chesterfield. "Let's hear some suggestions."

They mulled for a moment.

"Urethra Dejeuner," Julian offered.

"Darling," Wil said. "As delightfully French as that sounds, I don't know that I want to be known as Pee-hole Lunch, but I suppose it's a start."

Violet set down her spoon as she pondered further. "How about Veneria Dungbottom? You could be V.D. for short."

Wil frowned. "Sounds a little too folksy for me."

"Play off the red hair," Julian suggested. "Go with something blatantly Irish, like Jiggles McTavish."

"Too ethnic," was all Wil replied.

"Genitalia Finkelstein," Moxie said, starting to settle into the rapid-fire discourse enough to add her two cents.

Violet seemed pleasantly surprised at her participation. "No, I knew a Genitalia Finkelstein in high school. She might sue."

"Pity," Moxie replied in amusement, sipping her absinthe. "It's such a pretty name."

"Yes, and she was a lovely girl. But she was far too sensitive."

Everyone laughed loudly.

Moxie let the fast-paced, witty mood wash over her, flush with the revelation that the banter was even more enjoyable when you were a direct participant. "So what is this movie you're off to make?"

"It's called *Manhattan Rhapsody*," Violet replied. "It's a Pinnacle picture."

Moxie giggled. "You're going all the way to California to make a film about New York?"

"Apparently most of Manhattan can be reproduced on the back lot. They just rub it with a little filth and, presto—instant New York."

Wil set down her now-empty cocktail glass. "Well, darling, do let them know that I'm available anytime to be rubbed with filth."

Julian smirked. "That's common knowledge, dear."

"Pinnacle Pictures?" Moxie was even more in awe. "That's T. Z. Walter's studio, isn't it?" Violet nodded. "So what's it about?"

Violet's face lit up as she started to talk about her project. "Well, a wealthy socialite—"

"You," Moxie interjected.

"—loses everything in the stock-market crash."

"So it's a comedy," Julian remarked dryly.

Violet continued. "She has to learn how to do everything for herself, for the first time. So the audience gets the joy of watching her struggle."

"And in the end?" Moxie asked.

"I think she meets a rich man and marries him and her problems are solved...or some shit like that." She took a drink.

"I suppose that is the proverbial happy ending," Moxie argued weakly.

"What I'm hoping I can do, before the picture wraps, is to talk them into a better ending. One where a rich man offers to take her away from her poverty, and she gives him the finger and tells him, 'No thanks, Bub. I'd rather work for a living.'"

Julian took another drag on his cigarette. "So I was wrong. It's not a comedy. It's a fantasy."

"We're not all just aspiring to be bought and paid for," Violet countered. "Some of us are more than happy to be given a chance to succeed all on our own."

"Hear! Hear!" Wil said. "Though you might feel differently if you enjoyed sex with men."

"I can be kept just as easily by a rich woman as I can by a rich man," she explained. "So I don't know if I buy that argument."

"Ha!" Wil dismissed that assertion with a wave of her cigarette holder.

Everything was now clicking into place for Moxie. The long admiring looks from Violet, her compliments, the wry comments from the others. Perhaps everything she had heard about theater people was actually true—eccentric, hedonistic, sexually capricious devil worshippers. And while none of them had mentioned Satan all night, he could certainly still come up.

Violet was still trying to make her point. "Why is it acceptable for only a man to have ambition that doesn't include living off someone else's fortune?"

Julian scoffed. "And why should marrying well be a goal that only extends to women? Darling, find me a rich man and I'll settle down in a second."

"Whatever happened to true love?" Violet asked. "And what happened to integrity?" She turned to Moxie, who was unsuccessfully trying to look as though she weren't surprised at the disclosure that Violet was attracted to women. "Didn't you marry your husband for love?"

"Who? Oh, him! The husband. *My* husband. Yes, we're madly in love."

Violet cocked an eyebrow. "What's his name?" Her voice was tinged with suspicion.

Moxie searched her mind for an answer. "Filbert," she finally answered.

"Your husband is named after a nut?" Wil asked.

"Ha," she said awkwardly. "I suppose so."

As Violet studied her, Moxie was alert enough to realize she was clearly intoxicated and making an abominable attempt to perpetuate her earlier lie. Violet glanced at Moxie's left ring finger, which sported no wedding band. What could Violet be thinking about her? Would she jump to the conclusion that Moxie was deluded? Or would she simply write her off as a filthy liar?

"Darlings," Wil said. "I'm feeling a little restless. You know what I need?"

"Satan?" Moxie asked timidly.

Wil stared at her for several seconds. "Well, no. But if he pays his own way I guess you can bring him along. What I need is a touch of the white lady."

"I'll second that," Julian replied.

"Who?" Moxie whispered to Violet.

"It's more of a what, actually. And it means heading to Harlem—to a buffet flat."

"A buffet flat?"

"Come on along," she said. "If you think what you've seen so far is amazing, you won't believe this place."

❖

1:50 a.m.

"Where the hell are we?" Moxie asked as they made their way through a small crowd and into what was undoubtedly someone's West Harlem home. "Who lives here?"

"Two-finger Flossie." Violet placed her hand on Moxie's back and gently guided her through the house.

"She's only got two fingers?"

Violet leaned in close to her ear. "Flossie's famous for 'two fingers of gin and two fingers within.'" She waggled her first two fingers in unison as though to elucidate.

Moxie's brain wasn't working to full capacity. "She puts her fingers in the gin?"

"Under the circumstances, I sure as hell hope not."

Before Moxie could ponder Violet's meaning further, they arrived in the crowded parlor and stopped to observe the crowd. In the corner, someone was playing ragtime on the piano. The room was filled with people of all races dancing, drinking, and smoking. Two men sat on a plush love seat locked in a tight embrace and kissing deeply. A naked woman was balancing a half-full bottle of gin on her forehead, while several men crouched on the floor throwing dice for cash.

Moxie blinked several times, trying to take it all in. "Why are we here again?"

"We all have our reasons, sister," Wil answered as she pushed past them and disappeared into the crowd with Julian.

"What does that mean?"

Violet set her terrier on the floor. "Well, Julian's here to find himself a man," she explained. "Preferably one of his famous back-alley frolics. Wil's here to make a different type of connection."

"Oh?"

Violet looked somewhat sheepish. "She's here to get some cocaine—the 'white lady' she referred to. As you can see, you can get anything in a buffet flat."

"So why are *you* here? What's your vice?"

"Baked Alaska," she said, one corner of her mouth rising infinitesimally.

Moxie had lost the physical ability to hide her disapproval. Did these people have no scruples whatsoever? "Baked Alaska, the dessert?

Or is that code for something too? Like having flaming heroin blown into your ass with a straw?"

"No, it's the dessert." She paused conspiratorially. "But I like to eat it off a dead hooker."

"And cheesecake just won't do?"

"It's too heavy. Makes me feel bloated."

"Well, that's no good," Moxie said, laughter betraying her words. "You don't want to feel that way every time you come across a dead hooker."

"Exactly. That's a waste of a perfectly good naked carcass."

A tall, dark-skinned man dressed in women's clothes and dolled up to the nines approached them, his long false eyelashes fluttering like blossoms in a breeze. "Did I hear the word *naked*?"

Violet's face lit up and she kissed him briefly on the mouth. "Sweetie, you look fabulous!" she told him.

"As do you, sister." He traced her cheek lightly with his slender index finger. "How are things?"

"You know me. Everything's jake. Moxie, meet Lady Dulce La Boeuf. Lady Dulce, this is Moxie Valette."

He seemed to study her for a moment as he took her gently by the wrists. "Honey, I could just eat cobbler straight out of your ass with a spoon."

She froze at both his words and his appearance in a mixture of shock and confusion. "Is that a good thing?"

"Absolutely," he assured her.

"Don't knock it till you've tried it," Violet said with a wink. "So, what have we missed tonight?"

"You missed my singing, you silly bitch. But I suppose I'll forgive you."

Violet chuckled. "Moxie here is a singer too."

He tilted his head curiously. "Is that so? I like you already, doll face." Despite her initial misgivings, Moxie felt a bit more at ease upon hearing his words. Well, his words coupled with the fact that she was crazy about the beaded ivory dress he was wearing. "You know who's upstairs?"

"Who's that?" Violet asked.

"I was just heading up to see Smokey Bender."

Violet seemed interested and clapped once. "Let's go up and see him."

They started toward the staircase and Moxie leaned forward so Violet could hear her. "Who is Smokey Bender?"

"He's…a performer."

"Hmm, why did you hesitate?"

"Because he's an acquired taste, so I didn't want to call him an entertainer. You may not find him entertaining." They reached a room at the top of the staircase filled with people, and the three of them crowded just inside the doorway. "There he is. This will be a treat."

"Why is he taking off his pants?" Moxie asked in concern. A small, wiry man who appeared to be in his mid-fifties pulled his trousers down and stepped out of them, then folded them neatly and handed them to a woman to his left.

"You'll see," Lady Dulce murmured.

"Is this some genitalia puppet show?" Moxie was aghast as the man then did the same with his underwear, turned so he was facing away from everyone, and bent at the waist. He reached out again to the woman holding his clothing, and she handed him a lit cigar. The crowd seemed pleased, and some onlookers clapped and offered words of encouragement.

He inserted the cigar into his rectum and, to Moxie's amazement, began to draw and expel smoke. The applause grew louder.

Lady Dulce whispered conspiratorially, "How about that?"

"That is one unbelievable asshole," she answered.

"Wait until he blows the smoke rings," Violet added.

Moxie's current inebriated state, coupled with the parade of the bizarre before her, left her unable to distinguish sarcasm from the laws of physics. "Really?"

She laughed softly. "No, not really. But he will extinguish a candle in a minute or two in what will appear to be a very uncomfortable manner."

"Christ almighty," she whispered, watching him ignite a fart with a cigarette lighter.

Wil and Julian appeared in the doorway then, and Violet signaled them over. "Lady Dulce, you remember my wonderful friends Urethra Dejeuner and her fiancé Red Nobgobbler, man-about-town."

Lady Dulce was clearly amused. "How could I forget?"

Wil suddenly ducked and tried to hide behind Julian. "What is it?" he asked, scanning the crowd.

"It's D.B.," she answered softly, pressing her back up against his. Moxie looked at Violet. "Who's D.B.?"

"An old conquest of our gal here. Apparently it didn't end well and, really, when has it ever? Ah, there he is, by the window."

Moxie, Lady Dulce, and Julian immediately looked at him in interest, and when the gentleman saw that he was being stared at by not one, but a group of people, his expression changed to one of grave concern. He looked down suspiciously at his fly.

"I thought that man's name was Floyd," Lady Dulce said.

"D.B. is a special nickname Wil gave him," Violet explained, her voice breaking with a hint of laughter.

Wil cleared her throat. "It stands for douchebag, because sex with him felt a lot like being flushed out with a bag of lukewarm Lysol."

"Ouch," Lady Dulce whispered.

"I'm sure somehow he remembers your evening together more pleasantly," Julian said before taking a sip of his drink.

"It would be hard for him not to, I'm thinking," Moxie said with a wince. She looked at her new friend in drag. "'Dulce La Boeuf'? Is that Italian *and* French?"

"*Si* and *oui*. Loosely, it means sweet meat."

"Or sweetly, does it mean loose meat?" Moxie asked, drunkenly cackling at her pun.

Lady Dulce laughed too and brushed Moxie's elbow in a familiar way. "You want a drink, doll?"

"Only if it means I don't have to see Mr. Cavity here put anything else in his anus."

"You have a deal. Come on." He took her by the hand and pulled her out of the room and back downstairs.

Julian raised an eyebrow. "Are you just going to let your date leave with the first woman with a penis she meets?"

Wil was still hiding behind Julian. "Now, now, Jules. Not everyone can have the same appreciation of the anal arts that you do." She peeked around him to see what Smokey Bender was doing now. "Holy Christ, is that a weasel he's putting in there?"

"It's someone's mink stole," Violet explained flatly.

Julian grimaced. "Does Smokey reimburse for the cleaning bills?"

Violet wasn't paying much attention anymore. "So what do you both think of Moxie?"

"She's charming." Wil stole a look to ensure that D.B. had not spied her from across the room.

"I'm sure her husband thinks so too," Julian said.

"Oh, darling," Wil said. "You can't possibly think that girl is married."

"No?"

"Absolutely not. She just wanted to make sure Vi here didn't cop a feel."

"That's what I was thinking too," Violet said. "Her husband is awfully convenient."

Julian raised an eyebrow. "Or maybe you just don't *want* to believe it."

She sighed in frustration as she idly watched Smokey Bender launch a cocktail wiener across the room and the crowd rapidly part to avoid it. "I don't know, Jules. There's something about her that fascinates me."

"Her jugs, perhaps?" he asked. "After all, what can be more fascinating than a pair of perfect jugs?"

"No," Wil said. "It's her ass, isn't it? Wait, no. Her gams. I vote for the gams."

"Besides all that," Violet explained, "I feel drawn to her."

"And her jugs, ass, and gams," Julian added glibly. "Understood."

"Well, sister," Wil said. "You only have tonight to make it happen. So why are you standing here watching some fella push hors d'oeuvres out his fanny? Go find her."

❖

2:40 a.m.

"Where the hell did she go?" Violet asked herself in frustration. She and Clitty had been through every room in the house at least once and didn't see Moxie anywhere. Based on how many people were milling about, however, she wasn't close to panicking. It would have been easy to miss her in the crowd.

Wil approached her in a room where people were gathering to watch a couple have sex on the floor. "Hey, Jules seems to have found himself a human almond frappe—all nuts and foam."

"Is that so? Is he somewhere shamefully lying about how much money he makes?"

Wil propped her hands on her hips. "Well, I'm fairly certain he can't be saying too much, what with that fella's dick in his mouth and all."

"I suppose that's a good way to avoid awkward conversation."

"And I found your gal while I was at it," Wil said.

"Tell me she isn't trapped under a cluster of fornicators."

"Even better than that," she replied blithely. "She's downstairs singing a duet with Lady Dulce La Boeuf."

Violet stared at her in disbelief, searching for some sign that she was putting her on. "Seriously?"

"I wouldn't miss it, if I were trying to seduce her."

"Point taken." She snapped her fingers to call Clitty, who—along with Wil—fell in step behind her, and headed downstairs. As they rounded the corner at the foot of the stairs, first she heard Moxie, and then she actually saw her. She and Lady Dulce were standing near the pianist, who was playing a song that Violet had never heard before. Their harmony was impressive, even if the lyrics weren't.

Don't dare call me a flapper.
Fitzgerald's not my man.
I'm wallowing in the crapper,
because my stocks are in the can.
Now I want to survive,
though I don't mean to be crass.
It looks like to stay alive
I'll have to peddle my ass!

Can't bear to stand in a breadline.
Hoover's just not my guy.
I'm living off of moonshine,
How else will I ever get by?

Now I want to survive,
and don't think that I don't have class.
But it looks like to stay alive
I'll have to peddle it—
Don't belittle it.
Won't you diddle it?
That should settle it—
Have to peddle my ass!

On the final note, both Moxie and Lady Dulce spanked themselves, and the rowdy audience applauded enthusiastically. Violet walked toward Moxie, clapping and nodding her approval. "Well, that was quite a tearjerker."

Moxie's cheeks were flushed, and Violet had no doubt that she'd had more to drink since she'd last seen her. "I love ballads," she replied, her brown eyes sparkling.

They stood mutely for several moments, until Lady Dulce gave Moxie's back a playful push, sending her only inches from colliding with Violet. "Take a break, doll," he said, nodding to the pianist. "I've got this number." The dulcet tones on the piano began, and he started singing Irving Berlin's "What'll I Do?"

"Dance, sailor?" Violet asked.

"You…and me?" Moxie looked self-conscious.

Violet took a step closer so their chests were nearly touching. "You and me." She held her hands out, offering to lead. Moxie looked around at the crowd nervously. "If you think you're going to get stared at here, sister, you're sadly mistaken. You could sodomize a monkey right in this room, and all you'd get from these folks would be pointers."

Moxie laughed and shrugged off her discomfort. After all, having seen a man do magic tricks with his rectum, dancing with another woman not only seemed innocuous, it felt as respectable as holy sacrament. She placed her right hand in Violet's outstretched left one, and when Violet grasped her waist and pulled her closer, her breath caught. At some point, Moxie realized that her feet were moving and that she was, in fact, dancing. But she was so tipsy her head seemed filled with a thick fog.

"Out of courtesy, I'd recommend that you stay away from the cocktail wieners," Violet suggested.

Moxie was confused by the unusual advice. "I'll do that. You know, you're not too bad at this."

"I do have other talents besides acting."

"I've noticed."

"Is that so? Do tell."

Moxie felt herself blush slightly as her body swayed against Violet's. "Well, you're quick-witted and intelligent."

"A clever ruse—nothing more."

"And you can certainly put away the booze."

"Now *that's* a talent to speak of. But please note that you have had much more to drink this evening than I have." Violet's right hand moved on Moxie's hip ever so slightly, but the light caress both startled and excited her.

"I—I have?"

"Yes," she whispered provocatively near her ear. The sensation gave Moxie chills. "Anything else you want to give me credit for?"

"Isn't it my turn yet?"

"I suppose so. You have a beautiful voice," Violet said, her mouth so close to Moxie's neck that she could feel her warm breath.

"Oh."

"And you have got to be one of the sexiest women—who doesn't realize she's sexy—that I've ever met."

"Can I add what a smoothie you are to your list?" Moxie's voice sounded deeper and throatier than she would have liked.

"Me?"

"Oh, most definitely you. You have more lines than a telephone operator."

Violet pulled back to look into her eyes. "While that may be, you really are beautiful."

"Thanks." It was a moment before Moxie realized that Lady Dulce was no longer singing and the song had changed to something upbeat and jazzy. Her head was spinning.

"Are you all right?"

"I think I need to sit down."

Violet led her back to where Lady Dulce and Wil had perched on a plush leather sofa, preparing even more drinks. Moxie sat next to them, feeling self-conscious that she had just been so intimately entwined with Violet. She slouched into the cushions uneasily. Violet sank into an armchair and snapped her fingers for Clitty, who trotted over and curled into a ball at her feet.

"So, that was nice," Wil said, her voice thick with innuendo. She offered Moxie a glass of an alluring amber liquid. "And so is this."

"What is it?"

"A sidecar," she explained. "You'll love it."

Violet looked cautious. "You know, it may be a good idea to stop drinking."

"This *is* good," she exclaimed, drinking some more of the tart cocktail.

Violet sighed.

"And you said you're not a drinker," Wil said, tapping glasses with her. "Even I'm impressed, kid."

Lady Dulce chimed in. "That says a lot. I've seen her drink for over twenty-four hours straight."

Wil chuckled. "Remember that time the coppers gave us the buzz?"

As Wil began her tale of bold, drunken debauchery, Moxie's attention kept drifting elsewhere. Her eyes settled on Violet, who had a rather nice profile, she decided. She really did look like a beautiful movie star. Her face was so striking and expressive, and her light eyes mesmerized Moxie.

What was going on? How did this woman, a stranger, really, draw her in this way? Why was she having to force herself not to stare? Why had she enjoyed that dance more than her last dozen dates? Well, she really hadn't had much of a sexual history, she mused. It wasn't like she was able to properly compare the sensations that Violet elicited to the ones her old beaus evoked.

Hell, it had been well over a year since she had even gone on a date. Most of the time the fellas were so dull she didn't even bother to accept their invitations. The ones she had gotten involved with seemed attracted to her initially, but somehow the relationships always culminated with them pulling out their dick, usually in the most inconvenient locations. Sometimes it took a few weeks for it to happen, sometimes just a few minutes. Every man she had known seemed like a large jack-in-the-box. If you decided to play, at some point it would come flying out at you. And even though you knew what to expect, it somehow *always* startled you and, in her case, left her wondering what to do with it.

She gazed again at Violet. Was she so different from those palookas Moxie had dated? Violet seemed just as intent on making time with her as all the others had, though she was a slightly better dancer than most.

Good Lord, was she actually considering Violet as a prospective lover? Had the drink, coupled with her abysmal love life, somehow skewed her perspective? When she got up this morning, she knew two things—she was not cheap, and she was not a lesbian. What odd turn of events would make those two certainties blur from fact into ambivalence in the span of a day?

Julian reappeared and took a seat across from Violet. He now looked somehow rumpled, and Moxie wondered if he had found what he came here for.

She glanced back to Violet and watched her index finger ever so lightly trace her lower lip as she seemed to take in Wil's anecdote with interest. Somehow the thought of the touch of that hand, combined with the feel of those lips, intrigued Moxie. Violet was nothing if not sexually charged, and in some way distractingly magnetic.

"So what's it like to kiss a woman?"

All conversation stopped and everyone stared at Moxie with expressions that ranged from amusement to stunned surprise.

Violet's eyes twinkled as she played with her necklace idly. "Well, based on present company, I'll assume that question is directed to me."

Lady Dulce and Julian looked at each other and shrugged in unspoken agreement.

"Not so fast, darling," Wil said, taking a drag from her Chesterfield. "I'm sure I've kissed a lot of women."

Violet was struggling to stave off laughter. "And do you remember any of them? Or is this based on what people tell you the next day?"

"Ah, yes. Good point." Wil took another sip of her drink and sat back again. "Go right ahead, then."

"Kissing a woman is a lot like kissing a man, with the exception of a few fundamental improvements."

"Like what?" Moxie took another sip of her drink.

"You don't need to worry about being chafed by stubble."

Wil licked the rim of her glass briefly. "Not from kissing her on the mouth, anyway."

"You're getting way ahead of yourself, toots." Violet looked back at Moxie. "Women also have a certain softness." Her gray eyes took on an intensity that made Moxie's stomach flutter. "They tend toward more of a slow burn, while men are like dynamite. Once you light the fuse you have maybe ten seconds before they explode."

"I take umbrage at that," Julian said.

"Which part?" Wil asked. "The metaphor, or how long she gave you till detonation?"

"All of it," he replied. "Some of us have a slow fuse."

"That's right, honey." Lady Dulce patted his knee supportively.

Violet put up her hands in mock defense. "Now, now, boys. You can't help the way you're designed—with all your wares on the outside." She gestured vaguely toward their laps.

"Very true," Wil agreed. "It's a bit like having a live grenade in your pants all the time." She looked up to see D.B. approaching her. "And here comes my little bombardier now."

"Wil, is that you?" He appraised her and stood with his mouth open in poorly feigned excitement.

She looked downcast for the first time all evening. "Unfortunately, yes."

"How have you been? It's been ages since we've caught up."

She eyed him suspiciously. "If by caught up you mean fucked, then yes, it has been a while."

He laughed a deep, forced-sounding guffaw, but when he saw that no one else was joining in, he immediately stopped. "Say, what are your plans for the rest of the night?"

"Plans?" Wil looked desperately to the other members of her party. "My plans for the night."

Moxie tried to look earnest. "You did want to go home soon and apply that ointment the doctor gave you."

"Yes, that's right," Violet added. "Before the blisters start to ooze."

Wil smiled at their quick thinking. "And how have you been, Floyd? Has anything been red or inflamed?"

His face fell. "What?"

Wil lowered her voice to simulate discretion. "Does it burn at all when you pee?"

He looked stricken. "No. Are you saying—?"

"I thought the doctor told you that men don't always show symptoms," Moxie said, unable to stanch her curiosity regarding how far they might be able to take this charade.

Wil turned to the man and looked reassuring. "I'm sure you're fine. You look plenty healthy."

"Good night," he spat hurriedly, darting out of the room. They could hear him not too far away shouting, "I need my hat and coat *now!*"

Wil seemed impressed by Moxie's clever stratagem. She raised her glass in a toast. "Quoth the douchebag—"

"Nevermore," they all answered happily in unison, clinking their glasses together.

❖

4:05 a.m.

"Come on, tomato. We're almost there," Violet said as she managed to nudge her apartment door open without losing hold of Moxie, who was so incapacitated from drink that she couldn't stand unassisted.

"Where are we?"

After Clitty darted inside, Violet closed the door behind them with her foot and made her way into the bedroom, her arm around Moxie's waist. "We're in my suite at the Algonquin."

"Al...gone...what?"

"It's a hotel, darling. I live here."

"Is this a come-on?"

Violet struggled to prop her up so that she was seated on the edge of the bed. "And what would your husband say to that? What was his name? Pistachio?"

"I don't have a husband," Moxie said, seeming confused.

"Well, earlier you said you did." Violet knelt to remove Moxie's shoes.

"I think you're mistaken." She wiggled her liberated toes for a moment. "That feels *so* good. I love toes."

"Yes, they're the unsung heroes of our feet. Turn around, so I can get to your buttons."

"I think you're trying to undress me, Miss London."

"*Trying* being the operative word. You could actually help a little, you know."

"I'm not a whore."

Violet sighed. "Which is truly a pity, because I could easily run and get my checkbook." She reached around Moxie and unbuttoned her blue evening gown down to the small of her back. She pulled the stitched fabric forward and Moxie's arms slipped out, but she now sat on the rest of the dress from the waist down. "Hmm…Lie back for me, darling. This will only take a moment."

"What about your slow burn?" She sagged back across the width of the bed.

Violet tugged the gown from under Moxie's bottom, over her shapely legs, and then draped it neatly over a chair. When she turned back around, she froze at the sight of Moxie in her chemise, garters, and stockings. "Damn, damn, damn," she mumbled. The most beautiful woman she'd ever met was lying across her bed in her underwear—very sexy silk, no less—but she was too drunk to actively participate in anything. As though this wasn't cruel enough, Violet's train left at 7:45 a.m. "Let's get your head up on the pillow."

"I can't move."

Violet lay down on the bed next to her. "You need some help?"

"Possibly."

"Well, you don't want to sleep lying across the bed sideways like this. Come on, just shift a little." Violet moved over her to guide her up to the head of the bed.

Moxie wrapped her arms around Violet's neck provocatively. "I like you."

She smiled. "I like you too."

"I had a really good time tonight. *Really good*. The best."

"Remember that tomorrow when it feels like your head has turned inside out."

"Thanks for showing me the town."

"Thanks for coming."

"Come here," Moxie whispered.

Violet chuckled. "I *am* here."

"No, closer. I have something to tell you."

Violet moved her face within inches of Moxie's, and Moxie unexpectedly kissed her. It was slow, deep, and passionate, and Violet enthusiastically kissed her back. The eroticism of Moxie's movements against her, coupled with the sweet taste of her mouth and the feel of her tongue, was driving Violet mad with hunger.

Abruptly, Moxie pulled away. "You're right. That was *much* better than kissing a man."

"Uh…you need to do any more research on that?"

"I feel funny."

"So do I," Violet said, throbbing with unrealized desire.

"Is the bed spinning?"

"No. But let's get your head on the pillow." She grabbed Moxie and shifted her so that she was lying lengthwise on the bed. Then she kissed her forehead softly before she stood up.

"Don't leave me," Moxie murmured with her eyes closed.

"You've got me for a few more hours, doll."

Within minutes, Moxie was asleep.

CHAPTER TWO

When Moxie finally awoke, she was racked with a throbbing headache, cottonmouth, nausea, and a generous amount of confusion.

"What the hell?" She looked around and saw this was definitely not her apartment. She was in a large, rumpled bed. A closer inspection revealed that she was in her underwear. She slowly sat up. This room did not look familiar at all, and she didn't detect another sound from the next room. "Hello?"

No one replied.

She struggled to her feet and saw that last night's clothes were folded neatly on a chair by the window. As much as she wanted to be dressed again, the bright sunlight through the window currently repulsed her. She mulled on the most painless way to get to the garments, finally settling on turning her head, closing her eyes, and flailing her arms wildly at the drapes to force them closed and shut out the light.

When she was satisfied that a fair amount of sun was blocked, she grabbed her clothes and headed back to the bed. Resting on top of her rolled stockings was a sealed envelope with her name written in flamboyant cursive.

For some reason, the handwriting instantly made her think of Violet, and snippets of the previous evening flooded her brain in no particular order. She sat on the edge of the bed, laid her clothing down, and ran her finger under the flap of the envelope.

Moxie,
    I hope you are neither too terribly hungover nor

filled with drinker's remorse. Sadly, I had to make my train this morning, so I wasn't able to wait for you to wake up. I very much wished we could have had breakfast together.

There's no hurry on when you need to leave. The apartment's paid up through the end of the day. Stay as long as you'd like. I've left a couple dollars for you to get a cup of coffee, a bite to eat, and a cab ride back to your place.

Just so you know, last night was one of the most amazing evenings I've had in quite some time, and I'd give anything to kiss you again.

It's my dumb luck that after six years in this goddamned city, I'd meet you on my last night in town. You are an astoundingly beautiful and sexy woman.

I'll write you from the train.

—Violet

Moxie dropped the letter in shock and watched it slowly drift to the floor.

"Holy snappin' assholes!"

❖

On the train to Chicago, Violet was utterly distracted. It seemed that nothing could take her mind off the festivities of the previous evening and a certain fair-haired singer who spent the night in her bed.

She sighed and looked out the window as Clitty twitched in his sleep in the seat beside her. Though she was exhausted, every time she closed her eyes, she imagined that kiss again. The memory of it made her stomach drop like she was on a ride at Coney Island.

Naturally Moxie would kiss her like that and then pass out. It was just her luck. Overcome with sexual frustration, she had gently removed Moxie's stockings and garter belt, though she *might* have taken her time, lingered a bit. She fought off a grin at the thought.

She had curled up next to Moxie for a couple hours of sleep, and the feel of her body had been arousing, yet blissful.

"She's a mystery, Clitty."

The terrier continued to dream, his paws jerking unconsciously and his breathing ragged.

"No, don't try and talk me out of it," Violet said. "I know you think I can't get serious with anyone, but this jane's different. She sings in that provocative voice and then smiles at me like she's an ingénue. She goes out of her way to tell me she's not interested by making up a husband and then hits me with that sockdollager of a kiss."

She picked up the business card for the thirtieth time and started flipping it over in her hands. On one side it read Cotton G. McCann, Professional Entertainment Agent, Twelve Years Experience. On the other side, Moxie had written her address and a phone number. GRamercy 5-9881.

"Well, Clitty, she's not heard the last of us."

Moxie tried to open the apartment door as quietly as she could, in hopes that Irene was distracted and she could slip in unnoticed. She peeked around the edge of the door and saw her roommate sitting on the sofa holding a book and now staring at her.

"Jeepers, Moxie. Where have you been all night?"

She sighed in resignation and entered the room fully, shutting the door behind her. "Hey, Irene."

"You look terrible."

"I guess that stands to reason. I feel terrible." She sat next to Irene on the couch forlornly.

"What happened? Were you hit by a freight train?"

Moxie rubbed her forehead with her hand. "I don't think so."

"What do you mean? You can't remember?"

"I remember *some* of it," she said, feeling defensive.

Irene eagerly curled her legs up under her on the sofa and got comfortable. "Well, start at the beginning and I bet it'll all come back to you."

"A group of people were in the club—a couple of Broadway

actresses and their friend—and they invited me out for drinks with them."

"And you went? But you don't drink." The volume of her voice rose shrilly.

"Shh," Moxie hissed, putting her finger to her mouth and wincing.

"Oh, you went." Irene rolled her eyes. "You *definitely* went. Who were the actresses?"

"Violet London and Wil Skoog."

"Never heard of them. What are they in?"

Moxie squinted as she tried to remember the name of the play. "Um…*Scandals and Lies*."

It was apparent from Irene's expression that she was not familiar with it. "So where did you go?"

"A thousand places, it seemed. We drank champagne at the Luna. We had absinthe at some speakeasy, where Violet and Wil got into a fight with a lady critic. Then we took a cab to some place in Harlem called a buffet flat, where I drank sidecars, sang with a man in a dress, taunted a douchebag, and watched a fella smoke cigars with his ass."

Irene seemed stricken mute for a moment, and her mouth hung open. "Wait, you're saying there's more that you *can't* remember? Those are just some random highlights?"

Moxie considered exactly how she wanted to say this. "I think I slept with Violet." Irene sat agog and blinked, but said nothing, her face unreadable. When at least a minute of silence passed, Moxie felt compelled to say something else. "Are you okay?"

"You slept with a woman?"

"Maybe?" she replied timidly.

"You aren't certain?"

"I don't remember doing anything with her—well, besides dancing."

Irene appeared confused. "So what makes you think anything else happened?"

"Waking up undressed in her bed, with this note."

Irene took the paper and read it, her lips moving ever so slightly. When she reached the part about the kiss, her eyes opened as big as dinner plates—titillated dinner plates—and her hand flew over her mouth. "Hotchy botchy!" She looked back at Moxie as though she had just suddenly remembered she was there. "Oh, sorry. What's the last thing you remember?"

Moxie closed her eyes to think. "Taking a taxi with Violet after the others all left to go home."

"Did you have clothes on in the taxi?"

"Of course I did. What kind of question is that?"

"I'm trying to piece it together deductively, like Nancy Drew would. So you remember being dressed in a cab with this Violet woman."

"Yes."

"Was she dressed too?"

"Yes."

"Was her tongue in your mouth?"

Moxie scowled. "No." A glimpse of her wrapping her arms around Violet's neck and beckoning her to come closer flickered into her mind, then disappeared again. Had that actually happened? Or had she dreamed it? "Well, not in the taxi."

"But it did happen somewhere?"

"Um…I'm not sure. It seems like I kissed her. We were on the bed, I think."

Irene's eyebrows arched and she fanned herself with the letter. "My goodness. So, how was it?"

Moxie shook her head and ran her hands through her hair. "Considering how blotto I was, I'm figuring it was horrible for her. No wonder she got on that train without even trying to wake me."

Irene cleared her throat. "I meant how it was for you. What was it like?"

"Oh." Moxie stopped to consider that question.

"As in, if you hadn't been lit, do you think that you would've… you know…done it? If you saw her again, what would happen?"

"Are you asking me if I'm a lesbian?"

Irene tried unsuccessfully to look nonchalant. "Nancy Drew would recommend that we stick to the known facts."

Moxie sank into the back of sofa, dejected. "Besides, she left this morning for Hollywood. I'll probably never see her again."

"Hollywood? As in, to make movies?"

"Yes." Moxie wished her mouth didn't taste like wallpaper paste. She pondered why that might be and if she had performed some sordid sex act that had that effect.

"You got nookie from a movie star?" Irene's face lit up.

Moxie was confounded. "Does that change something?"

"You bet your Sapphic ass it does. Now we know a star."

"We?"

"Sure. I mean, why shouldn't something good come of last night?"

"And what *good* are you referring to?"

"Well, everyone in the city says you need to know someone to get a break. Now we do."

Moxie massaged her temples in pain and frustration. "Irene, I need a bath and some time for my head to stop pounding. It would be nice in the meantime if you could stop plotting how to turn my drunken night of lesbian sex with a stranger to your advantage."

"Sorry."

"I doubt Nancy Drew would do that."

"Like in *The Midnight Muff Caper*?"

Moxie groaned and reclined slowly into the sofa cushions. "Remind me to sock you in the jaw when I'm feeling better."

❖

As Moxie started to sing "What'll I Do?" into the microphone, she couldn't help but think of the dance she had shared with Violet as this song played just two nights before. She tried to focus on the lyrics, the low murmur of soft conversation coming from the crowd, the piano—anything besides that provocative memory that gave her a rush of adrenaline.

As she struggled to get past the sad sentiment of love lost, her stomach lurched when she recalled moving slowly against Violet's body. She shut her eyes tight as her mind again wandered to what their night of intimacy must have entailed.

Lyrics, for God's sake—focus on the lyrics. You're performing, after all.

She opened her eyes to look at the patrons. A few tables back she spied Julian, seated with a rather attractive-looking fellow. He nodded at her in recognition and sipped his drink.

When the song ended, the applause was generous.

"Thanks so much," she said. "I'll be back for more soon." She took a few more bows and headed over to Julian's table.

"Hey there, hotsy," he said affably as he motioned for her to join them. "Get that extra set that you wanted?" He motioned for her to sit.

"I did, yes. Just today, actually." She pulled up a chair. "I'm up to three a night now."

"Well, Violet must have more pull than I thought. Gary, this is Moxie, singer extraordinaire. This is Gary, master sodomite."

She examined Gary as she smiled politely. "Nice to meet you." He had chestnut hair and wore spectacles, and his jaw was prominent and chiseled.

"Enchanted," he replied, flashing his perfect white teeth.

Moxie thought she saw Julian's chest swell a bit with pride—having someone so clean-cut and handsome for his date. "What do you mean about Violet having pull? Are you saying she had something to do with it?"

"I know our girl had a chat with the owner about you the other night, to put in a good word. It could just be a coincidence, but I'm sure having a Broadway actress sing your praises can't hurt. Unless, of course, that Broadway actress is Wil." He tapped a cigarette on the back of his hand before lighting it.

She supposed she owed Violet her thanks, if only she was able to tell her. "So where *is* Wil tonight?"

"We just came from seeing her in *Scandals and Lies*. She was very nearly sober—"

"You really had to pay attention to tell that she wasn't," Gary added.

"And she wasn't *completely* unintelligible."

"Oh dear," Moxie said, rubbing her chin. "As good as all that, huh?"

"Which was a profound improvement from last night's show, where she shouted out the word *fuck* when she tripped over a piece of stage furniture."

"An ottoman," Gary said helpfully.

"Inconsequential." Julian waved his hand. "Let us just say that she's still settling into the role, and that may require a bit more time."

Moxie narrowed her eyes. "And is the producer willing to give her this settling-in time?"

Neither man answered right away.

"I suppose we'll see," Julian finally said. "You seem to have fully recovered from the other night." He looked at Gary for a moment. "She bravely decided to go out on the town with Wil, Vi London, and myself. She was a real trouper."

"Yes," she said, with some degree of embarrassment. "I'm sure you'll razz me for this, but yesterday all I managed to swallow was a handful of saltines and some water."

Julian chuckled and shook his head. "But you're better now?"

She knocked on the table. "It's all silk so far."

"Hmm, what you needed was one of Wil's eye-openers," Julian said. "That would have set you straight."

"And what exactly is in her eye-opener?"

Julian began counting on his fingers. "Seltzer, lemon, sugar, and gin."

Gary looked perplexed. "Isn't that a gin fizz?"

"That sounds more like an eye-closer," Moxie said.

"Well, it depends on how many you have. If you have three or less, it's an eye-opener."

"Tell me, Julian," she asked cautiously. "What business are you in that you can see Wil's play every night of the week?"

"I'm a freelance writer." He lightly flicked the ash from his Lucky Strike.

"Which means he's unemployed," Gary said.

"I have a story coming out in *Harper's* next month." His voice dripped with smarmy defensiveness. "So I'm not unemployed. If you're good enough at what you do, you can get by doing a ridiculously negligible amount of work."

Gary squinted at Julian. "Says you. Sounds like laziness to me."

Julian coughed indignantly and stared at Gary for what felt like a very long time. Finally, he turned back to Moxie. "So have you heard from our gal Vi?"

She fought to hide her sudden discomfort. "Nope. Is she in California yet?"

"I don't think she's due to arrive until tomorrow afternoon, but I'm sure she'll be in touch."

"You seem pretty sure of that." She avoided his gaze.

"She seemed dizzy with you, darling. I'm sure you noticed. I mean, you did give her your address and phone number, after all."

Time seemed to come to a screeching halt. "I did?"

❖

Irene ran the scalding iron over the peach skirt that was stretched over the ironing board. "So then the bastard leans his chair backward and tries to grab my costume as we're all starting the finale."

Moxie flipped idly through a movie magazine as she listened to her roommate's story. "No kidding? What did you do?"

"Well, I was already doing a high kick. So I just kicked a little more to the left. I got him right in the jaw."

"Holy Toledo! What happened then?"

"He spat out a little blood and scooted his chair back. I never even missed a beat."

"You slay me, sister," Moxie said appreciatively. "Who knew that being a chorus girl would be such a hazardous job?"

"Well, the owner told me not to kick anyone else in the face. He said it goes against the *highbrow atmosphere* that he's established." She slid the skirt around on the board to iron the other side.

"Then why did he name the place Jughead's Joint? To pull in the opera crowd?"

"And how," Irene replied with a sigh.

There was a knock at the door, and Moxie rose to answer it, not wanting Irene to have to set the hot iron anywhere. Mrs. Bennington, the landlady, stood in the hallway looking irritated.

"Good mor—"

"You got a letter," the woman blurted out between loud hacking. "Here." She pushed an envelope so close to Moxie's face that she reflexively drew back.

"Oh, um, thanks." She took it from Mrs. Bennington, who turned and left with no further pleasantries, the sound of her wet cough echoing down the stairs.

The door shut quietly and Irene mumbled, "She's such a people person. I can see why she chose to be a landlady. Who's it from?" She looked over her shoulder. "Hey, Beethoven, didn't you hear me?"

Moxie stood stunned, staring at the name in the upper corner of the envelope. "It's from Violet."

"Bunk," Irene declared, carrying the iron with her to look over Moxie's shoulder.

Moxie held the letter up to her. "See?"

Irene whistled a low tone. "Let's give it the dust," she said. "Open it."

Moxie took a deep, calming breath, tore it open, and began to read silently.

"If you think you're not going to have to read that out loud, you have another think coming, sister."

Grudgingly, Moxie cleared her throat.

Moxie,

As I write this, Clitty and I are bound for Chicago and hoping you are well and have bounced back from your night of overindulgence. Clitty, cheeky bastard that he is, was concerned that your hangover would be so colossally debilitating that you would be unable to function for days. But I reminded him that he is, after all, a dog, and therefore not an expert on these things, though I'm sure he has seen things that would make some church-going folk spontaneously combust. To his credit, he is very discreet.

With any luck, by the time this reaches you, we'll have arrived in Los Angeles and I'll be on my way to securing a permanent address. Once I have that, I'll send it along to you in the hope that at some point you'll send me a sassy reply.

Let me know if you want any film-star autographs. I imagine I will meet a few celebrities at the studio, though I can't guarantee that any of them will be worth a tinker's damn. (I did promise Clitty that I would help him get a snoot full of Rin Tin Tin, though he may have to settle for Irene Dunne. If so, I would certainly understand his disappointment.)

I've been told that the nightlife in Hollywood makes

New York City seem like a convent, so I can't wait to see how people on the West Coast slowly kill themselves. They say everything out there is grander—so I imagine grand venereal diseases, grand delirium tremens, and an overall grand absence of scruples. How can I possibly be either disappointed or bored?

You know, even though this trip westward makes me feel like I'm on the precipice of something remarkable, I can't seem to reconcile that I felt the same way when I was with you.

Well, I'll sign off before any further confessions are breached. Do take care.

Thinking of you,
Violet

Once Moxie finished reading the letter aloud, she started rereading it to herself.

Irene walked back to her ironing board slowly, as though she were contemplating the contents. "She has a dog named Clitty?"

"Yes."

"Does that mean what I think it does?"

"Yes."

"So one of her clitties talks? Is that something you can shed some more light on?"

Moxie glared at her. "Go climb up your thumb."

Irene just laughed.

CHAPTER THREE

When Violet and Clitty finally disembarked the train in Pasadena, it was early afternoon. She stood on the platform and inhaled the smell of orange groves, unable to remember the last time she was overcome by nature. It certainly wasn't any time in the last six years. She inhaled again. "Well, I'll be damned."

"Miss London?"

She turned and looked over her sunglasses at a short, sweaty man in a white linen suit. "Yes?"

He extended his hand formally. "Shep Abrams—assistant to T. Z. Walter."

"Nice to meet you." She returned his handshake.

"I trust you had a pleasurable trip?" Before she could reply, Shep became completely engrossed in summoning a porter to transport Violet's luggage.

"Are we in a hurry?" His sense of urgency puzzled her.

"*You* are. You need to check into your new apartment, then change and be at Mr. Walter's estate at seven for dinner."

She whistled in surprise. "Anything else I need to squeeze in tonight? Perhaps bake a seven-layer cake? Broker world peace?"

He squinted at her, seemingly caught off guard by her sarcasm. "Hmm" was his only reply.

"Is this a formal dinner?" Violet asked. "I'm not sure I have anything packed that's terribly fancy."

"It's Mr. Walter's standard Tuesday-night dinner party, so it's only semiformal."

This new hectic pace already irritated her. The porter arrived with her trunks stacked on a luggage cart, and she slipped him a healthy tip.

The ride in Shep's roadster from Pasadena to Hollywood lasted forever, and though Violet tried several times to spark healthy discourse, he was not what she would deem a sparkling conversationalist. When she asked about where she would be staying, he merely said, "The Garden of Allah," nothing further. He was probably being sarcastic and could just as easily have said "the moon," "purgatory," or "my ass."

Additional questions yielded one-word answers, including those about his employer or lighthearted inquiries about himself. Exasperated, she gave up and concentrated on the scenery, which really was lovely.

When Shep pulled off Sunset Boulevard into a complex, Violet was stunned to see it actually *was* called the Garden of Allah—a dizzying series of Mediterranean-style bungalows with red tile roofs and an elaborate swimming pool. He informed her that a car would be around to collect her at 6:40, then drove away, leaving her outside the main building with her luggage and her terrier.

Clitty barked sharply as they watched the dust from his wake settle. "I agree, boy. He is a tit-faced bastard."

She turned back to look at the main building, which was a little dark and foreboding for a hotel. Perhaps it would grow on her. She left her trunks where they were, picked up Clitty, and walked into the office.

Inside, a friendly-looking fellow wearing an odd hat of some kind greeted her. As she reached the front desk, she was surprised to see that his headwear was actually a belted sanitary napkin, cocked like a jaunty chapeau.

"Greetings," the man said. "Checking in?"

Violet scrutinized him. He was portly and perhaps in his late forties. More important, he seemed oblivious to the fact that he was sporting a feminine hygiene product on his head as though it were a festive fez. "Um…yes. I am checking in. You work here?" She looked around, hoping someone would appear and explain that this man was an escaped mental patient who had wandered in, or maybe the owner's son who, after haphazardly falling off the roof many years ago, had never been right since.

His pupils dilated, and he excitedly flipped open the register. "Yes, do you have a reservation?"

"Currently, I'm having a number of them."

"What's your name?"

"London."

"Ah, yes. Miss London, you'll be in bungalow eleven."

Before he could start checking her in, a beautiful young woman with dark red hair entered the office. "Hey, Lyle," she said.

Violet was perplexed that the odd headgear didn't seem to faze this young lady. She acted like it was nothing out of the ordinary.

"Afternoon," Lyle answered cordially.

"My fridge is on the blink again," she said, drumming her fingers lightly on the desk.

"What's the problem now?"

"Same as last time. It's not cold inside."

Lyle looked momentarily confused. "You went inside it?"

Again, this show of peculiarity didn't seem to shake the woman. "No, but my corned beef did. It mentioned it in passing."

"I see. I'll try to find the name of that repairman. Excuse me, I'll be right back." He disappeared into a room behind him.

"Should I assume this is his usual state?" Violet asked her. "The sanitary fedora or the talking food don't seem unusual to you?"

"Oh, that's just Lyle," the redhead said calmly. "He's a little daffy sometimes, sure, but he's a good egg. Nothing to worry about."

"So he won't sneak into my bungalow at night and try to make a lampshade out of my lower intestine?"

She smiled. "He may come in and politely *ask* you for your lower intestine, but it would be only in the most courteous way."

"That's good news. I'm Violet London, checking in." She extended her hand and the redhead's strong handshake surprised her.

"Nice to meet you. I'm Ginger Rogers. My mother and I live in bungalow six."

"I'm in eleven."

"Singer?" Ginger raised an eyebrow appraisingly.

"Actress. You?"

"Actress-dancer-singer."

"That certainly improves your odds," Violet said.

"I do whatever it takes. If they told me I needed to learn how to juggle live animals, I'd do that too."

"Well, based on what I've both heard and seen regarding some casting directors, there are those who might consider that live-animal juggling."

"You can say that again, sister."

Violet studied her for a moment. Ginger was striking, and if she had met her a week ago, redheads would no doubt be her new favorite thing. But all she could think about now was Moxie—the way she sang, moved, and looked. "Have you ever considered going blond?"

Ginger seemed to ponder this suggestion. "You think it would make a difference?" She unconsciously ran her hand through her hair.

"It would be very striking with your features."

Lyle appeared from the back with an index card, presumably with the information of the refrigerator repairman on it. "I've got it, Miss Rogers. I'll give him a call presently."

"Thanks, Lyle. You're a doll." She turned to Violet before leaving. "I appreciate the tip. I'll think about it."

"Anytime," Violet replied. Lyle held her key out to her and handed her a sheet of paper. "What's this?"

"The hours and specials of our restaurant. How long will you be staying, Miss London?"

"I'm not sure." She was still wary. "At least five weeks. I'm shooting a picture at Pinnacle."

"That's exciting." He straightened his belted pad so that it tilted even more daringly to the left.

"Yes. Well, thanks. I need to mail a letter." She scrutinized Lyle. "Can you take care of it for me?" She had serious doubts, but Ginger seemed to trust him.

"Absolutely. I just need two cents for the stamp."

After hesitating, Violet produced her letter to Moxie, composed over the last couple days on the train. "Say, what's the address here?"

He flipped a book of matches over and set it in front of her so the address was prominently displayed, and she picked up a pen and wrote her name and the Garden of Allah as her return address on the envelope. "And you're sure you can take care of this for me?" She held the sealed letter out to him.

He nodded violently, and she handed it over in concern, then fished two pennies out of her handbag. "I'll give it my utmost attention," Lyle assured her.

"Can someone get my bags?"

"I'll have the bellboy do it and take them to eleven."

"Wonderful, thank you." She paused on her way to the door. "Lyle, you have a little something right here." She touched her index finger to the left corner of her mouth.

He rapidly produced a handkerchief and wiped his face. "Did that get it?"

"Yes," she lied. "Much better."

"That would have been embarrassing," he said, adjusting his sanitary-pad belt.

"Glad we avoided that!" She saluted him as she turned to leave.

❖

After checking in, Violet unpacked, showered, and changed into a light blue frock. She then fed Clitty and bathed him in the sink, and he was nearly dry when she heard a car pull up outside. Thankfully a well-built chauffer driving a red Cadillac Fleetwood appeared, rather than monosyllabic Shep.

He opened the rear door for her, and she and Clitty bounded into the backseat. "How are you?" she asked as he nodded politely, closing the door.

He slid into the driver's seat and started to pull out into the street. "Does Mr. Walter live far from here?"

"His home is up in the Hollywood Hills."

"Uh…and where are we now?"

"Sherman. Don't worry, it's not far."

As the car wended its way into the hills, dusk began to settle over the scenery, and Violet took it all in with moderate awe. Everything she had seen of California so far was impressive, and the beauty of the undeveloped hills certainly fell into that category too. She had never lived outside the city, and so much unspoiled countryside made her feel as though she were in a foreign land.

How high would this winding road take her? They seemed to have been heading straight up for quite some time. At a certain point, the dirt road led them to a set of elaborate, heavy iron gates with a large filigree *W* inscribed into them.

"Does the *W* stand for 'What the hell?'" she joked.

"Close."

"You fellas aren't big on the chitchat out here, I'm noticing."

He glanced in the rearview mirror and their eyes met for a moment. "We're the hired help, miss."

"What's your name?"

"Fitzhugh." He slowly pulled up the long, circular driveway.

"Well, Fitzy, don't let them treat you like shit. I have yet to see money make someone a better person. In fact, it seems to do the opposite."

He politely declined to comment as they slowed to a halt in front of a massive Tudor-style mansion. He exited and came around to open her door.

Clitty trotted out and went to sniff the grass, and Violet rose and stepped out. When Fitzhugh refused to make eye contact with her, she kissed him quickly on the cheek.

He smiled ever so slightly. "Don't let him get the better of you, miss," he whispered.

"No chance of that, Fitzy."

She approached the mammoth double doors, scooping her dog into her arms on the way up the steps. Before she could ring the bell, the wood creaked open and an older, balding butler appeared.

"Please enter, miss," he croaked.

"Thanks."

"Mr. Walter is entertaining in the parlor. Follow me."

She did so, scowling at his humorless demeanor. She hoped this wouldn't be the general mood of the evening, but she supposed they could be as grim as they pleased. That certainly didn't mean that she had to be that way too.

At the butler's direction, she entered and he announced her arrival loudly. Three people sat inside the lavishly decorated room, drinks in their hands. One she immediately recognized as an actress—a petite ingénue who was a crowd favorite. The other two were unfamiliar gentlemen.

"Hello," Violet said, approaching them. She set Clitty down on the rug.

"Hi there, I'm Sylvia King," the woman said, rising. She wore a shiny cream-colored silk gown and held a long ebony cigarette holder in one hand and a glass of booze in the other. "This is director Henry Childs, and this is the leading man of my next picture, Rex Kelly."

Violet nodded politely. "Nice to meet you all."

"Goodness," Sylvia said. "Is that your little dog?"

"Actually," Violet replied, "he's the talent. I'm just tagging along."

"Oh?" Rex asked curiously.

"He's a ventriloquist," she answered. "He's actually doing all the talking. I'm just moving my mouth." She walked over to the bar and poured herself a drink.

Rex appeared offended. Sylvia looked confused and kept glancing back and forth between Violet and Clitty. Henry was the only one of her three new consorts who looked amused at all.

She took a sip of scotch and sighed. This might prove to be a very long evening.

"Not so fast," Henry said, approaching her and pointing at her with his cigar. "I saw you on Broadway in *The Green Hat*. You were wonderful."

"Thanks. And I saw your film *Never Too Late*, which was marvelous."

"Ooh," Sylvia said shrilly. "A *Broadway* actress. Well, la-di-da."

Violet looked at her and blinked. "And I saw you in *The Foreign Legionnaire*. You should probably stick to comedies."

"What?" Sylvia barked, her once-delicate face now twisted into an angry sneer.

"Just my opinion, dear," Violet said, feigning a smile. "You have such a comic gift."

Henry tried to stifle his laughter with his martini glass.

Before anyone else could comment, T. Z. Walter swept into the room, wearing a monogrammed maroon smoking jacket. "Ah, I see you've all been getting acquainted."

He looked like Violet had imagined him—stout, spotty, and balding. She also assumed he was one of those men who felt that scads of money would counteract any and all shortcomings and character flaws.

"Good evening, T. Z.," Sylvia cooed, her anger instantly replaced with consummate bootlicking. "It's swell to see you." She kissed him on the cheek.

"Sylvia, you're looking lovely tonight." His eyes traveled to Violet. "You must be Violet London."

"I am," she replied with a genial smile.

"I hope you're worth what we're paying you," he said, snorting in amusement.

Violet's inclination toward pleasantries quickly evaporated.

Sylvia rolled her eyes. "If it's more than a nickel and a stick of Juicy Fruit gum, I'd say you got rooked, T. Z."

Violet fixed her with a look of utter insincerity. "Everything they say about you is true. What a pity."

Rex exhaled cigarette smoke through an expression of derision. "Be happy you don't have any scenes with her where you have to pretend to be in love with her."

"Thanks for the perspective," Violet said.

T. Z. was clearly amused. "Are we ready for dinner?"

Violet's host certainly wasn't very interested in keeping the peace. "If it's going to move this evening along, then absolutely."

As they walked to the dining room, T. Z. noticed the terrier following Violet closely. "What's your dog's name?"

"Clitty."

He looked baffled. "That's an unusual name. Is it Norwegian?"

"Yes, it is. He's half elkhound, actually."

T. Z. cocked an eyebrow. "Really?"

These people were so wonderfully gullible. "On his father's side. His mother was a hamster." She paused for effect. "It was a very difficult breeding, as you can imagine. A bit like trying to thread a needle with a sausage."

All three gentlemen laughed, but Sylvia crinkled up her nose in disgust. "Animals are filthy."

"Yes," Violet replied. "But we'll let you eat with us anyway."

"T. Z., are you going to let this guttersnipe speak to me like that?" Her hands moved to her hips indignantly as she reached the dining-room table.

"If the conversation stays this funny, I will."

Sylvia looked upset, but clearly not enough to challenge the head of the studio. She meekly sat and spread her linen napkin across her lap.

A server appeared and began pouring wine for everyone.

"So, Violet," Henry said. "I'll be directing you in *Manhattan Rhapsody* come next week."

That was the best news she had received since she arrived in California. Henry was the least offensive person in the room. "That sounds wonderful. I assume the male lead has been cast."

"We tried to get Gary Cooper, but he was already committed to another picture."

Violet breathed a small sigh of relief. Cooper's acting was rather wooden and stilted, and a production was only as good as the weakest link. She didn't need to be filming the majority of her scenes with someone whose acting might distract her from her own performance. After all, she had a lot riding on this first film. "So who did you get?"

"Rex here," T. Z. answered.

"What?" Sylvia looked very unhappy. "Rex is supposed to be filming *Love Comes Running* with me in two weeks." She looked across the table at the actor. "Rex? Do you know anything about this?"

He gazed back at her through half-lidded eyes and sipped his glass of wine. He appeared to loathe her, and Violet understood that feeling completely.

"Rex?" she implored again. "Answer me."

"Sylvia," T. Z. said, ringing the bell to signify they were ready for the first course. "Rex will make *Manhattan Rhapsody* with Violet."

She looked as though she would weep. "So who's starring in *Love Comes Running* with me?"

"Frank Thatcher," T. Z. said calmly. The server appeared and started ladling out creamy bisque.

"Frank Thatcher?" she snapped. "That mook? He looks like a harelip troll!"

Violet was amazed at how this young woman carried on. The New York theater scene would swallow her alive. "Now, now. I'm sure poor Frank is just as unhappy about the whole thing as you are, Sylvia. Have a little sympathy."

Sylvia's eyes flashed. "Look here—"

T. Z. calmly held his palm up. "Sylvia, you'll make this picture with Frank. That's how it will be. And if I say you'll do thirty more with Frank, you'll do that too. Now eat your goddamned soup."

The air was filled with nothing but the sounds of clinking spoons on china and slurping. Violet grinned mischievously. "This is *good*," she said, pretending to be talking about the soup.

❖

As the butler held open the front door, Rex, Henry, and Violet, with terrier in tow, walked outside.

"So, Rex," Violet said, "I suppose I'll see you at the studio in the morning for wardrobe fittings."

Rex blew cigarette smoke out his nostrils and tossed the lit butt on the ground. "Yes."

Sylvia walked briskly past them all, clearly still irritated. "Well, enjoy that. Good night." She stepped into her waiting car, and they watched it drive away down the winding road.

"What an absolute festering cunt," Violet said, unable to keep her feelings to herself any longer.

Henry chuckled. "She's just as pleasant to direct, let me tell you."

"Whenever I have to kiss her," Rex added, turning up the collar of his jacket against the evening breeze, "I imagine that I'm actually strangling her. It makes being that close to her much more bearable."

"You're my hero," Violet said, brushing his shoulder.

For the first time all evening, Rex smiled.

"We should have a good time on this picture," Henry said, walking toward his car. "I'll see you at the studio in the morning and give you the newest revision of the script, Violet."

"See you then."

Rex walked to where his driver stood with the car door propped open. "Good night."

She strolled over to Fitzhugh, who dutifully stood near the Fleetwood. "I understand you are to be my driver, Fitzy. You didn't tell me that."

"Yes, miss." He closed the car door once she and Clitty were safely inside. "I work for the studio, and you're my assignment. So I'll be chauffeuring you around until they tell me otherwise." He got into the front seat and started the car.

"Good. I have to be at the studio at nine in the morning."

"Very well," he said, pulling out slowly from the circular drive into the street. "What time shall I collect you?"

"How about seven thirty?"

She could see his look of confusion in the rearview mirror. "The studio is closer than that, miss."

"Call me Vi, Fitzy. I was thinking we could stop somewhere and have breakfast on the way."

"Breakfast?"

She took a deep breath. "Look, it seems I'm in for one hell of a roller-coaster ride. It would be nice to have someone come along with me."

The silence was palpable as he maneuvered the hilly dirt road.

"There's a little place right up the road from where you're staying that poaches a mean egg," he said softly.

"Sounds wonderful. Now let's talk about where to find some booze."

CHAPTER FOUR

Violet's first day at the studio was tiring, but interesting. Henry, true to his word, delivered a finalized script to her just after she arrived. And praise the gods that he had, because she had so much downtime in between the wardrobe fittings and the hair and makeup tests that she was well on her way to memorizing most of it.

Fitzy had dropped her back off at the Garden of Allah in the late afternoon, and while he was apparently warming to her, he was still far too concerned with propriety and decorum—two words that Violet had little use for.

Oh, her family had tried to get her to curb her natural enthusiasm for both eccentricity and the consecrated wonder that is the female breast, to settle into a life of mundane heterosexual tedium. They had put a great deal of effort into that endeavor, but had ultimately failed. Both of her parents had made it abundantly clear that while she continued to indulge in what they deemed her unholy excesses, they would neither accept nor acknowledge her.

They had magnanimously appended their condemnation by assuring her that once she repented and came crawling back, ready to renounce her religion—Our Lady of the Miraculous Jugs—and her lifestyle, and accept instead their more upstanding credo filled with temperance, obedience, and feigned orgasms, they would again welcome her into their home. What a horrible fucking place to live. She shuddered at the thought of returning.

Bored by the script and craving something engaging, she walked Clitty around the grounds. Ginger was playing Ping-Pong by the pool with another young woman.

Violet waited until the point was over. "Hi, Ginger. Are you winning?"

"Hey, Violet. I am now. This is Mabel, from bungalow fifteen. Mabel, this is Violet London."

"Nice to meet you," Mabel said with minor interest.

"You playing the winner?" Ginger asked.

"Hmm, I suppose it's not bad exercise." Violet spoke her thought aloud.

"I'm working up a sweat," Mabel complained.

"Then it's definitely out," Violet said. "The last time I did something that was good for me, I regretted it for weeks. I'll just watch from an unhealthy distance, thanks."

"Suit yourself." Ginger served the ball.

Violet ambled over to the very large and odd-shaped swimming pool and tried to make out what it resembled. She tilted her head to the side as she took it in.

"It's supposed to be the Black Sea," someone behind her said. She turned to see a man lying in a deck chair by the pool regarding her with what seemed to be amusement. He looked to be of an imposing stature, but reclined as he was, he was anything but. His terry-cloth robe was pulled closed tight, all the way to his neck.

"And how do you know that?" She took a few steps closer to him.

"The woman who had it built told me." He sipped something from a martini glass. "Do you know who that is?"

She shook her head.

"Alla Nazimova."

Violet studied his elaborately waxed mustache as it curved upward in a friendly way. She was both impressed and surprised to hear the name of such a renowned thespian. "Really?"

"It's true. This used to be her home. When she went broke in the Crash, she sold it and they turned it into a hotel."

Violet mulled on that notion for a moment, saying nothing.

"You can walk all the way over here," he said, apparently mistaking her silence for apprehension. "I'm quite harmless."

"That's what they all say." Violet raised an eyebrow. "I'm beginning to question whether anyone in Hollywood is harmless." She closed the distance between them.

"Well, luckily you have a guard dog with you."

Violet glanced at Clitty, who had chosen that very moment to sit rather indelicately on her left foot and stare up at her adoringly. "He's not my guard dog. He's my agent. He told me to pack up my things and head west, and here I am."

"You always take his advice?"

"Absolutely. He hasn't steered me wrong yet, unless you count the time he talked me into perpetrating the St. Valentine's Day massacre. That may have been a little"—she stopped and whispered the rest, as though to be discreet—"well, heavy-handed, if you ask me."

He smiled. "You know, I do remember thinking that those killings were so dark and grisly that only a woman could have committed them."

"Someone sounds married." She sat on the deck chair beside him.

He sighed. "Guilty as charged. Peter Easton." He offered his hand.

"Violet London, and this is Clitty."

"So not only is he a very sadistic dog, but he's a naughty one as well." He rubbed the dog between the ears.

"I actually may have him beat in the *naughty* arena, but we try not to be too competitive. So you live here with your wife?"

His expression immediately darkened. "Good Lord, no. Hollywood is a cesspool of sin and depravity. My wife and children are back in Boston, amongst good God-fearing folk."

"But the sin and depravity—"

"Are just fine for me, yes. Martini?" He pointed to a cocktail shaker beside him and a couple of empty glasses on a tray.

"Love one, thanks. What is it that you do out here, Mr. Easton?"

He shook the concoction, poured the chilled liquid into a glass, and offered it to her. "I have the dubious distinction of being a screenwriter. My *raison d'être* is taking an abysmal script and making it borderline mediocre."

"Hmm, I may have seen a few of the films you've worked on, as they were all exceedingly mediocre." She took a sip of her drink and gasped. "Great grandmother's balls! This may be the driest martini I've ever had. Have you ever heard of a little thing called vermouth?"

"I've always been of the mindset that the proper ratio of vermouth to gin is achieved by running one's hand over the label on the vermouth bottle just prior to filling the glass fully with gin."

"Then why call it a martini?"

"My good woman, a martini is a drink of distinction, while gin is something slurped noisily by hobos and bootleggers."

"By that logic, why not just refer to what you're drinking as the queen's vagina? That sounds frightfully regal and is almost *never* slurped noisily by hobos or bootleggers."

He looked at her, his eyes filled with laughter. "Then the queen's vagina it shall be. I'm having a party in my bungalow this evening, which makes it much like every other evening. Perhaps you'd like to stop in and enjoy the queen's vagina with us."

"Mr. Easton, how can I turn down an offer of such prim grandeur? I haven't tasted the queen's vagina in days."

"Splendid. I'm in bungalow sixteen. I hope to see you this evening, and frequently after that."

Violet liked this man quite a bit. "I believe that can be arranged."

❖

Moxie shuffled up the steps to her apartment building, utterly exhausted. It was after three in the morning, and she had sung her ass off all night. She unlocked the front door as quietly as she could and slipped through the darkened communal parlor.

The only people permitted to live at Mrs. Bennington's building were unmarried women, a rule she made very clear when Moxie moved in. About sixteen of them resided there, all aspiring actresses, singers, and dancers of some kind. Some were earning their way as waitresses or cigarette girls until they could get a paying gig, so Moxie felt fortunate to have even secured a job singing.

The one thing Mrs. Bennington wasn't too picky about, however, was the hours people kept. So as long as Moxie didn't wake anyone, she could come and go as she pleased.

She paused at the foot of the staircase before beginning her long, tiring journey to the fourth floor. As she stepped, she tried to avoid creaky areas and was fairly pleased that she was, for the most part, successful. Finally at her apartment door, she unlocked it and opened it slowly, in an attempt not to wake Irene.

The dim light from the hallway cast a faint glow into the darkened room. On the small dinette table a few feet in front of her she saw a letter, and her mind lurched for an instant. Could it possibly be from Violet?

She turned on a small lamp and closed the door behind her, striding to the table to examine it. Her name was on the front, written in Violet's ornate handwriting, and she couldn't fight the broad smile that came over her as she tried to open the envelope as silently as humanly possible.

This letter was longer than the last, and Moxie sat excitedly at the table and angled herself so that the dim beam from the lamp shone directly onto the paper.

Moxie,

Greetings from the westward-bound Chief. I believe as I write this, I am somewhere outside of Kansas City, but I'm not completely certain.

How is life treating you? I do hope things are going well at the Luna for you.

By the time you receive this missive, I'll be thoroughly ensconced in the Hollywood zeitgeist, though I plan to keep my eyes open and my mouth shut (as opposed to keeping my mouth open and my eyes shut, which is a much more common way to work your way to the top in this industry but, sadly, just not my style).

Actually, come to think of it, I've never been terribly good at the mouth-shutting part, but as I get older, I am getting better at the part where I at least regret whatever I just said that was either very inappropriate, scandalously untoward, or, in some particularly candid moments when the planets are aligned, both of those things. Remorse must count for something, right? Perhaps not enough to negate the verbal atrocity, but it's certainly better than nothing, I would think.

I have to say that I am finding rail travel particularly tedious. For example, no one has publicly launched anything from their anus this entire trip, though, for a time yesterday in the dining car, it did sound as if an elderly man a few tables over was making a valiant attempt to. Nor has anyone engaged in any type of spectator sex act, not even the garden-variety, humdrum, man/woman kind.

The people onboard seem quite dour, actually. This morning at breakfast, I sat with a woman who for some reason did not want to hear my story about the night that Wil got so drunk that when she was overcome inextricably in a fit of laughter and unable to catch her breath, she peed herself. The woman just kept mumbling something into her pancake stack and asking me to be quiet. I found it all exceptionally rude, as I hadn't even reached the part about her stripping down naked and trying to play the spoons with her ass cheeks, which really is the highlight of that story, as you can probably well imagine. The ass is, after all, a remarkable piece of engineering, but its musicality lies elsewhere. It's simply not designed to play the spoons—or even the tuba, for that matter.

Clitty, however, seems to be taking this high-speed jaunt in stride. He has gone out of his way to try to make eye contact with every poor bastard in the dining car every time we pass through, in the hopes that they will share a morsel with him. I swear to God, earlier today I could have sworn I saw him suck in his cheeks in a superficial attempt to look like a hungry stray. When no one fell for his ploy, he promptly shat, as though editorializing what was clearly the breakfast of the walking dead. I, for one, applauded him.

Goodness, there has been a great deal of ass-talk in this letter. I would apologize for it, but upon rereading, those seem to be the best parts. Instead, I'll advise you to wallow in the delicious assiness of this correspondence. Let it enfold you in its warm embrace.

Have you noticed that I'm just prattling on about nothing now? When all sense and courtesy should have dictated that I close this letter long before the mention of public sex acts, asses playing tubas, or Clitty's act of civil disobedience, I clearly chose to continue.

Why, you ask? Well, I suppose that I'm having a hard time telling you good-bye.

Since I left New York, our communication has been, by necessity, one-way. I'll not mail this without including my new address on the envelope, in the hopes that you've been thinking of me even a fraction of the amount that I've been reflecting on both you and the night we met.

If you haven't been, and if my letters to you have become a nuisance, this is your chance to say so. I won't contact you again unless I first hear from you. If you want to continue this correspondence and see where it may take us, you need only reply to this letter. To be certain, I would be elated if you chose to do so.

I do miss the sound of your voice and the gentle ease of your laughter. I hope to hear from you soon.

Violet

Moxie set the letter down as she finished reading and stared for a moment at the wall. What the hell was happening? Why was she so euphoric to hear from Violet?

She had, after all, spent only one evening in this woman's company. It wasn't as though they had known each other for years.

She drifted back to that night, now exactly a week ago. In fact, it was probably right around this time of morning when they had…well, when they had done whatever it was that they did.

Moxie flinched again at the realization. She had mentally pictured every imaginable sexual act and position, trying to spark some shred of a memory from that evening. Honestly, she was a little concerned at how much time she was spending pondering that event. Her imagination lingered there more and more.

She closed her eyes to replay a few of her favorite scenes. She imagined Violet over her, undressing her as their mouths met hungrily.

In a flash, they were both naked and glistening with sweat as Moxie rode Violet, their bodies moving rhythmically and with tremendous urgency.

Another flash and Moxie was lying on the bed, her legs dangling over the side, as Violet knelt on the floor before her, bringing her to climax with the prowess of her nimble mouth.

Her eyes flew open as her own carnal visions shocked her back into reality.

"Christ," she whispered, putting her face in her hands. She was becoming an emotional mess. True, those thoughts highly aroused her, and she was slowly beginning to accept that fact. But these ruminations had begun to intrude frequently into her consciousness, and they were astoundingly distracting.

She had always been a romantic and had cared more for love than for sex. It was just unfortunate that love had never happened—nothing beyond fleeting infatuation or fancy. Perhaps she had sabotaged herself with her natural standoffishness. But despite her reclusive disposition, Moxie had never wanted anything as much as she had wanted to be cherished.

Instead, Moxie had been an object of lust. The dates in her past had been filled with stilted conversation, punctuated by awkward sexual fumbling. In fact, her minor experiences with sex didn't merit any fantasies or daydreams. They simply hadn't been that great. Now she found herself compulsively cycling through various erotic mental interludes with a woman she had spent only a matter of hours with. It was as though Violet had turned on a switch somewhere inside her.

If only she could remember what they did when they slept together. At least then, she wouldn't have to speculate. What if she continued to guess like this? Soon she'd be imagining one of them bound and swinging from a chandelier while the other smeared her own body with maple syrup and Sen-Sen.

She closed her eyes to mull on this scene further, then slapped her forehead in irritation. She cursed this new low threshold for titillation she had developed.

Picking up the letter, she began to read it again. She chuckled as she counted just how many references to ass there *had* been in the letter, and she let it enfold her in its warm embrace—well, as much as that was possible.

She examined the return address that looked to be hastily scrawled.

"The Garden of Allah," she muttered. What an intriguing name. She brushed the lettering with her fingers and contemplated what would happen if she did reply to Violet, as well as what would happen if she didn't.

CHAPTER FIVE

Violet poured brandy, triple sec, and lemon juice into a cocktail shaker over ice, covered it, and shook it vigorously.

"Good Lord, Vi," Peter said. "You're not mixing that drink, you're thrashing it."

She poured the frothy concoction into a glass. "I like my sidecars somewhat demoralized."

"Exactly how I like my women," Peter murmured into his gin.

"That says so much about you."

Fitzhugh sat in a chair in the corner of Peter's bungalow, smoking a cigar with great zeal, and Violet turned her attention to him. "Did you want a refill, Fitzy? I made plenty." She rattled the ice in the shaker at him as an added temptation.

"I don't think so, Vi," he answered. "Any more of those, and I won't be able to drive the car back."

"Fair enough." She stepped away from Peter's makeshift yet fully stocked bar and took a seat in the armchair between them, feeling momentarily pleased with herself. In ordinary circumstances, these two men would probably never have drinks together, but now, thanks to her, the class system was momentarily suspended. Violet always liked things best when everyone was on equal footing. She had been in town for just under two weeks, and she already felt like the great regulator. "So, Peter, did you actually go to work today?"

"I did. You'd have been proud of me." He looked out the window at the last vestiges of sunlight hanging in the sky. "But of course it just brought regret."

"What happened?" Fitzhugh asked, leaning forward.

"You'll never believe the script I've been assigned. It's a complete travesty."

"*The House at Pooh Corner*?" Violet asked.

"If only it were that good. They have given me *Husbands and Wives*, apparently the next vehicle for William Haines. I'm just not sure if he's cast as a husband or a wife. I'll have to march in tomorrow and tell them I won't do it."

Violet's good humor started to fade. "Why on earth not?"

"Please, Vi, the man's a degenerate. I won't be able to write dialogue that's supposed to come out of his mouth. God only knows what, or who, he's had in there."

She blinked at him for a moment and drew in a deep breath. "You complete fucking hypocrite."

He appeared stunned. "What?"

She looked to Fitzhugh, whose expression had rapidly changed to alarm and concern. He'd just have to be concerned, damn it. "Peter, do you really think you have the moral high ground here? Let me make sure that I have the complete picture. You sit here in this bungalow, living the life of a bachelor, with your dick in every mid-priced whore and naïve starlet who's simple enough to believe your empty promises of furthering her career, and you—*you* dare judge someone? With your wife and children sequestered three thousand miles away and your liver full of gin, you honestly hold your lifestyle superior to a homosexual's? You think you're too good to write for someone because of the kind of sex he has? Let me explain a few things to you, Mr. Easton. It would benefit you to start measuring people by the things that really matter. Are they honest? Compassionate? Trustworthy? Or are they bigoted, close-minded, and cruel?"

She stood, setting her drink on the coffee table gently and straightening her dress with her palms. Clitty rose too, poised to go wherever she did.

"Vi—" Peter began.

"Mull on that." Her extended palm signaled that she was done listening to him. "And do make sure you take into account that, by your definition, I too am a degenerate and apparently therefore worthy of your scorn and derision. So go ahead, but I refuse to sit here for it."

She strode to the door and opened it. "I hope to see you bright and early Monday morning, Fitzy. Good night, gentlemen."

The door shut softly, leaving the two men to ponder her disclosure.

As Violet walked rapidly back to her place, she was livid, completely incensed that someone she had been developing such a pleasant friendship with had said something so callous and intolerant. She wished she had shouted everything she had just said, but that wasn't in her. When she was happy, she was lighthearted and calm. When she was angry, she was stoic and grave.

She did possess the passion to really scream at someone. Somewhere along the line, no doubt amongst the many altercations with her parents, she had learned that it was better to simply shut down emotionally and walk away. That was how she was able to deal with most things. To become enraged would give people power over her. To look them squarely in the eye, tell them "bullshit," and then leave gave her the upper hand.

As she entered her bungalow, she saw a piece of mail had been slipped under the door. A closer look revealed it was from Moxie, and she was unable to suppress a smile. "Your timing's getting a whole lot better, toots."

She sat on the sofa, and Clitty jumped up to sit beside her. Slowly, she slid her finger under the envelope flap and prepared herself for whatever Moxie had decided to write.

Violet,

To say that I've thought about writing you a hundred times may be an understatement, so let's agree that the number is somewhere between a hundred and five thousand. Every time I considered not replying to your last letter, I experienced an overwhelming sadness. And every time I considered replying, I wondered what I would say and exactly what it would mean.

The truth is that I want very much to correspond with

you. I love getting your letters. I've never really received mail before so, yes, it has a certain novelty. But the stories of your comically tawdry exploits must unquestionably surpass what passes for a standard letter these days.

This may shock you, but most of us just muddle through our lives without a constant parade of anal artists, public fornicators, ass musicians, and pancake-eating corpses vying for our attention. I'm still not certain exactly what quality you possess that attracts these kinds of people, but it wouldn't be truthful if I said that I didn't find it fascinating, in a bizarre, carnival-sideshow sort of way.

I suppose I should try and catch you up on things here. Julian has started coming into the Luna a couple times a week. He's almost always on the arm of a fella named Gary, who's fairly easy on the eyes.

According to Julian, Wil is a hair's breadth away from getting canned from _Secrets and Lies_. Apparently her drinking (and God only knows what else) is becoming increasingly detrimental to her performance. She drinks to steel her nerves, does poorly because she's sozzled, and then gets even more nervous for the next night's performance, so she has a little more. I don't know if you've spoken with her since your arrival in California, but perhaps you could contact her and offer her some consolation or advice. It's ironic that a woman who seemed so self-possessed when I met her can deep down be filled with such self-doubt.

I got my third set at the Luna, and I hear that I may

have you to thank for that. I appreciate anything you may have told my boss to make him consider it. So far, things are going well. While I'm busy now, and the money's better, I worry that I may be running myself ragged. Cotton, my agent, says he's trying to get someone from the Kasbah to come out to see me perform in the hopes that I can transition from upscale juice joint to upscale supper club. It would be fantastic if that happened, if just for the shift in clientele— to work for people who weren't <u>necessarily</u> criminals. After the supper club, who knows? Perhaps I could even put out a record.

For the first time I'm starting to feel like my life may not have limits. Things are really looking up for me, and somehow meeting you seems to be a part of that sensation— perhaps the catalyst.

I do think of you, quite a bit, and I recall our night on the town every day in some fashion or another. I'd be a fool to say that I completely understand my feelings for you, but I do know that somewhere mixed in with the trepidation, anxiety, and confusion is a good deal of appreciation, elation, and amusement.

In no way could I consider you a nuisance. There is a strange void that your letters somehow help to fill. They make me laugh and feel significant, so please keep writing them.

Tell me how the film is going and how your co-stars are. How has Clitty been enjoying it out there? (I mean the dog.) Have you been able to convince the powers that *be to modify the ending? When might you be coming back to New York? Anytime soon?*

Well, I'll close this. I'm apparently finally running out of words.

Regards,
Genitalia Finkelstein

Violet sighed and leaned back on the sofa. "Clitty, I'm falling in love with this woman." She reached over and scratched his back. "What the hell am I going to do?"

❖

After Violet mailed her reply to Moxie, she and Clitty spent some quality time playing fetch amongst the jacaranda trees outside her bungalow.

In her peripheral vision, she saw Peter approaching her, and she sighed loudly, not wanting to reopen that particular can of worms.

"Vi?"

She turned to him, feeling a mixture of irritation and dread.

"Pardon me," he said softly. His eyes nervously darted from her face to the ground and back again. "I need to get this off my chest. You owe me nothing, but I'd appreciate it if you'd let me apologize."

She took the ball from Clitty and tossed it again, and the little dog took off after it. "Give it a try. I'm mildly curious."

"Thank you. First, let me say that I have never felt quite so small as I did after you left last night. I've always considered myself to be both liberal and humane, and you showed me that I am neither. If I made you feel ashamed, I'm sorry."

She squinted at him as Clitty dropped the ball at her feet. "I don't feel ashamed, Peter. That seems to be the critical point you're missing." She threw the toy back out past the trees. "I don't have anything to feel ashamed about."

"Yes—"

"Shame should be reserved for occasions when you've hurt

someone. I'm just living. I don't have time to worry about what some homespun, folksy neighbors think about my choices. I mean, God only knows who's sucking Pastor Stevenson's cock when his wife is at the temperance meetings, and who's spanking the schoolmarm with a steel-wire brush. What even remotely gives them the right to judge me?"

He cleared his throat nervously. "I have worded it poorly."

"You have, yes."

"What I meant was that I had no right to say such things, to belittle you in that way."

"Agreed, though obviously it's not just me who's belittled. It's everyone who gets lumped into a category for one thing or another and then treated like utter shit for it."

"Understood. I am very sorry. I behaved terribly."

"I mean, how would you feel if everyone judged you because of your dreadful mustache?"

"I love my mustache," he said softly, beginning to stroke it gingerly with both hands.

"And as a consenting adult, you should be permitted to do so in the privacy of your own home, without anyone casting aspersions on you for it."

He seemed to relax slightly at her humor. "You really think it's dreadful?"

"It resembles the tightly packed bundles that Clitty pushes through his colon. But I only share that observation because you asked. I'm far too polite to simply volunteer something so tactless."

"Clearly." He paused. "Can I buy you a drink, Vi? Make it up to you?"

She smiled. "I believe you may, sir."

❖

Cotton took a long drag on his cigar. "Look, this is no easy feat, kid."

Moxie looked at him closely, in the hopes of determining if he was lying. "But it's just taking so long. I mean, how much coercion does it take to get a fella to go see a show? It's not like you're trying to talk him into castration."

"Shh." Cotton brought his flattened hand down slowly, signaling for her to lower her voice.

Moxie looked around the parlor of her apartment building where they sat. No one nearby seemed to be paying them any attention whatsoever. Was this one of Cotton's many ploys to regain control of the conversation? "What?"

"Look, you act like I haven't been on my dogs all day and night working to get you places. I got you that third set at the Luna, didn't I?"

She studied him suspiciously. "Hmm, how'd you do that, anyway?"

"With my nose to the grindstone, that's how. I campaigned for weeks on your behalf with the management there. They didn't tell you?"

"Must have slipped their minds," Moxie said in a monotone. The more Cotton talked, the more she wished he'd stop, and the less she tended to believe him.

"Look, I've got Brown's word that he'll be by the Luna to see one of your sets next Saturday. He's going to be out of town this coming weekend. That's the only reason this is taking so long."

"Okay, Cotton. I'll be ready for him." She was starting to wonder if getting the manager of the Kasbah to come by and see her perform would ever happen, and she was quickly tiring of this conversation with her self-congratulatory agent. Cotton represented a number of people now, and he had more clients to consider than just her. But lately, even though he seemed to be putting less effort into her career, he still managed to take credit for anything good that came her way.

"Make sure you wear a fancy dress that knocks him on his ass."

"How fancy?"

"As high class as you can stand, sister. You've got to really get all dolled up, you know? You need to *look* upscale if you want an upscale gig."

Now she was officially irritated. "I don't look upscale?"

"You look like a singer in a gin joint. You need to seem like you just dropped in from a swanky dinner party at a Manhattan penthouse, like you shit diamonds."

"And will you be fronting me the jack for said diamond-shitting dress?"

He looked put out. "What, you can't borrow one from someone? There must be fifty dames living here with you."

She sighed. "Sure, Ebenezer. I'll just ask the countess on the third floor if I can borrow her tiara while I'm at it."

Mrs. Bennington approached her, making a disgustingly vile sound as she snorted something from her sinuses into her mouth. Moxie tried to ignore it.

"You got another letter," she rasped, tossing the envelope into Moxie's lap where she sat on the divan.

"Thanks," she murmured, though the woman had already turned to leave.

Cotton's brow furrowed. "Who is that from?"

She smiled as she regarding the writing on the outside. "A friend of mine out West."

"Since when do you have friends out West?"

"Why do you want to know? So you can figure out what I can borrow from her? Want me to see if she has some upscale shoes?"

He rolled his eyes. "You know, I don't get any kind of gratitude from you. If it wasn't for me, you'd be mopping up urine in a clip joint in the middle of nowhere." He expelled cigar smoke dramatically.

Moxie was no longer interested in this conversation. She had a letter to read, after all. She decided to just skip to the end of this all-too-familiar conversation in order to speed things along. "Yes, Cotton. You are wonderful yet I mistreat you. I am a selfish bitch, and you ejaculate rainbows. I get it."

He stared at her. "Ejaculate rainbows?"

"Or something like that, yes. I'll find something to wear before next Saturday." She stood and kissed him on the cheek. "Thanks for stopping by." She scurried up the staircase, leaving him alone in the parlor looking completely bewildered.

Once she was contained within the relative safety of her apartment, she opened the letter.

Miss Genitalia (Genny) Finkelstein,

I received your letter tonight and I was touched and delighted by both the gesture, as well as the sentiment within. I've been holding my breath since I mailed that last letter to you, wondering if I would hear back. And while things have obviously progressed here—the shooting is more than half completed now—with regard to you, time has stood still for me.

So let me catch you up on the last couple of weeks here in Hollywood. The accommodations that the studio arranged for me are a perfect match—private bungalows nestled amidst nature and lunatics, which happen to be two of my favorite things to sit and observe.

The front desk is diligently manned by Captain Napkin, as I call him, and I'm sure that over the phone, without any visual cues, he may come off as only slightly deranged. Good for him that he doesn't allow his dementia to interfere with his conscientiousness. He is a very hard worker; it's just that sometimes his "work" includes wearing menstrual accoutrement on his head or periodically liberating pieces of garbage from the residents' trash, burying them in shallow graves, and performing tiny funerals. I caught him saying a few words over an empty anchovy tin and some coffee grounds the other day.

Incidentally, I don't know what you mean when you say that I attract odd and eccentric people. Perhaps you can provide an example?

Other residents here have shown themselves to be both kind and unkind to varying degrees, which makes them very much like New Yorkers, but with a healthier glow about them.

Manhattan Rhapsody is progressing ahead of schedule. My leading man is Rex Kelly, a fella who might be slightly more engaging were he not abusing morphine so regularly. The director, Henry Childs, is marvelous, though he wasn't exactly sold on my suggestion that my character have an epiphany, renounce her worldly possessions, and devote the rest of her life to working for charities. When he said we would need to gin up that ending a bit, I suggested that perhaps in addition to her work in soup kitchens, she could have lots of anonymous, back-alley sex with random hobos. Remarkably, he seemed to consider this possibility.

It's astounding to me that a protagonist who embarks on a long spiritual journey is only considered interesting while she's sucking someone's cock. I can't wait to see what Hollywood adds to a film of Helen Keller's life story. Perhaps they'll try to imply that her blindness was brought on by syphilis, the deserved precipitant of an infancy filled with immorality and depravity. Surely you know how promiscuous babies raised in the South can be.

Regardless, it's safe to say that the ending of the film is still very much in question. At this point, I'd settle for my character to merely not end up with some rich douchebag, to coin Wil's term of endearment. I mean, what personal progress is there in that?

Speaking of Wil, I'm concerned about her, based on your updates from Julian. I'll try to get in touch with her before she slurs (or urinates) herself right out of the best job she's ever had. But I find that Broadway actresses are a difficult species to get hold of, especially the ones who spend a good deal of time unconscious in random places. This habit makes them much less inclined to answer the phone.

I know it may not seem like it, but Wil really does want to be a success. I think she battles self-doubt more than she would ever admit and, worse, that self-doubt wins a hell of a lot of the time. Should you hear anything else, or actually see her, please let me know how she's doing.

Congratulations on getting that third set. I'd love to take credit for it, but all I did was talk to the manager and tell him how fabulous you were. You're the one who actually went through all the effort of being fabulous— much more difficult in my mind than just talking about it.

Keep me posted on what happens with the Kasbah. But remember that you've got "it," doll, that special something that sets you apart. You have a face like an angel and a singing voice that could give a jellyfish a hard-on. I can't imagine there's anyone out there who wouldn't be able to see and appreciate that fact.

Lord knows I've been missing both your face and your voice, and all the delicate goods stowed below them. I have to confess that I think about you a great deal as well. And while I can't really say that trepidation and confusion were even remotely what I hoped to conjure in you, it warms me no end to know that thousands of miles away, you may be looking into the same night sky that I am, wishing just as much that we were in the same place.

I'd love to take this opportunity to continue fawning over you, Moxie, to tell you how absolutely amazing and beautiful I think you are, but I worry that I'll just exacerbate your anxiety and perhaps drive you away. Do know that as much as you enjoy getting my letters, yours evoked the same feelings in me, and it cheered me at a particularly low ebb. It was more helpful than you know.

I'm not sure when I'll get back to New York, but at this point I hope it's soon. With at least two more weeks of shooting, I already feel as though I've been here for ages. All I know for certain is that I can't leave until filming concludes, so I just try to make no mistakes in the hope that will move things along quicker.

Clitty misses you (and so does the dog).*

Thinking of you fondly,
Vi

*I simply couldn't let you be the only one to use that joke, and I must admit that I laughed so hard when I read it in your letter that I very nearly spotted. Consider the above usage to be just a humble homage to yours.

Moxie laughed and brought the stationery to her nose, inhaling deeply. She wasn't sure what the paper smelled like exactly, but it contained a faint trace of something floral.

When Irene suddenly walked into the apartment, Moxie self-consciously jerked the letter away from her face and tried to look nonchalant.

"What are you doing?"

"Nothing," Moxie answered quickly. "Just reading."

Irene cocked an eyebrow. "Did you get another letter?"

"I did."

Irene scurried eagerly to the sofa to sit beside her. "Ooh, let's see."

"It's kind of personal."

"Personal? Are you kidding?" Irene looked more surprised than hurt.

"Well, it's just that I wrote her—"

"You did?"

"And this is her reply."

"Moxie, what gives? Are you and this dame getting serious?"

"No...maybe. Oh, I don't know!" She ran her hand through her hair in frustration. "Irene, I don't know *what's* going on, except that I love talking to her and struggling to keep up with her breakneck quips. She's fun and smart, and I really like the way she makes me feel."

Irene whistled a long, descending tone. "You're a real mess, sister. You know what you need?"

"A manicure?" She glanced at her fingernails.

"Close. You need a man."

Moxie scoffed. "What are you talking about?"

"Look, if you're really worried about how you feel and which path you might be taking, then you should walk down both roads before you decide, right?"

"I'm worried where your road may lead me, Irene. Perhaps into the woods at night."

"Aw, applesauce," Irene said with a dismissive wave of her hand. "Before you decide that men aren't your cup of tea, you need to suck on the teabag a little."

"You use the most disturbing metaphors."

"Well, you get my meaning. Look, I've got a fella who's perfect for you."

Moxie rolled her eyes and groaned. "Here we go."

"He's a friend of Tom," she said, referring to the gangly man she sometimes went out with. "We could double-date, if you like. It doesn't get any safer than that."

"I'll think about it. But first I need a pen and paper."

CHAPTER SIX

Moxie sat at the table with her chin in her hand, pushing the food on her plate around idly with her fork as the man across from her, her date for the night, continued to drone on. She glanced back up to him politely, feigning interest, before she looked over at Irene, who clearly was avoiding looking her in the eye.

She wasn't sure how she had let Irene convince her that this double date was a good idea. She had insisted that Tom's friend Noel was a wonderful match for Moxie, that he was a smart, engaging gentleman. Now she was starting to realize that Irene based her definition of a gentleman solely on where he peed. If Noel had to choose a public restroom, he was more likely to visit the one that read Gentlemen than the one marked Ladies.

She glanced back at him.

"And so I told him no dice," he was saying as she started paying attention again. He laughed awkwardly.

"Then what happened?" Moxie asked.

"What do you mean?"

"After that, once you said no, what did he do?"

Noel seemed confused by this line of questioning. "Um, he walked away."

"Oh. So that was the *end* of the story."

"Well, yes," he stammered. "I must have told it wrong." The scraping of utensils on plates punctuated the awkward silence among them. "So, what is the name Moxie short for?"

Moxie wondered if she had misheard him. "What?"

"I'm sure it's something exotic," Noel said, cutting his meat with his knife and fork. "Is it something foreign?" He suddenly looked horrified. "You're not foreign, are you?"

"I sure am," she said. "My full name is Sharamoxatolia." She made sure to trill her tongue as much as possible.

"Goodness! Where are you from?" Noel was plainly stricken by the notion that Moxie might hail from some barbaric locale beyond the States, and she found it telling that he made no attempt to hide his rampant prejudice. If Violet had been there, she would have mocked him mercilessly for his jaundiced eye.

"Istanbul." Moxie lacked both the will and the desire to stop making him uncomfortable. Who else might he find threatening in a foreign sort of way? It came to her in a flash. "Just like Theda Bara." She watched excitedly as his face registered the dismay she had hoped for at the mere mention of the famous film star known as "The Vamp." Just a few years prior, Hollywood moguls had labored to ensure that Bara represented everything they thought was wrong with Eastern countries, and clearly Noel had been paying attention.

"Wow," Noel said. "Do you know her?"

Irene looked disgusted. "I thought Theda Bara was from Cincinnati." She looked to Tom, who, as usual, said absolutely nothing.

Moxie ignored Irene's contribution to the conversation. "Of *course* I know her. Our parents were friends. Theda showed me how to fry cats."

Noel's face seemed to drain completely of its already pale color. Moxie could barely keep a straight face.

"And she was why I got a bone in my nose," she added, taking a sip of water. "All the neighborhood girls wanted to be like her."

"They do that in Istanbul?"

"Noel," Irene finally interjected, "jump on the trolley and stop being so gullible."

He looked at Moxie suspiciously. "Oh, I get it. You never had a bone in your nose at all, did you?"

She put her hands up in surrender. "You got me. We didn't pierce our noses, but every summer solstice, we did sacrifice a goat to Kreplik, the god of thunder."

"Excuse us, fellas." Irene stood suddenly. "Miss Turkish Delight and I need to powder our noses. We'll be right back."

The intense focus in Irene's glare impressed Moxie, who rose to follow her toward the ladies' room. Just before they went inside, Irene spun to face her and unloaded. "What are you doing? You're toying with Noel like a cat with a mouse. This is *not* what we agreed to."

Moxie had reached her breaking point. "Yeah yeah yeah, 'sampling the tea.' Well, let me tell you something, sister. This guy's teabag tastes like ashes and ass crack, and I'm sending it right back to the kitchen."

"You're not giving him a chance."

"Are you *kidding* me? If I wasn't giving him a chance, I wouldn't have listened to his sixty tedious stories, not one of them with a beginning or end. I would have gone home after he implied that all women in show business are whores. And I most certainly would not have pretended *not* to be livid when he told me that I had no right to mourn my father's passing because Jesus knows best and the Lord is my daddy now. I've given this man more of a chance than he will ever deserve over the course of his lifetime. I can't believe I'm wasting my night off with this...this douchebag." Vi was right. That really was the perfect word.

Irene seemed stunned, her anger defused. "Okay, so this particular tea is a little bitter. But just because you have one bad mouthful, don't throw out the teacup."

"But I shouldn't have to keep slinging it back either." Feeling empowered, Moxie stood up straight. "I'm leaving."

"Wait, you can't just leave us all here at the restaurant. What will Tom and I say to Noel?"

"Tell him I don't feel well and need to go home. It's all true."

"But we didn't even get to dessert."

"You know, there are a million things I'd rather be doing than sitting here trying to force something that doesn't feel right. I appreciate you trying to help me get my head straight, Irene, but this isn't making anything better." She smiled and kissed her on the cheek. "I'll see you at home."

Moxie walked out without even a backward glance.

"Shit," Irene muttered. Moxie was right about Noel. He certainly was irritating and dull. But she had hoped Moxie simply needed to get back on the horse, so to speak—back out into the dating world—and that might end this troubling obsession with a strange woman living on the other side of the world.

She shook her head and tried to imagine what it would be like to meet someone and, in the course of a single evening, be so powerfully drawn to them that she completely lost her marbles. That had certainly never happened to her, but she wasn't convinced that it couldn't. And as much as she was worried about Moxie and concerned about her choices, she couldn't help but feel a small sense of wonder at the sheer romanticism of her situation.

Of course Moxie and Violet would probably never see each other again. Things never happened like that, at least not to anyone she knew. She just needed to be there for Moxie. Maybe Noel was a complete washout, but New York was a big place and must have a fella or two who could make Moxie feel the way Violet did.

Irene might have been a lot of things, but one of her *good* adjectives was *devoted*. She'd try to make sure Moxie worked through all this. And she'd do her best to ensure that Moxie received all the consideration, respect, and class she was due.

She clapped her hands and turned to go tell Tom and Noel that Moxie's period had come unexpectedly; she'd just bled through the ass of her dress and had therefore gone home.

❖

Home from the studio earlier than she expected, Violet walked eagerly to the front desk, wondering what Lyle might be doing—perhaps conspicuously sporting a dildo that protruded from his forehead as though he were a plump sex unicorn. She was thoroughly disappointed to see him doing nothing of the sort and wearing a well-pressed suit jacket and tie.

"Good afternoon, Miss London."

"Hello, Captain. I was wondering if I got any mail today."

"Actually, you did." He turned and poked through a small stack of papers, retrieving a letter in a familiar-looking envelope. "Here you are."

She verified the return address and was thrilled to see it was indeed from Moxie. Not wanting to waste any time, she walked to the divan in the front office and got comfortable, then tore open the envelope impatiently.

Vi,

I received your latest letter today, and I have to say it was a wonderfully welcome distraction from talking to my agent, Cotton. He has finally managed to get the manager of the Kasbah to agree to see one of my sets next Saturday night, but I somehow have to come up with a dress that makes me look like I don't <u>need</u> a gig at the Kasbah—a predicament that strikes me as nothing short of ironic.

At any rate, wish me luck that not only can I find something absolutely breathtaking to wear for about a nickel, but that I also don't fall on my face when the music starts. I almost wish I didn't know he was coming. And the fact that I have over a week to stew on it is making me a nervous wreck.

Your description of the place where you're staying was absolutely hilarious. It made me wish I was there to see the nature, the morbid employee with the menstruation fetish, as well as, of course, you.

My roommate Irene is, at this very moment, lecturing me that I'm letting myself get too drawn into your "dark, Sapphic charms" and that I should be more interested in finding a nice fella who'll want to treat me to dinner. She insists she has the perfect man for me, but it's hard to take Irene's counsel after having met her beau, Tom. I've seen him many times and he has yet to do or say anything that would imply that he has even a spark of a personality. I think she likes Tom for letting her always be the center of attention, almost as much as she likes having someone to take her out places and pay. But I can't imagine that they have much to talk about, just as I am unable to understand what would possibly make her willing to have him touch her. I mean, if Tom's kisses are as exciting as he is, she must worry about nodding off while they're necking, though politeness forbids me from asking her that question. However, if she continues haranguing me, that may change.

I'm sorry to hear of your difficulty finding someone in Hollywood who isn't more interested in salacious titillation than telling a story that could be considered inspirational. I was inclined to send someone out your way who could show the corrupt studios what it was to have principles and conviction, someone who could bring some sincerity and ethics to that town, but then I remembered that I'm in New York City, and there's no one like that here either.

That being said, at the risk of contradicting myself, I _so_ want to see the movie about the woman who has a generous heart of gold by day, but by night has copious indiscriminate sex with a parade of random hobos. You've definitely piqued my interest, and I think you may have been holding out with that particular gem. Who wouldn't be instantly drawn into the humanity of a story like that? This gal sure is.

I did notice that your last missive had some small pockets of sentiment that were both sweet and plaintive, and those seem to be the parts that I keep rereading for some reason. If those are your dark, Sapphic charms that I've heard so much about recently, then perhaps they <u>are</u> dangerous. If nothing else, the words certainly steal my breath, and I find myself wanting to believe them, yet wanting not to at the same time.

Of course, there are the other parts of your letter that go beyond sweet, past flirtatious, and dive right into bawdy. And yes, I reread those passages too. I may not know entirely what I want, but I'm no fool, for God's sake. I've never had anyone say those kinds of things to me before, and if you're worried they're driving me away, then this prompt reply to you should confirm that's not the case.

It wholly puzzles me that I can feel like I miss you when I've really spent only a matter of hours in your company. But many times over these past few weeks I've wished that I could meet you for drinks, though perhaps coffee would be safer. And I imagine that if you hadn't already shared that you are, in many ways, feeling the same, I would likely have questioned my sanity.

After all, I don't have a lot of ties with people. I have no living family members, no lengthy friendships or suitors. It's completely beyond my nature to trust easily and even more so to put credence in something like chemistry or kismet. I therefore remain bewildered and doubtful, though less so, I find, with each successive note from you.

So I'll take this opportunity to cynically ask that you please not view me as some type of grand sociological experiment or, still worse, as a challenge to be conquered. If you are ever not utterly certain of your words, please *don't write them. Though I have never known you to show me anything but the utmost regard, I simply need you to understand that whatever this is that we're sharing, it's more to me than a trifle.*

Well, I've gone and gotten serious, which was the last thing I intended when I sat down to pen this letter. I do hope that things are going well for you and that your film finishes both soon and to your liking.

I'm looking at the night sky and thinking of you,

Moxie

Violet stopped reading and stared at the floor. Moxie had chosen to be remarkably candid, even though she had probably a thousand reasons not to be. As a result, Violet's pulse beat loudly through her body like a tympani.

"Hey, Captain," she finally said to Lyle. "I need to make a long-distance phone call."

She smiled wryly when he came around the desk and she saw that he wasn't wearing pants.

CHAPTER SEVEN

It was still what Moxie considered to be early in the day when Mrs. Bennington pounded on her apartment door. Within a moment, both Moxie and Irene had thrown on their robes and anxiously darted to answer it and see what was wrong.

"Mrs. B." Irene yawned. "Is anything wrong? What time is it?"

"It's ten a.m.," she answered gruffly. "And there's a colored lady downstairs who says she's your tailor, Moxie. Says she has some dresses to bring you. But I wanted to check first, 'cause something about her don't seem right."

Moxie tried to blink away the sleep so she could process this odd situation. Perhaps Cotton had come through for her after all. "This must be for Saturday night," she said. "Please have her come up, Mrs. Bennington."

The landlady was clearly still not completely at ease with this course of action, but she snorted in acceptance and shuffled back to the staircase.

"You have a tailor?" Irene asked, shutting the door.

"I knew Cotton was being purposely obtuse." She hastily changed out of her nightgown and threw on undergarments and a light frock that she'd be able to easily slip in and out of, if she should need to try things on for size.

When another knock came, Moxie nearly ripped the door off its hinges in her excitement. In the doorway stood Lady Dulce La Boeuf, in glorious drag, holding at least half a dozen evening gowns on wooden hangers.

"Sweet meat!" she said, immediately hugging Lady Dulce tight.

"Hiya, doll face." He seemed just as happy to see her as she was to see him and rubbed her back with his free hand.

Irene reappeared newly dressed and seemed completely flabbergasted by the sight in her entryway. She appeared ill at ease with their visitor, and her gaze darted skittishly back and forth between Lady Dulce's face, large hands, and still larger feet. "Wow."

"What are you doing here?" Moxie asked cheerfully, ushering her guest inside.

Lady Dulce looked coy. "I got a call last night from someone who said you had something special going on Saturday night that you need to look absolutely divine for. And as we all know, divine is right up my alley."

Moxie tried to suppress her smile but assumed she was failing. Why had she even considered this was Cotton's doing? This was a wonderful, thoughtful surprise—not his style at all. No, this little endowment absolutely screamed of Violet.

"Um, hello," Irene mumbled meekly, still looking baffled.

"Where are my manners?" Moxie asked. "Irene Cavendish, my roommate, confidante, and general nag, this is Lady Dulce La Boeuf, chanteuse extraordinaire and master of part-time femininity."

"Enchanted," Lady Dulce said with a coquettish tilt of the head.

"Ditto," was all Irene managed in response.

"So you're up early." Moxie took the gowns and hung them on the door trim. "How about I make us all some coffee?"

"Doll, I'm not up early, I'm up late. So a cup of joe would be great, thanks. This is a cute little place you have."

"Thank you. Have a seat while I start the percolator."

Both Lady Dulce and Irene sat in the front room as Moxie busied herself in the small kitchenette.

"So, how do you two know each other?" Irene finally asked.

"Two-finger Flossie's."

Moxie chuckled as she eavesdropped on them, realizing that Lady Dulce's answer only begged more questions. An even longer silence ensued.

"She only has two fingers?" Irene finally asked, just as Moxie rejoined them.

"That's what I thought when I first heard of her," she said. "You'd probably be happier not knowing the real answer."

Irene looked out blankly, seeming to consider this option. Suddenly her face registered complete shock. "Ohh," she murmured.

"I appreciate you stopping by," Moxie said. "Especially since you haven't even been home yet."

"I thought about going home, but being here in this outfit made more sense. If a skinny colored man showed up here with dresses for you, they probably wouldn't let me up."

"And for future reference," Moxie asked, "what name does he go by?"

"Milton," he said flatly. "Frankly, he's a little boring, which is why it's so much more interesting to be Lady Dulce."

"I'm sure I'd like Milton just as much," she said, putting her hand on his and looking at him with affection.

For an instant, he appeared touched, then somehow uncomfortable. "Yes, well, while that coffee's brewing, let me show you what I brought you." He stood and went back to where the gowns hung. "I had a bit of a challenge finding something your size. As you can see, I'm a bit more...statuesque."

Moxie laughed and gestured toward her breasts. "True, but I've got these to help keep a dress up."

Lady Dulce paused dramatically. "You're a little bitchy when you first get up, aren't you?"

Irene huffed. "Trust me, it's not just when she first gets up."

❖

When Saturday finally arrived, Moxie was still nervous, but she had to admit that with the shimmering ice blue dress on loan from the lovely Lady Dulce, she felt like a million bucks.

She did her best to perform as though it was any other day and no one in particular was in the audience. It pleased her when Lady Dulce's male persona (aka Milton) slipped in and took a seat at Julian's table during her final set. She had begged him to come, since he was so instrumental in helping her get prepared. He had been noncommittal, but she gave the doorman a heads-up to expect him, just in case.

As far as her performance, it had gone very well. The audience picked up on the energy in the air and was more attentive than normal, speaking less during her vocals and supplying plentiful applause.

When she finished, she was overwhelmed with relief that she had nothing to be nervous about any longer. She scanned the crowd, generally pleased at both the enthusiastic response and the fact that some of her friends had come to cheer her on, something she was not accustomed to.

The only thing amiss was Violet's absence, and though Moxie tried to push that thought aside, not wanting to sour the sweet taste of the moment, she felt it was wrong that she wasn't there. Violet was the one person whom she really wanted to share this moment with and wanted to make proud.

"Moxie," Cotton said, breaking into her thoughts. "I'd like you to meet Theodore Brown, manager of the Kasbah." He extended his hand to lead her from the stage and to their table. "Theodore was very impressed with your singing."

Theodore Brown was younger than Moxie expected, and while he was a bit swarthier than she had pictured him to be, he was attractive. Unfortunately his expression didn't convey the kind of admiration for her that Cotton had just verbalized. In fact, he looked as though he smelled bad cabbage. "Nice to meet you," she said unsurely.

"Yes," he replied briefly, his countenance impassive.

"Excuse me," a man in a gray pinstriped suit interjected. He extended a business card to her that read:

EDWARD PHELPS
TALENT SCOUT, PINNACLE PICTURES
NEW YORK, NEW YORK

"Um, hello," Moxie said, unable to contain her surprise. She handed it to Cotton, whose eyebrows arched.

"I'd like to talk to you, young lady," Phelps said. "I think Pinnacle might be able to make you a very attractive deal."

"Then you'll want to talk to me," Cotton said quickly. "I'm her agent."

Theodore cleared his throat in a very affected way, no doubt to remind everyone that he was still standing there. Cotton seemed to regard him in a slightly different way now and patted his back dismissively. "Yes, it was good to see you, Theodore. We'll catch up later." When Theodore did not immediately leave, Cotton extended their contact further by actually shoving him away.

Phelps looked amused. "Why don't you both step over to my table so we can talk?"

❖

The next day, Moxie was still elated. As she folded her clothes, she hummed a cheery tune.

"Hey, Moxie," someone called from outside her door.

She poked her head out to look into the hallway and saw a resident from a second-floor apartment. "Hi."

"Telephone's for you."

Like most apartment buildings, Moxie's had a single telephone that everyone shared. Theirs was in the parlor downstairs, and she energetically headed down the four flights of stairs.

She picked up the candlestick base and held the receiver to her ear. "Hello?"

"Hey, tomato. I hear you knocked them on their asses last night."

The familiar voice made Moxie's stomach lurch, and she instantly sat in the armchair behind her. "Vi?"

"Yes, it's nice to hear your voice again."

Moxie was ill equipped to handle Violet's provocative tone, and she closed her eyes for a moment to help her focus. "Yours too. Last night went really well. It seems I'm forever owing you for something or other."

"You don't owe me a thing, toots. All I did was make sure your talents were suitably showcased."

"Oh, they were showcased, all right," Moxie replied with a sultry chuckle. "You definitely would have approved of my dress."

"Hmm…I wasn't talking about *those* talents, but while we're on that subject, what *did* your dress look like?"

"Ice blue, beaded, low-cut, thigh-high slit up the side."

Violet gasped at her stark description, which pleased Moxie. She was brazenly flirting with Violet, but it made her feel so damn sexy, she just couldn't resist. After all, she and this woman had already made love, she kept telling herself. Her aptitude for affecting Violet both empowered and excited her.

"Shall I assume that you approve?" she asked seductively.

"So very, very much," Violet answered hoarsely. "My spies tell me you got an offer from Pinnacle."

"Yeah, about that. It's a remarkable coincidence that the night I planned to be all dolled up and singing my heart out, a scout from your studio just *happened* to be in the audience."

"I had less to do with that than you might think. I heard one of the joes on the set talking about casting a singer for a small role in a new picture. They wanted someone with a fresh face and gams from here to there and back again, and I immediately thought of you."

"And did he pick Saturday night on purpose? Or was that just chance?"

Violet's voice took on a sheepish quality. "Well, it seemed like a good time for them to stop by, and I figured if he didn't think you were right for the part, he could just quietly leave and you'd never know the difference. You'd have someone else in the audience who might make you an offer. But clearly that wasn't the case. You obviously bowled him over as much as I expected you to."

"I guess so," she said, unable to hide her glee. "They want me to travel to Hollywood for a screen test. I leave in a week."

"Congratulations. I can't think of anyone who deserves it more."

"Thanks, I'm a little nervous," she whispered. "Traveling all the way to California and then performing for studio executives."

"You'll be great."

"When are you coming back to New York, anyway? You won't be arriving just as I'll be leaving, will you?"

"I'll wait for you," Violet said softly, and the words gave Moxie a sudden chill.

"Really?"

"I wouldn't want you to be out here all alone. You can stay here at the Garden of Allah…with me." Moxie suddenly couldn't swallow. "Provided that's what you want," Violet added.

Moxie recognized the familiar anxiety fluttering through her gut that she had been dealing with on and off for the last month. "Well, it would be nice to spend some time with you."

"*Manhattan Rhapsody* should be done filming in a few days, so I can show you around town."

"We can see the sights?"

"Absolutely."

"Like what?"

"I'm sure there are some things. I've spent most of my time either at the studio or at the Garden."

Moxie laughed. "And the city hasn't asked you to do any tourism radio spots yet?"

"Hmm, it is odd that I haven't heard back from them, now that you mention it. And the Temperance Union isn't returning my calls either."

"Perhaps for the same reason. That would be like making you the national spokeswoman for penises." A woman who lived on the fifth floor, sitting within earshot, suddenly looked at Moxie in horror. "What?" she asked her confrontationally. The woman turned away, but still looked disturbed.

"Speaking of penises," Violet was saying.

"What an unexpected way for you to start a sentence."

"I don't like it any better than you do, but your last letter said your roommate was trying to set you up with a fella."

Moxie winced. "Ah, yeah."

"I couldn't help but wonder if she convinced you."

"She did. It didn't go well."

"Oh? Care to share the details?" Violet sounded interested, but Moxie couldn't read anything else into her question.

"He was a sap through and through, and I couldn't stand his company one more minute, so I actually left the three of them at the restaurant and came home."

"That is particularly bad if you didn't even make it through the meal. I suppose next time you could always try Wil's method and feign death."

"I'd prefer there not be a next time."

"If you want to get technical, so do I."

Moxie grinned. "Is that so?"

"I'd be lying if I told you it didn't bother me."

"I suppose you're leading a monastic existence out there amidst all the movie stars and beautiful dames?"

"Actually, I am."

"No young ingénues to educate?" Moxie asked playfully. "No sun-kissed breasts to fondle?"

The woman from the fifth floor was staring again. "What?" she barked.

"Not a one."

"I'm shocked."

"I know, I know. But see, I've met this incredible woman back in New York who has me completely dizzy. I can't concentrate on anything but her."

Moxie's pulse started to race, but she couldn't resist seeing where this conversation would go. "Do tell."

"She's gorgeous, with a voice so sultry that when she speaks, I melt like butter. She's all I think about."

"And what kind of thoughts are you having?"

"About how her dark eyes sparkle when she finds something funny, and the sexy way her lips move when she sings."

"Vi—"

"Her wonderful sense of humor, her silky blond hair, and how her perfume smells like bergamot. How her mouth tastes sweet, like cherry brandy. And God, the way she kisses. She's an exceptional ki—"

"My, but you *have* been deep in thought, haven't you?"

"More than you know." Violet's voice had become so deep and tinged with arousal that it threatened to seep through the phone and be Moxie's undoing.

"No wonder you can't concentrate." Her voice cracked. "You must be taking thirty cold showers a day."

"It is somewhat debilitating. So you have no such distractions? You don't think of me at all?"

"I wouldn't say that."

"So what *would* you say, Moxie? Do you ever imagine me touching you?"

Her mouth was suddenly parched and somewhat numb. "Yes."

"And do you sometimes think about touching me?"

"Yes." Moxie's answer was barely a whisper.

"What about me tasting you?"

"Oh, God, yes." The bitch from the fifth floor glared at her again.

"Do you mind?" she implored in irritation as she put the phone to her chest to muffle her voice.

"That's nice to hear," Violet said softly. "I'm relieved I'm not the only one who's sexually frustrated."

"Well, I was just fine before you called. So it's clearly all your doing."

Violet laughed. "And I was fine before I met you, so I have to disagree. But I challenge you to try and prove your case."

"I'm sure you'd like that."

"That I can't deny. But as much as I'd love to sit here and continue to listen to your voice become more and more seductive, I have to meet a couple of friends for a round of golf."

"You play golf?"

"Not well, but I've tried a time or two, yes. I find it's even better when I take my hip flask."

"You might say that about just about anything."

"Very true."

"I'm glad you called," Moxie said sincerely. "I've missed talking to you."

"That's very mutual. When I see you, I owe you a bottle of champagne to celebrate your success."

"Hmm, it seems to me that's how all this got started."

"We can celebrate that too."

Moxie cleared her throat. "I'm planning on staying sober, just so you know."

"That's admirable," Violet said, her amusement audible. "It's important to have goals."

"Have a good golf game."

"And you have a nice trip out West."

"I'll write when I have my itinerary, but Cotton says I'll probably leave next weekend sometime. Will you meet me at the station?"

"I'd meet you anywhere, doll."

Moxie felt jittery again. "Thanks."

"And feel free to wear that dress from last night the day you arrive."

"I'll think about it."

"So will I, sugar. That's part of the problem."

"I'll see you soon. And thanks again."

"You're welcome."

"Bye, Vi."

"Bye."

Moxie hung the receiver up and sighed deeply. The whore from the fifth floor was finally gone. Pity she hadn't left before all the steamy talk.

She fanned herself for a moment with her hand. The effect Violet had on her was inexplicable. And while she was impatiently looking forward to seeing her again, the notion of being alone with her in a bungalow with a bottle of champagne absolutely petrified her.

CHAPTER EIGHT

"And that's when I told him to pipe down and kiss my ass," Irene said, a trace of the bitterness still in her voice.

Moxie whistled a descending tone in surprise as she wrestled with her false eyelashes in the mirror. "Jumping cats, sister. How long did he suspend you for?"

"A week. I guess I'll be living on rainwater and dust until then."

"Next time, try to think of that *before* you crack wise to the boss."

Irene looked disgusted. "It would be a hell of a lot easier if he wasn't such a—"

"Douchebag?" Moxie suggested helpfully, watching Irene in the reflection.

"Exactly! Cold, unpleasant, *and* intrusive—that's him to a T."

"I'll make sure I pass along to Vi and Wil that you heartily approve of their term. Though I'm proud to say that I met the original douchebag. The others are just pale imitations."

Irene's expression changed slightly. "What's your plan when you get to Hollywood? Are you going to…look…her…*up*?" The intent of her inflection was obvious.

"She's picking me up at the station."

"Wow, you didn't waste any time, did you? So are you two…?"

Moxie sighed and faced her. "I've asked myself that question about six thousand times, and the best that I can tell is, I don't know the answer."

"Well, what do you want? You must know that."

Moxie paused to consider Irene's question. "I want things not to be so complicated. I want to be able to meet someone and then actually spend time *together* to determine if they're the one for me or not. I want to not question my sanity when I feel a spark of attraction for someone." She paused again before she continued with more conviction. "I want to *remember* any sexual encounters I have—fondly, I might add. To not spend my time trying to imagine what naughty thing got done and to whom. To make up my mind between either trying to control my body and its reactions or just giving in and letting whatever this is overtake me. Mostly, I want to keep feeling the way she makes me feel."

Irene scowled. "Why, when you speak from the heart, is it some poetic monologue, and when I do it, I get suspended from work for a week?"

"What am I ready for? Perhaps that's the more important question I need to answer."

"Ooh, good one. So?" Irene got comfortable on the sofa as though preparing for an engrossing ghost story.

"I'm not sure. She affects me. Just hearing her voice over the phone the other day made me a total wreck. I feel like I *have* to see her again, if nothing more than to see if this is real or not."

"And what if it is? Real, I mean?"

Moxie shrugged. "I haven't worked all that through yet." She turned back around to apply her eye shadow. "Maybe I need a chaperone, so things don't end up like they did last time."

"Well, I'm free for the next week."

"Would you really want to go?"

"To Hollywood? Are you daffy? You bet your ass I would! Just give me twelve seconds to pack."

"I don't have the jack for your train ticket, but if I did, I'd definitely be dragging you with me in the morning." Irene looked dejected. "But why don't you come with me tonight to the Luna? I can at least pull that off."

"Yeah?"

"Sure. It'll cheer you up. I'll even buy you a drink."

"You sound like a movie star already. What should I order?"

"Hmm, do you like licorice?"

❖

Wil sat in her small apartment, taking long drags from her cigarette and staring at the red neon sign outside her window as it perpetually flashed "vacancy." How could anything be so monumentally and constantly vacant? She snapped back to reality long enough to realize that she had not been listening to the radio program that was playing, and she contemplated standing and crossing the room to turn the goddamned thing off, but that seemed like so much trouble when she could just keep ignoring it.

A knock at the door made her rethink the effort of rising. "Who is it?"

"Your fairy godmother, child," a muffled female voice said.

"Julian?" She walked to the door and opened it, surprised to see Violet leaning in the door frame, her arms crossed and her terrier at her feet. "Where the fuck did you come from?" Wil blurted, looking out into the hallway to see if anyone else was waiting there to surprise her—perhaps her dead grandmother.

Violet seemed amused. "Well, my parents like to tell a story involving a stork, but personally I'm dubious."

"No, I mean I thought you were in California. Did they kick you out?"

"Of the entire state? Based on the Californians I've met so far, I can't fathom what I'd have to do to make that happen. Thanks," she said, pushing her way into the unkempt apartment. "I'd love to come in. Good God, Wil, is the maid buried in here somewhere?"

"Is that what that scratching sound was?" Wil shut the door after Clitty pranced inside behind his master.

"This must be what they mean when they say good help is hard to find. Check under that pile of shit in the corner."

"Have a seat," Wil said in resignation. She watched as Violet tried to find a piece of furniture not covered with rumpled garments, papers, or piles of trash.

"What guarantee do I have that there's really a chair under there?"

"Is my personal deep-seated suspicion good enough?"

"Has it ever been?" Violet unceremoniously shoved a heap of junk from the armchair onto the floor, then sat. "I'd like to ask how you're doing, but my keen sense of intuition has answered that for me."

Wil grunted in response.

"You spending the evening alone?"

"Just me, Amos n' Andy."

Violet's expression softened. "What happened to *Scandals and Lies*?"

Wil took a deep breath to steady herself. "That asshole director recast it."

"Why?"

She drew in the last bit of blaze from the remains of her cigarette, exhaled through her nose, then stubbed the butt out brutally in the ashtray to her left. "I fucked it all up."

"How do you mean?"

"I mean I balled up everything, but good." She was frustrated and more than a little embarrassed. "I spent so much time blotto that I couldn't remember my lines. And after getting shown the door there, I can't get an audition anywhere else in town."

"So you're in a bind, huh?"

"I don't know what I'm going to do, Vi." She ran her fingers through her hair.

"I do."

"What do you mean?"

"Look here, sister. You're Wil Skoog, one of the best goddamned actresses I know. You're not going to let this get you down."

"I'm not?"

"Absolutely not. You're going to take this personal setback and learn from it."

"I hate learning."

Violet's eyelids dropped slightly. "Which is why you're living in this life-size anus with just a radio for company. Surely you must see the correlation."

"Can you please get to the point? You're cutting into the time I set aside to wallow in self-pity."

"Look, Wil, I'm here to make you an offer."

"What kind of offer?"

Violet removed a train ticket from her handbag. "This is a ticket for you to leave with me on the morning train to Chicago, then on to Hollywood."

Wil was stunned—unable, for possibly the first time in her conscious life, to speak.

"But here's what I need from you," Violet continued. "You need to pull yourself back together. If you come with me to Los Angeles, you're coming to act, not to see what your body's saturation point for cocaine and gin is. You need to remember how talented you are."

"You're taking me back with you?" she finally whispered, feeling more emotional than she could remember being when it wasn't written into stage directions.

"Yup, you're stuck with me, toots."

"You already knew about the play?"

"I talked to Julian, yes. He's very worried about you."

"I've been such a dope. I can't tell you how much I appreciate this, Vi."

"Good. Now get packed. When you're done, we're heading to the Luna. There's a certain blonde there I mean to surprise."

Irene sat at a table near the stage while she waited for Moxie's last set to start, as pleased as she could be that she was seated with Mr. Cotton McCann. After all, if he was able to get Moxie an audition for a movie in Hollywood, why couldn't he do the same for her?

"Do you know any movie stars?" she asked, trying for what felt like the hundredth time to start a conversation with him.

"I haven't done much in the film industry," he said. "Personally, I think it's on its way out."

"Yeah?"

"Come on, now, movies with sound?" Cotton scoffed as he lit his cigar. "Just a flash in the pan. It's only a matter of time before America tires of film and goes back to its true love, vaudeville."

Irene furrowed her brow as she considered this possibility. "Gee, I sure hope not," she said without thinking. When he glowered at her, she played with the stem of her fancy champagne glass. She had drunk only one glassful all evening, but could easily see how Moxie had overindulged the night before she had awoken a lesbian. Was there a connection between those two occurrences? She eyed the stemware suspiciously.

The club was filling up quickly, and Irene did a double take when a woman with a dark bob sauntered in holding a terrier. She and her red-haired friend sat at a table toward the back, where a plump man with a mustache and a nice-looking fella with spectacles were already seated.

"Nah," she muttered aloud. "It couldn't be."

❖

"Vi, you made it after all." Julian rose to kiss her cheek. "And you brought a creature of the night."

"Yes, on both counts," Violet replied. "Thanks for getting me Moxie's itinerary."

"It was simple, darling. She can't shut up for a second about this trip. By the way, Violet, this is Gary."

"Nice to meet you." She extended her hand.

"What can I get you?" a waiter asked.

"Where's Fred?" Wil questioned. "I'd like to see his perfect little ass. Can that be arranged?"

The waiter looked uncomfortable. "Fred's off this evening, ma'am."

"Well, then, let's see your ass. Spin for me, darling."

Violet smiled, feeling encouraged by the return of Wil's playfulness, then completely amused when the lad did hesitantly turn around, his arms stretched out awkwardly.

"Splendid," Wil said. "You'll more than do. What's your name?"

"Um...Ira."

"How wonderfully Jewish. Tell me, are you circumcised, Ira?"

Violet intervened, marveling at how quickly *playful* inevitably seemed to cross the boundary to *inappropriate*. "Ira, might you bring us a bottle of champagne and four glasses?"

He nodded and darted away.

"Celebrating?" Gary asked.

"I hope to be soon," Violet replied. "You boys don't mind drinking champagne with us, do you?"

They both shook their heads. "Good God, Vi," Julian said over the rim of his rickey. "You look absolutely tanned. How the hell did that happen?"

"Pass out naked by the pool just once, and this is what you get."

"That sounds absolutely decadent." His voice was tinged with titillation.

"If only it were true."

"Damn," Julian murmured.

"The truth is they have a fat load of sun there, and it bakes you like a soufflé. There's no escaping it, even at night."

"That sounds horrible." Julian shook his head.

"It's not as bad as all that. California is bright, clean, and unspoiled."

"So it's the exact opposite of Wil," he added, unable to stanch getting his amusement at her expense.

"My, my," Wil said, eyeing Julian warily. "You've been such a busy bee, Jules. Providing itineraries and reporting to everyone on my state of well-being."

His amusement vanished. "Do you intend to tell me that you'd rather be back in that rat's nest, living on potted meat and Chesterfields, than here with us, planning a trip to Hollywood?"

"Well, if by *with us*, you mean with *you*, then I might have to consider that option for a moment."

"Come on, Wil. You're not really upset, are you?" he asked.

"I would have appreciated you talking to me first. Instead of having Vi travel a million miles on a camel's back."

His expression softened. "Darling, accept that sometimes talking to you is neither appealing nor productive."

"Thank you, you fat-assed queen."

"You're welcome, you insufferable cunt."

Violet glanced at Gary, whose mouth was hanging open and who seemed completely bewildered by this strange amalgam of thoughtfulness and abuse. "So touching," she said. "If one of you strikes the other, I may not be able to suppress my tears."

The lights dimmed, and the stout emcee appeared. As he began to introduce Moxie, Violet realized her hands were trembling. Over five weeks had passed since they had seen each other. What if things were completely different now?

When the spotlight hit Moxie, Violet's breath caught in her chest. She was as beautiful as her memory had attributed, perhaps more so, in a candy-apple red dress with fringe and black fishnet stockings. Moxie signaled to the pianist and started to sing a slow, sexy number.

The mention of your name
Makes my temperature rise;
And you fan the torrid heat
With the look in your eyes.

I watch you lick your lips
As you stare at my mouth;
And my stomach does flips
When your gaze travels south.

How you melt my resolve,
I'll never know.
My reservations dissolve
For wanting you so.

When your hand brushes mine,
My pulse gets to racing,
Like I've had too much wine,
I'm dizzy and aching.

How you melt my resolve,
I'll never know.
My reservations dissolve
For wanting you so.

When the music stopped, the place broke into enthusiastic applause, though Violet found herself somewhat catatonic.

"Violet." Julian strained to be heard over the crowd. "You look like a wolf ready to devour a sleeping lamb."

"Is it wet in here, or is it just me?" She saw no empathy from anyone at the table. "I really need to start socializing with *someone* who's attracted to women. When did the champagne arrive?"

"Right after your jaw hit the floor, darling," Wil said, pouring Violet a glass.

"She's absolutely gorgeous, Wil." She took a sip.

"I've heard this number before, sister—in this very place. So do what you need to do to get her out of your system."

"I'm not sure I *can* get her out of my system, but I can't think of anything I'd rather do than try."

❖

Several songs into her final set Moxie thought she caught a glimpse of Violet in the audience. At first, she assumed her mind was playing tricks on her. The table was in a dark corner, and while she could clearly make out a woman with a black bob and straight bangs sitting there, she decided that lots of women wore their hair that way.

A short time later, she realized that Julian was sitting at that same table with Gary. Coincidence? After all, Vi was in Hollywood. And was that fourth person sitting with them Wil? Was it possible that black thing in the brunette's lap was a terrier and not a fuzzy handbag?

When the redhead slapped the waiter's ass, Moxie had no more doubts. Her stomach sank, and she found it difficult to concentrate.

She closed her eyes and started to sing "But Not for Me."

How did Violet get here? Was everything all right? Why had she traveled all the way back to New York without telling her she was coming?

She forced herself to push those thoughts aside and focus on what she was doing, though even without consciously considering Violet's presence, she felt different performing for her—somehow electric, bolder. She let her voice get a little throatier and lightly traced her neckline as she sang. Moxie sank into the eroticism of performing for her lover, and she wondered if it showed.

CHAPTER NINE

Cotton was agog.

He wasn't exactly sure what had happened to Moxie over the course of the evening, but the Moxie of her earlier sets had *nothing* on this gal. Sure, she had been entertaining before, even exceptionally good, but now she was on fire.

She radiated a sexuality that was provocative and captivating. And clearly he wasn't the only one who was transfixed. All eyes were on her through each and every song.

Her hips slowly gyrated. She pulled her hands through her hair passionately. And Moxie, perhaps unconsciously, at times slowly and softly stroked the microphone as though she was urging it to ejaculate.

When she finished her final song, people leapt to their feet and applauded loudly. Some were whistling, and the energy in the air was palpable.

Moxie's roommate—what was her name?—was standing and clapping vigorously as well. "Wasn't she great?" she shouted toward him. He nodded in response, but didn't rise, instead twirling the cigar in his hand idly.

When at last the adulation ebbed, he stood to politely welcome her to the table, but instead she made a beeline for a table somewhere in the back.

"Where's she going?" he asked no one in particular, standing now for no reason and feeling quite foolish.

"Oh, wow," the roommate said.

"Wow, what?"

"I guess that *is* her at that table—Violet London, I mean. The Hollywood actress."

This wasn't making any sense. "Who is?"

"At that table back there. The one with the dark hair. She's been writing Moxie from Hollywood."

"So that's the friend out West?"

The roommate nodded.

He scrutinized this woman closer. She had a real Hollywood look about her, all right. From her sleek yellow dress to her little dog, this London dame seemed all bathtub gin and quiff. He instantly disliked her. "Where did they meet?"

"Here, I think." She was eyeing their reunion closely for some reason. Something didn't feel right.

"Say, what's the deal with this doll, anyway?"

The irritation in his voice must have startled her, because she suddenly snapped her head back nervously. "I dunno. It's not like they're having sex or anything." Her face then went through about six emotions in a few seconds. What looked like shock became mortification, then embarrassment, irritation, anger, and finally shame.

"What the hell are you gabbing about?" he barked.

"I mean, how *could* they have sex?" she stammered, then laughed awkwardly. "What would they do, right?"

Her discomfort and her veiled attempt at muddying the waters set off all kinds of warning bells in Cotton's head. He needed to break this up, whatever it was.

❖

As Moxie made her way across the floor to the table in the far corner, she couldn't hear anything but her pulse roaring in her head. It seemed to take forever to navigate the length of the room, and as she finally got close enough to see Violet's gray eyes, she shuddered as she realized they were staring, somewhat hungrily, into her own.

She stopped just in front of where Violet was standing, and for a moment, she couldn't say anything. She bit her lower lip as she struggled inwardly for just the right pithy quip to break the ice. She wanted to say something smart and sassy that would leave Violet breathless.

"Hi," Moxie rasped, the beginning *h* sound seeming interminable. She internally cursed just how far from smart and sassy she had deviated.

"Hey there," Violet replied, her voice brimming with sensuality. "You were amazing."

The compliment, and perhaps the way it was delivered, meant more to Moxie than she anticipated. "Thanks." She nodded amiably to the others seated around the table. "Vi, what are you doing here?"

Violet smiled. "Everyone keeps asking me that. But I think I know the answer." She placed her index finger to her lower lip in mock contemplation. "Is it because the concept of my *not* being here is illogical?"

"How did you know I wasn't on my way already? My itinerary must have arrived long after you left."

"A magic fairy told me."

Wil turned to Julian. "You're *magic* now?"

The corners of his mustache shifted upward slightly. "Did I forget to mention that?"

"So I guess you're not picking me up at the station," Moxie said.

"Even better," Violet replied. "Now Wil and I can just ride the train west with you."

"Wil's coming?"

Wil looked only slightly offended. "I'll do my best not to embarrass you, darling."

Violet turned to Wil. "Whatever you do, try not to shit in the dining car. They really take issue with that."

Wil scowled. "Should I be writing all this down?"

"So," Moxie said slowly, "when things get dull, just pack up the carnival and take it along with you?"

"Perhaps I had other, ulterior motives." Violet's eyebrows twitched twice suggestively.

"Oh? Like what?"

Violet abruptly changed the subject. "Did I mention that your opening number, your whole show really, was quite—"

"Provocative?" Julian suggested.

"Arousing?" Wil proposed.

Gary decided to give it a try. "Jazzy?"

Everyone turned to him quizzically.

"Jules," Wil asked, "where did you find this guy, the Salvation Army?"

"It's closer to the *salivation* army, darling," he answered smugly. "You should stop by sometime and pick up a saliva soldier for yourself."

Moxie was anxious to bring the conversation back to where it had been a moment ago. "So, the song, the show, you were saying—"

"It was very, very sexy." Violet's words were little more than a throaty whisper.

Moxie was pleased at that observation, and her face was radiating heat for some reason. "Noticed that, did you?"

Violet took a small step toward her, so they were dangerously close. "I did. Every bit of me noticed."

"Is that so?" She felt an unfamiliar mixture of excitement and fear. Looking into Violet's eyes, she saw what she could only interpret as intense desire.

"Can I buy you a drink?"

"I might be amenable to that," Moxie said as she pulled up a chair at the table. "But only one this time."

Wil frowned. "You sadden me, darling. I saw such potential in you."

"Well, the last time we all went out, things kind of got away from me."

"We refer to that phenomenon as vespers," Julian explained.

Wil poured a glass of champagne for Moxie. "Mostly because it's punctuated by lying prostrate at the toilet and periodically calling out to the Lord."

Moxie took a sip, enjoying its effervescence. "Oh, well, perhaps I wasn't as bad off as I thought I was."

Violet covered Moxie's hand with her own. "It's very good to see you."

The intimate contact between them was unsettling, yet thrilling, and Moxie turned her hand over to caress Violet's palm with her own. "I've been thinking about our phone conversation."

"So have I." Violet's index finger slowly traversed the valley between Moxie's middle and ring fingers, through the sensitive center of her hand, and down to her wrist. Her touch was one part tickle, one part heat, and three parts erogenous stimulation. Or maybe it was four parts. Hell, her ability to do simple math was clearly a goner.

"Shit." Her attraction had overpowered her.

Violet seemed to be studying Moxie's response closely. "Do you have any plans tonight?"

"Sorry to interrupt, but Miss Valette needs to cut this evening short."

Moxie looked up to see Cotton standing at the table, and she jerked her hand away from Violet's reflexively. "I do?"

He looked at her sternly. "Yes, it's getting late."

"Everyone, this is my agent, Cotton McCann. Cotton, this is—"

"Yes. Enchanted." His disinterest was evident. He pulled her to her feet. "But we really must be going, since we have such an early departure tomorrow morning."

"We?" Moxie asked suspiciously.

"Yes, I'll be joining you, and so will Ida."

"You mean Irene?"

"The one I've been sitting with. Whoever she is."

Moxie was confused. "When did you decide this?"

Cotton stared at Violet in what appeared to be a silent challenge. "Recently. It's best for you to be surrounded by people who are looking out for your best interest."

Wil polished off her drink. "Just a li'l tip from me to you, mister. I hear you should avoid shitting in the dining car." She winked at him.

He seemed disgusted, but Moxie wasn't sure if it was what Wil said or how she said it that generated his disdain. "Go get changed, Moxie."

When Violet looked to Moxie to gauge her response, Moxie discreetly motioned back toward the stage. This either meant that Violet should venture backstage to meet her or that she had a neck disorder. Violet dropped her chin to show understanding.

"Okay, thanks again for coming out, everyone," Moxie said before departing.

Violet studied this man, this Cotton McCann. She tried to suppress her anger, but that had never been her forte.

He was still trying to stare her down for some reason. "You'll find I'm very protective of my clients, Miss London."

It interested her that he knew her name without first being

introduced. "That's an admirable quality, unlike pomposity or antagonism, which are decidedly less so."

His eyes narrowed. "You look like one of those Hollywood deviant types to me."

"Looks can be so deceiving," she replied with a calm that belied her emotions.

"Yeah?"

"Absolutely, because you look like a fat, manipulative, bombastic chiseler, but I'm sure you simply make a terrible first impression."

Wil beamed. "I love it when she gets like this."

"I can see why," Julian replied. "Even I want to fuck her right now."

A muscle in Cotton's cheek began to spasm. "Look here, you cheap piece of Christmas trash—"

"No, Mr. McCann, stop right there." Violet had now officially reached her breaking point. "I don't know who you think you are or how you cultivated such an asinine and misguided sense of entitlement. You think you can just pull out your dick and swing it around like a hammer—"

"Nice metaphor," Julian interjected.

"—and everyone will kowtow. But this Violet isn't shrinking, if you get me, not by a long shot. So go flex your muscle for some meek tomato who's too enraptured by the promise of stardom to care that you are a complete ballsack. And when you're done with all that, jump up my ass."

A look of incredulity washed over Cotton's face, no doubt exacerbated by Wil, Julian, and Gary all spontaneously breaking into applause.

"Thanks," Violet mumbled, picking up her dog. "Now, if my adoring public will excuse me, I need to take Clitty to the little terrier's room."

She walked off, headed toward the restrooms, and, feeling fairly certain that no one was looking, she ducked back toward the dressing rooms. There seemed to be only two rooms dedicated to the entertainment staff. One was empty, and the other had the door closed. Feeling lucky, she set Clitty down on the floor and knocked.

Before she even had a chance to pull her hand back completely, the door flew open to reveal Moxie, wearing a blue silk peignoir—

implying to Violet that underneath, the dress was gone and who knew what she had on now. Moxie smiled and tugged her into the room by the hand. As Clitty followed, she checked the hallway suspiciously before shutting the door and locking it.

"Expecting G-men?" Violet asked.

"No, but I wasn't expecting you either, and look what happened." Moxie boldly closed the distance between them.

"I'm like a bad penny." Violet tentatively reclaimed Moxie's hand. "Where were we?"

Moxie's tone took on a more seductive quality. "Let's see. You had told me how sexy I was."

"I had, yes." Violet moved closer, and now their faces were only inches apart. "And you were saying you'd been thinking about that day we talked on the phone."

"You were very naughty."

"You seem to bring that out in me."

"Why is that exactly?"

"Because I want you so much."

"Oh, baby." Moxie's words were nearly a whisper, but they were all the invitation Violet needed, and she leaned forward and kissed her.

What started as gentle and hesitant rapidly became urgent and all-consuming. Moxie's right hand moved to the nape of Violet's neck, while the other one slid around her waist. Their tongues moved against each other as Violet reached beneath the blue silk, praying to God that Moxie really was naked under there. Almost as tantalizing, Moxie had stripped down to her underwear, and Violet's finger brushed the satin of a stray garter belt.

When Moxie moaned, Violet thought she would explode from the sexual energy coursing through her. "God, you smell so good."

"Twilight Moon," Moxie murmured, her mouth beside Violet's ear. "My perfume. You said that you liked it."

"Know what else I like?" She nibbled on Moxie's neck, and the sound of her ragged breathing told her that the enjoyment was mutual. Emboldened, she brushed her thumb over Moxie's breast lightly through her brassiere and the nipple stiffened instantly.

"Mmm. I love how you touch me."

"I haven't even started yet." Violet kissed her again, consumed with hunger.

A loud knock startled them both, and they separated.

"Moxie? It's me, Cotton. Can I come in?"

Moxie looked panic-stricken. "Um...just a moment." She readjusted her dressing gown, glanced in the mirror, and wiped off her smeared lipstick with her thumb.

Clitty, on the other hand, was completely confounded by the disembodied voice behind the door and pawed at it before letting out a staccato yip.

"What was that?" Cotton asked.

Clitty yipped again.

Violet bent down and picked him up to silence him.

"Hiccups," Moxie called, wincing immediately at such a horrible lie.

"Can I come in yet? I need to talk to you."

Moxie put her finger to her lips silently, then slipped out into the hallway, shutting the door behind her.

"Why are you out here not completely dressed? Let's go back in the dressing room, for God's sake."

"You don't want to go in there. I'd hate for you to see what the other girls have done. It's a real mess. Lots of...period things everywhere."

"Oh." He appeared repulsed. "Look, I think I've gotten rid of that London woman for the evening."

"You have?"

"I don't know what you're thinking, falling in with a group of queers and boozehounds, but luckily for you, I was here to step in. You have a career to think of, after all."

"I realize that, but—"

"Don't ruin it before it even gets started. You were fantastic tonight. Better than I've ever seen you. You're on your way up. Eileen said—"

"Irene."

"—she thought that woman might even be on the train tomorrow."

"She might."

"Which is exactly why we're coming along too. You need to focus on your screen test and think about your future. Now finish changing and meet me out front. I told Iris—"

"Irene."

"—that I'd take you both home."

She blew her bangs out of her eyes while she considered this predicament. "And if I asked you not to go to any trouble?"

"I saw how that woman was pawing you. If I left you here, I wouldn't get a bit of sleep tonight."

"Neither would I," she muttered in frustration.

"Exactly. I'll see you out front. And get a wiggle on."

She watched him walk away and tried to collect herself. "Shit." She took a deep breath and reentered the dressing room, where Violet sat, her dog in her lap and her chin in her hand. "Did you hear any of that?"

"Not really. Something about periods and boozehounds. The rest was a bit muffled."

"Just as well."

Violet stood and deposited Clitty in the chair. "Why, oh why, is your agent such a bastard?" She let her hands rest on Moxie's hips as she kissed her throat.

"He thinks he's looking out for me."

Violet continued tasting her neck and earlobe. "More like looking out for his vested interest in you."

"Mmm…what?"

"I said come back to my hotel with me."

Moxie's head was spinning and her groin was tightening. She had never felt this kind of raw desire before, and it was debilitating. "I can't."

"Why not?"

"Cotton's driving Irene and me home. He's waiting for me outside now."

Violet's tongue probed Moxie's ear, and her whispered reply gave Moxie chills that vibrated throughout her body. "I'll send a taxi to your place to get you after he drops you off. He'll never know."

She struggled to form words. "Except he's also picking me up in the morning to take me to the train. God, your tongue is so…mmm."

"This tongue can be yours for the rest of the night, and it takes requests."

Moxie tried to snap out of the erotic fog that was wrapping around her and clouding her mind. "That's a very attractive offer, to be sure. But I can't tonight."

"Moxie—"

"Shh." She traced Violet's lips lightly with her fingers. "Things are moving a little fast for me. In the last half hour I've discovered that you traveled across the country and were in the audience without telling me, that my agent doesn't approve of you or anyone you know, that both he and my roommate are now coming along on my train trip to Hollywood—but only to keep me from you—and, most importantly, how very much I love your mouth. That's quite a bit for me to absorb, wouldn't you say?"

Violet nodded slowly.

"Then give me tonight to work through everything, okay? We have the next three days together and, after that, however long I'm in Hollywood."

"I'm sorry. I didn't mean to make you crazy."

"You can't help it," Moxie joked. "It's just something you do."

"I guess I'll go, then, and see you in the morning." She kissed Moxie once more, this time softly and reverently. "Good night."

Before Moxie could catch her breath and even consider replying, Violet and her dog were gone.

She sat down and rubbed her forehead with the heel of her palm as she pondered the unexpected turns the evening had taken. As right as being with Violet felt, she couldn't shake the fear that there was some truth to what Cotton had told her. He was an opportunist of epic proportions, that was certain. But he had also pulled her out of obscurity in that lousy Nebraska dive and pointed her toward success.

Maybe she *did* need to focus on her future and her career first.

But holy crap, Violet got her so hot. When she was with her, she couldn't think about anything but the surging waves of arousal that Violet evoked, and how wet and tingly she felt. She wanted her so badly that she was amazed she had the resolve to send her away. Or was it fear?

She started to change her clothes, all the while wondering what the hell she would do when morning came.

CHAPTER TEN

"All right," Cotton said authoritatively. "I'm going to go get tickets for Ivy—"

"Irene," Moxie and Irene said in unison.

"—and me. Don't go anywhere. Don't talk to anyone. Just wait here until I get back. Got me?"

Moxie rolled her eyes, nodded, then took in all the activity in the bustling concourse of Grand Central Terminal. Even though she had been in New York City over seven months, the grandeur of the architecture and the size of the crowds awed her as much as they had the day she arrived.

She casually scanned the crowds for a glimpse of Violet. "I can't believe you sold me out," she muttered to Irene. "Coming along on this trip so you can spy on me for my agent."

"I'm not spying. Mr. McCann says he only wants what's best for you. And just last night, you said you didn't know *what* you wanted."

Moxie winced. Irene had a point. "It would be nice to be treated like an adult able to make her own decisions and not like some fat girl who can't be left alone in a sweet shop because she might fondle all the fondant." She wiggled her fingers.

Irene cocked an eyebrow. "Well, perhaps you *would* be treated like someone who could make her own decisions, if you'd make one."

"Look, this is a little more complicated than deciding which shoes go with which bag."

"Are you the shoes or the bag?"

Moxie glared in response until a tap on her shoulder prompted her to turn.

"Hey, tomato," Violet said with a grin.

Moxie felt her face light up. "Hey, yourself. I was worried you wouldn't make it."

"I had a little problem getting Lady Chatterley here up and dressed this morning." She motioned to a very weary-looking Wil. "It seems she and a certain waiter had an illicit encounter last night that has made her a little, shall we say, sleep-deprived."

"A waiter from the Luna?" Moxie asked conspiratorially. "Which one?"

"The circumcised one," Wil replied. "And let me go on record by saying that he has completely reformed my perception of Judaism."

"So he made you see Moses?" Violet asked.

"That may very well be what happened, though we may have broken a commandment or two."

"Well, if it was only two, that's a slow night for you, sister," Violet said.

"Holy cats." Irene's shock was evident.

"Oh, sorry. Wil, Violet, this is my roommate Irene."

"You're the spy?" Wil blurted.

"I'm not spying! I'm just here to help...and to get a free trip to Hollywood." She looked at Wil and Violet. "I'm really not a bad person." Her attention moved to the floor, where a little brown dog sat staring up at her attentively. "Is this Clitty?"

"His reputation precedes him, apparently," Violet said. Irene knelt down to pet him, and Violet took the opportunity to share a smoldering look with Moxie. "You look lovely."

"Thanks. You look hungry."

The left corner of Violet's mouth rose slightly, but her gaze stayed smoldering. "Yes, I was just imagining warm, moist flapjacks."

Moxie surged with heat from this provocative playfulness. "The kind that are sticky and sweet?"

"Definitely that kind. So messy you have to lick your fingers when you're done."

Wil groaned. "Good Lord, all this pancake talk is making me horny. Can you two just fuck and get it over with?"

"Hotchy botchy!" Irene stood up quickly.

"What's all this?" Cotton said, returning to the group with a sneer. "I thought I said not to talk to anyone."

"Wil and Violet aren't just *anyone*," Moxie replied in irritation.

"Yes," he snapped. "They're, in fact, the ones I wanted you to avoid."

"But—"

"Come on." He pulled her toward the train by her forearm. "This is precisely why I'm here. Let's board now."

Moxie turned and looked at Violet apologetically as she was briskly led away.

"Hey, wait for me," Irene called. "It was nice meeting you," she said awkwardly as she hurried after them.

"Wow," Violet said as she watched them board the train.

"You know what that was?" Wil asked.

"What?"

"Douchebaggery, of the highest degree."

"I would have to agree."

"It looks like you might have to work a little for this one, sister."

"Hmm, and you might have to help me." She picked up her dog.

"Well, I *do* owe you. And you know I can't tolerate douchebags."

"You can't cotton to Cotton?"

"Count me in, doll."

Violet smiled. "I was hoping you'd say that."

❖

Moxie was chagrined, though not at all surprised, that Cotton had made sure she and Irene were sharing a double bedroom. She had surmised that Irene would be her constant chaperone.

Nonetheless, the way she was being treated still bothered her. Sure, Cotton kept droning on about what was best for her career and how she'd thank him later. But she was still reconciling the astounding effect that Violet's presence had on her and the novelty of this kind of powerful desire. It was rather comical that after years of singing songs about passion and longing, she had never felt what she had been crooning about, until now.

What had she felt with her old beaus? It didn't remotely compare to this. Back then, she found it harder to say yes to them than no. She had to really concentrate to rebuff Violet's advances and then almost immediately experienced a series of regrets that oscillated between hunger and misgiving.

She dutifully spent the first couple of hours of the trip in the communal drawing room that all four bedrooms in her railroad car shared. But after she realized she had read the same page of her book about sixteen times and still didn't have a damn clue what it said, she sighed and stood.

"What?" Irene asked.

"I'm just jittery. I need to go for a walk."

"Oh, no, you don't. Mr. McCann said we're supposed to stay here."

Moxie put her hands on her hips. "What did he promise you?"

"Huh?"

"Don't play dumb with me, girlie. What did Cotton offer you so you'd stick to me like glue?"

Irene's face fell. "He said he'd get me a screen test when we got to Hollywood if I kept you and Violet apart." The words spilled out as though the confession was a relief.

"And you believed him?"

Suddenly something slid under the door.

"What's that?" Irene picked up the envelope. "It's for you."

"Is that from Violet?"

"No." She flipped it over and read the name on the back. "It's from someone named Fanny Hertz." She handed it over to Moxie, who was laughing. "What's so damned funny? Who's Fanny Hertz?"

"Mine does." She tore the missive open and slid out the folded paper inside.

Darling,

I realize that you're sequestered, but I miss your company terribly. Could you possibly slip away? I'm in bedroom 8, and Wil is next door at 7, but I'll be getting a bite in the dining car soon.

Come by to see me, or meet me for lunch. Your choice.

Vi

"What does it say?" Irene asked.

"Nothing." Moxie folded the note back up and slipped it under the neckline of her dress. "Just welcoming me aboard. But I'm getting hungry. Let's change and head over to the dining car in a bit."

❖

When Irene and Moxie arrived at the dining car, it was apparent that idea had occurred to many of the other passengers as well.

"Wow, it's packed in here," Irene said.

"There's Vi. Let's sit with her." She pulled Irene across the car.

"Are you sure it's food you're hungry for?"

"Violet," Moxie said in feigned surprise. "What a coincidence. Is it okay if we sit with you?"

Violet looked up calmly from her newspaper, a copy of the *New York World-Telegram*. "Certainly, ladies," she replied, almost in disinterest. "Ah, the crossword puzzle."

As Moxie took the seat next to Violet, she was surprised and a little disappointed by Violet's cool response. She tried not to frown as she watched Violet borrow a pen from a waiter. "Where's Wil?"

"Sleeping," Violet answered as she started the puzzle.

"Recovering from last night still?" Irene took a seat across from them.

"Getting ready for tonight. There's a whole trainload of men she hasn't slept with yet, and Wil has very lofty goals."

"She's like a machine," Irene said, with a tinge of awe in her voice.

Violet looked at her in amusement. "She is—a well-oiled, foul-mouthed, gin-swilling, dick-licking machine."

"God bless her." Moxie touched her water goblet to Violet's glass.

"And God bless Tiny Tim," Violet toasted back, taking a drink.

Moxie coughed into her water. "Is Wil sleeping with him too?"

"To some, it's a crutch," Violet teased. "To Wil, it's a dildo."

The waiter took that very inopportune time to return to the table, but if he overheard the conversation, his expression didn't show it. "Can I get you ladies anything?"

"I'd like a cup of coffee," Irene said.

"Tea, please," Moxie added.

"And you, miss? Would you care for another lemonade?"

Violet nodded, though she grimaced slightly as the waiter departed.

"Not your first choice, huh?" Irene asked.

"Lemonade wasn't even in my first hundred choices, no. But sometimes you just have to make do."

Moxie lowered her voice slightly. "You and Wil didn't bring any libations with you?"

"You bet your ass we did, toots. But I'm saving them until I can really use them."

Cotton suddenly loomed over their table with a look of disapproval. "Ah, here you are. I should have known."

"Like now, for instance," Violet said matter-of-factly.

Cotton squinted at Violet. "Moxie, why is it that every time I turn my back, when I next see you, you're with this…person?" He gestured dismissively toward her.

"Thanks for acknowledging my species," Violet said, her voice devoid of discernable emotion. "It sounded like it challenged you."

Moxie huffed in annoyance. "As you can see, Cotton, it's very crowded. Violet was nice enough to let us sit at her table."

Cotton pulled out the remaining chair across from Moxie and got comfortable. "Where's the other floozy? The redhead?"

Violet didn't look up from her crossword puzzle. "Resting, but I'll make sure I convey to her your regards. She'll no doubt be touched to be in your thoughts so fondly."

He sneered. "Aw, applesauce."

Violet shifted to Moxie. "Say, are you any good at these?" She waggled the newspaper.

"Crossword puzzles? A little, I guess."

"This one—five letters, goddess of love." Violet paused for a moment and in the blocks wrote M-o-x-i-e.

"That doesn't seem right," Moxie said softly.

"I think it is, because from the *i* I get this." She wrote I-w-a-n-t-y-o-u in 19 Down.

"Ah" was all Moxie could rasp out. "I see."

"What did you order?" Irene asked as she perused the menu.

"Roast beef. I recommend it." Violet returned her attention to the puzzle. "So, a twelve-letter word that means a nighttime activity."

"Uh." Moxie was too distracted to process the clue.

She watched Violet write M-y-m-o-u-t-h-o-n-y-o-u in 24 Across. "There."

"Yes!" Moxie blurted a little too quickly. She was relieved to see Cotton and Irene were still discussing lunch options. "That's definitely it."

"Hmm, eight letters—a honey-like substance."

Moxie pulled the pen seductively from her hand and scribbled y-o-u-r-l-i-p-s in the blocks.

"You *are* good at this," Violet said.

"I hate to interrupt your literary consortium," Cotton said, "but do you know what you're ordering yet, Moxie?"

Violet ignored him, taking the pen back. "Twenty-nine Down. Nine letters, meaning ever-watchful." She filled the blocks with d-o-u-c-h-e-b-a-g.

Moxie struggled not to laugh. "Yes, Cotton. I do." She nodded.

"Good," Irene said. "Because I'm hungry."

Moxie reclaimed the pen and wrote S-o-a-m-I in 36 Down before handing it back.

Violet completed 42 Across with T-e-l-l-m-e. She extended the writing implement as though daring Moxie to take it from her.

Moxie was feeling up to the challenge, and she filled the puzzle blocks with Y-o-u-m-a-k-e-m-e-a-c-h-e.

Violet tore the pen from her hand and scrawled "Meet me in bedroom 8" at the top of the puzzle.

She wrote "I'll try" beside it, prompting Violet to jot "Try very, very hard" in a shaky script.

At that moment, Cotton sneezed.

"Fuck you," Violet said innocently.

"Thank…" He caught himself in the midst of reflexively thanking her for a blessing. "Never mind." He continued to glower, while Violet avoided his eye contact.

"So," Irene said awkwardly. "What's the news today?"

"Not much different from yesterday, I'm afraid," Violet replied.

"Poverty is still crippling the vast majority of the population, and shockingly, President Hoover's sage policy of telling people to pull themselves up by their bootstraps somehow still isn't working."

"You're blaming the president for the Depression?" Cotton asked, his voice laden with derision.

"No, but I am blaming him for not doing a goddamn thing about it, while around him, people are starving."

He sighed. "This is why women should never have been given the vote."

Moxie could feel it coming, and she inwardly braced for the gathering storm. "Oh, shit," she whispered, glancing nervously at Irene.

"Because you prefer empty-headed, closed-mouthed little dishes who fetch your pipe, bake pies, and lie back and daydream of someone more attractive than you—long enough for you to ejaculate into her orifice of choice? Does a woman who not only understands current events but has opinions about them really threaten you that much?"

"Me? Threatened by a woman? Ha!"

Her gaze narrowed. "Then why are you here, guarding Moxie like she's made of gold bullion?"

Cotton said nothing but looked livid as the waiter arrived with drinks and a plate of crusty bread.

"Bread," Irene proclaimed. "Thank God." When the waiter studied her strange response she added, "I *really* love bread." She stuffed a small piece in her mouth as though to further illustrate her statement.

"Yes, miss," the waiter said coldly. "Sir, may I get you a beverage?"

Cotton's head was in his hands. "I suppose a gin would be out of the question," he said weakly.

"They amended the Constitution because of dirty boozehounds like you," Violet snapped, waggling her finger at him. "Waiter, might I be moved to a different table, please? This man offends my delicate sensibilities."

"I'm sorry, miss. I don't believe there is anywhere else for you to sit right now."

"I understand," she said, touching the waiter's hand softly. "You've been very kind. Who would I speak to about having him removed from the train?"

"Hey," Cotton shouted.

"That would be the conductor, miss."

"Thanks so much. If he continues to bother me, I'll be sure to report him."

The waiter nodded and left the table hurriedly.

"What about my drink?" Cotton called after him. His attention snapped back to Violet. "Look here, bitch, that wasn't funny."

"It wasn't meant to be," she replied flatly. "It was meant to demonstrate two things to you. First, just because you're a white man of means, you're not superior to anyone. I don't answer to you, and you don't control me. If I want you gone, I can make it happen. Secondly, I don't like you. And the more time I spend in your company, the stronger that feeling gets."

"I will *not* be spoken to in this manner," he spat.

"You will, and you just were. Try to remember just how shitty it feels the next time you do it to someone else." Violet stood and picked up her dog from beneath the table. "Ladies, Clitty and I would love to stay and continue discussing politics with you, but your lunch guest is a hinky bastard, something Clitty has very little tolerance for. Good day."

As Violet walked out of the dining car, Moxie was crestfallen. So much for spending time together.

"If I'd known that was all it took to make her leave, I'd have been—what was it? hinky?—as soon as I sat down." He looked smug.

"Oh, you were," Irene said, stirring her coffee. "Trust me."

"What *is* hinky, anyway?" he asked her.

"A shifty ass," Moxie answered.

Cotton began to hum to himself.

When Wil finally stirred and ventured into her semi-private drawing room, it was well into the afternoon. Violet was slumped in a chair, dejected and bored.

"Good Lord, has some ecclesiastical militia invaded us?"

Violet shifted her eyes left, studying her for a moment, but otherwise did not move.

"Tsk, tsk." Wil sat across from her and began to brush her hair.

"I'll take a guess and say that things with Moxie have not progressed as you hoped."

"If that means not one damn bit, then your guess is right on the money, doll."

"Is she waffling?"

"Not that I can tell. It's her entourage that's gumming up the works. They're *always* with her."

Wil looked sympathetic. "And her agent seems to be a real rank piece of meat."

"I need to get them out of the way."

"Do you want to shove them off the train?"

"I do, though obviously that can't be the plan."

"It's exciting, though—planning to rub someone out. Makes me feel like I'm from Chicago."

Wil's elation bothered Violet. "Let's try and devise something slightly less lethal."

"Well, there's always the old standby."

"You mean fuck him?"

"Exactly! I'll charm his cock right into my hand."

"Hmm, I'm not sure you want that particular cock anywhere near you, Wil."

"Well, that's why I said my hand and not anywhere, you know, good."

Violet chuckled. "I don't doubt your seductive prowess, but earlier he referred to you as the other floozy. He may not be as willing as your average joe."

"What? Goddamn it, I'm *the* floozy, and he better believe it."

"Well, you may be handicapped by your association with me, coupled with his abysmal personality."

Wil looked resolute. "Madam, I have yet to meet a heterosexual man who doesn't want a slice of this pie, if you get me." She pointed to her genitals.

"Oh, I get you, all right. Subtlety is not your strong suit. Would you like to wager?"

"You know I would." Wil managed to look confident and promiscuous at the same time. "What are the stakes?"

Violet considered the question. "How about a night on the town?"

"Which consists of what?"

"Winner's choice," she said with a grin.

"That sounds very attractive. You have a bet, darling."

"Wil, you don't know how much I want you to win."

"Until you just proposed the stakes, I wanted *you* to win."

"Completely understandable. He is, after all, a douchebag of the highest degree."

"Vice-chancellor Douchebag," Wil announced regally.

"Is that higher than Monsignor Douchebag?"

"Yes, but below Cardinal Douchebag."

"So what's the plan, sister? All this waiting is killing me."

❖

Moxie flipped over three more cards and sighed. She wasn't even paying attention anymore, and how sad was that? What did it mean when you faked a game of solitaire, for God's sake? "C'mon, Irene. I'm dying in here. I just need a little walk."

"I know where you want to walk to. Nancy Drew has you all figured out."

"So you're not bored at all?"

"Are you fooling? I'm going out of my *flipping skull*." She blew her bangs out of her eyes dramatically.

There was a knock from outside, and Moxie practically tripped as she leapt up to answer the door. Opening it revealed Violet and Wil.

"Hi there," Violet said smoothly, lounging against the doorjamb.

"Hi," Moxie whispered, her voice suddenly leaving her.

Wil pushed the door open farther with her foot. "We thought it might be pleasant to pass the time with you three." She glanced into the drawing room. "Where's Prime Minister Douchebag?"

"In his compartment, one car back." Moxie happily stepped aside to let her guests enter.

"He has a bum stomach or something," Irene answered. "Apparently travel food bothers him."

"Pity," Wil said insincerely as she reached deep into her cleavage to retrieve a silver flask. "Because I brought some brandy."

Violet's eyes brimmed with amusement. "And she's warmed it already, for your convenience."

"No extra charge," Wil added. "I'm full service all the way."

"Who would dare dispute that?" Violet asked.

Moxie retrieved some glasses and set them in front of Wil, who began to pour.

"Gee, I've never had brandy before," Irene said, somewhat hesitantly.

Wil held a shot out to her. "Aphrodite's nectar."

She took it and stared into the amber liquid. "Sounds fancy."

"Nearly as fancy as we are," Violet said, holding her glass aloft.

Irene took a sip, and after a moment her eyes flew open wide. "Holy mackerel!"

"Now close your eyes," Wil advised, "and inhale through your mouth."

"Is it supposed to burn?"

Violet sat down and watched Irene intently. "That's a sign of quality, sister."

"Yes, the burn is bliss," Wil said.

Moxie leaned in closely to Violet so she could whisper. "You're not going to make her sick, are you?"

"No, Wil's just a distraction. Though admittedly, she tends to have greater success distracting those with a penis."

"As I would imagine."

Violet stayed close to Moxie's ear, but didn't speak right away, causing Moxie's body to react to her nearness. "You didn't come to my room," she finally said.

"I wanted to…want to."

"You know." The raspiness of Violet's hushed tone made Moxie's breath catch in her chest. "I'm fairly certain I've reached whatever my physical limitations are for sexual frustration."

"I know what you mean."

"What are we going to do about this?"

Moxie exhaled sharply. "I haven't a fucking clue, but whatever it is, it needs to happen soon."

Violet's expression fluctuated between humor and ardor. "Once Wil has entranced your gal with her booze and stories, let's slip out of here."

"Cotton will be by in a little over an hour to take us to dinner."

"I'll tell Wil to hurry."

CHAPTER ELEVEN

A nd he was so big, I had to tell him to scram," Wil said, sitting cross-legged on the floor.

Irene gasped. "That can happen?"

"Sadly, yes. And I'll have you know this snatch is not what most people would consider petite. I've had some fairly large things in there. Comfortably," she added with a nod.

"So what did you say to him?"

"That he was joking if he thought I had a goddamn orifice that could accommodate that. After all, I'm not a fucking manhole."

"You said it, sister," Irene said, sipping from the flask again.

Behind them, Violet and Moxie sat beside each other, waiting for just the right moment to slip out of the room.

"Come on," Violet said softly.

"Is it wrong that I want to hear the rest of this?" Moxie asked, intent on Wil's tale of enormous genitalia.

Violet snaked her tongue lightly up Moxie's ear. "It is, yes," she murmured. "So wrong that I think you may need to be punished."

"Let's go," she said suddenly, picking up Clitty in one hand and pulling Violet into a standing position with the other.

They crept out the drawing-room door, nearly colliding with an older couple who were on their way toward the rear of the train.

Politely letting them pass, Violet was suddenly panicked to see Cotton making his way through the same door they were en route to. Taking advantage of his distraction when he yielded to the old couple, she yanked Moxie in the opposite direction and through the door that led toward the front of the train.

As the door closed behind them, they froze. "Do you think he saw us?" Violet asked.

"If he did, we'll know in about ten seconds." Moxie looked around. "Where are we?"

"Looks like the baggage car." Violet took Clitty from Moxie and set him on the floor. She then tugged Moxie into the corner behind a large stack of luggage. Before Moxie was able to say anything, Violet covered Moxie's mouth with hers and laced her fingers through Moxie's hair possessively.

Their tongues entwined, and Violet felt a fresh rush of desire as the kiss deepened and became more urgent.

"We don't have long," Violet said quietly. "And there are so many places on you that I want to taste." She ventured down Moxie's slender neck and grazed the tender flesh there with her teeth.

"God," Moxie groaned, her fingers moving along Violet's waist. "Is this one of them?"

"Yes." Violet caressed Moxie's breast through her dress, and the nipple grew taut and erect beneath her palm. "And so is this," she added, bringing her mouth down to the breast to intensify the response. With the barrier of fabric in place, she boldly bit the soft tissue beneath to ensure that she got the reaction she wanted.

"Oh!"

Violet brought her face back up within inches of Moxie's. "Shh. You can't make any noise."

"But—"

"Silence." It was a whispered command, and coupled with Violet's ardent gaze, Moxie heeded her with no further urging. Violet deftly pulled up the linen of Moxie's dress to gain access to her thighs and marvelously round ass. Skimming over garters and stockings, Violet felt her heart nearly stop when she realized Moxie wasn't wearing anything beneath her garter belt, and she had full, unimpeded access to where she most wanted to be.

She guided Moxie back a step, so she was now pressed up against a large steamer trunk. "Sit up here," she commanded, and in one nimble movement, Moxie was seated before her, her dark eyes level with Violet's.

The kissing resumed with greater urgency as Violet moved her fingers skillfully along the inside of Moxie's shapely thighs and was rewarded with the most astounding wetness. Moxie's desire felt so hot and slick that Violet couldn't suppress a throaty murmur of approval. "I'd say you want this as much as I do," she rasped, continuing to stroke her.

Moxie nodded and ground her hips against Violet's hand.

This was certainly not how Violet had envisioned their first time— Moxie draped over some stranger's luggage in the baggage car—but at this point, she would take whatever opportunity she was given. God knew she doubted her ability to wait much longer.

Violet knelt and began kissing her way up Moxie's thighs. When her tongue reached their juncture, she couldn't suppress a smile at the way Moxie tasted, suffused with passion and need.

Moxie was obviously still trying to be silent, though she wasn't completely successful. As she gyrated against Violet's mouth her breathing was ragged, punctuated by soft staccato moans.

The sound of the door sliding shut startled them both.

"Hello?"

"Fuck," Violet mouthed, her frustration blurring with homicidal fantasies surrounding whoever that voice belonged to. She looked at Moxie and held up her index finger as a signal for her to stay still for a moment.

"Is anyone in here?" the male voice asked again.

Clitty barked happily. Violet rolled her eyes that her dog was so damn friendly.

"Well, hey there. Who do you belong to?"

Violet quickly stood as the sound of footsteps approached them, and she helped Moxie pull down her dress.

"Hello?" he asked again.

"So you see, rainbows are simply light refracted by moisture," Violet said in her best college-professor voice.

Moxie had her chin in her hand as she tried to feign fascination. "Wow."

"Oh," Violet said, turning to the train porter holding Clitty, who had appeared around the corner. "Hello. We didn't hear you."

"What are you doing in here?"

"We were just going over the basics of hydrometeorology," Violet replied.

He looked completely confounded. "Um, is this your dog?"

Moxie hopped up and took Clitty from him. "Yes, we came in looking for him. Thank you."

"You aren't supposed to be in this area." He scowled.

"We're *very* sorry," Moxie said. "We'll be going now. Thanks again for finding him for us."

Violet followed Moxie into the next car, and when she saw no one in the corridor, she backed Moxie against the wall and put her palms flat on the walls on either side of her.

"So you study science in your free time?" Moxie asked, her voice husky.

"Actresses aren't all fluff and quim, you know." Their mouths were excruciatingly close.

"Is that so?"

Violet smiled. "Actually, I have a photographic memory. If I read it once, it's with me forever."

"Really?"

"How do you think I remember all those lines? Now, would you like to tell me why you aren't wearing any underpants?"

"Well, since lunch, the crossword puzzle, I've been a little distracted."

"Uh-huh."

"And honestly, they just kept getting wet. So I took them off. I was hoping to cool off a little."

"That may be the best fucking reason for anything that I've ever heard."

"I love your mouth," Moxie said softly.

"And it loves your—"

The door of Moxie's drawing room flew open, causing them both to jump.

"There you are," Cotton announced, as he, Wil, and Irene stepped into the hallway. "I'm afraid to ask what you two were doing."

Moxie grinned weakly. "Hydronumeralzoology."

"Is that what the kids are calling it these days?" Wil joked.

"I needed to get something in the baggage car," Violet explained. And tragically, she *still* needed to get it, and badly.

"Goodness," Moxie said brightly, "is it already dinnertime?" She placed Clitty on the floor.

Cotton looked nonplussed. "I was only able to secure a table for two tonight. But I'm sure you ladies will fare just fine." He directed Moxie to head toward the dining car, and as she did so, he turned to glare at the remaining women.

Wil, Irene, and Violet stood with only each other for company as Wil sighed. "I want you to know, Vi, this bet is going to be *very* unpleasant for me."

"I understand," Violet said. "But you'd better get hot on it, sister, or I might just implode."

"Do you two have dinner plans?" Irene asked.

"My dinner plans were rudely interrupted," Violet answered in irritation.

Will looked pleasantly surprised. "Do tell."

"The appetizer was incredible."

Irene looked confused. "There's food in the baggage car?"

"Finger food?" Wil asked.

"That was just the first course. I was well into the second."

"You're making me hungry," Irene said dejectedly.

"Yes," Violet replied. "Unfortunately my appetite isn't sated either."

❖

Cotton sawed his knife through the piece of well-done steak on his plate while Moxie waited—waited for him to start lecturing her.

So far, they had been seated, had ordered, and been served their dinner without anything more than pleasant small talk about menu items and railway amenities. She knew something was brimming under the surface, and Cotton was no doubt biding his time for just the right moment to erupt.

"Moxie, we need to discuss your career."

Ah, here it was. She tried to stifle a smug smile as she loaded her fork with mashed potatoes. "Do we?"

"I was hoping I wouldn't have to spell all this out for you," he began quietly. "But obviously my subtlety has been ineffective."

"You were being subtle?"

He pressed on without responding. "I realize you're a young, Midwestern, homespun girl."

"Don't forget corn-fed."

"You've probably never been exposed to people like this before."
Moxie arched her eyebrows in curiosity and continued to chew.

"There are women out there, predators, who will want to do things to you." He dropped his voice to a whisper. "Sexual things."

She shifted in her chair, clamping her thighs together in the hope that things down there would stop throbbing and, with any luck, begin to air-dry. Cotton's mention of women wanting to do sexual things to her was not aiding her in this endeavor.

"I don't mean to offend or upset you," he said, apparently interpreting her fidgeting as discomfort with the topic itself.

"I appreciate that, Cotton." She needed Violet's mouth on her again. That had been the most incredible and erotic sensation she had experienced in her entire life. How did she *do* those things? It was like some of her body parts were enchanted. Oh, Cotton was still speaking.

"I believe this London woman to be one of these seducers."

"And what experience do you have with predators and seducers?"

He looked suddenly uncomfortable. "I'd rather not say."

"You're starting to sound paranoid."

His jaw tightened, and a muscle in his cheek twitched. "I'm speaking from experience. I know, because that's what happened to my wife."

"You never mentioned being married."

"I like to pretend that I never was." He continued cutting his meat and did not meet her gaze.

"What happened?"

He didn't respond right away, and Moxie simply waited.

"We were only married a few years. I traveled quite a bit for my job."

"Who was it?"

"My brother's wife."

"Oh, my. How did you find out?"

"One evening my train was canceled due to snow. I returned home and found them in the act."

Moxie pressed her legs together tight. She knew it was wrong to find her friend's heartbreaking story arousing. "What were they doing?"

she asked without thinking, in a voice that sounded too husky to be hers.

"What?" He seemed caught off guard by her candid question. "Well, they weren't playing pinochle. Let's just leave it at that."

"Perhaps there was an innocent explanation."

He scowled. "An argument that she tried to make. Cake frosting doesn't just *fall* into one's vagina. Such an action defies the laws of physics." He seemed to notice that he was speaking quite loudly and he shrank into his chair.

"Mmm, that is very tragic." She could not believe how wet she was. Just when she hoped she'd be able to concentrate on something innocuous, to force herself to think of something other than Violet's dexterous hands stroking her to wondrous climax, suddenly she heard stories of frosted lesbian muff parties. It was like a cruel conspiracy. If she hadn't been so incredibly horny, she might even have laughed about it. Her clit thrummed like a plucked bow string. "Shit," she murmured.

"At any rate, I think I know what I'm talking about."

"Perhaps they were just sharing a recipe."

"What they were doing was giving in to insanity."

"I don't know that cake frosting is *crazy*, per se. Messy, certainly—"

"I even offered to try and overlook her indiscretion, if she simply promised never to see my sister-in-law again. And of course get psychiatric care for her dementia," he added almost as an afterthought as he took a sip of tea. "She declined. Can you believe that?"

"Shocking." She hoped her incredulity had not seeped into the word as it fell from her lips. Moxie was now finding this conversation disturbing in a whole new way. "Cotton, I'm sure that was difficult to bear."

"Very."

"So you divorced."

He nodded.

"Perhaps you should have suggested the cake frosting first."

"I beg your pardon?"

"Well, then perhaps she needn't have looked outside her marriage for…baked goods."

"I'm a good Christian, I'll have you know." He appeared horrified. "That's no way for married people to behave."

"Yes, you wouldn't want anyone to enjoy it," she mumbled into her water glass.

"Moxie, I see you as the daughter I could have had, if my filthy slattern of a wife hadn't destroyed both our marriage as well as my brother's, by rutting with my whore of a sister-in-law."

"Um, thank you?" She supposed there had been a compliment in there somewhere, amid all the bitterness.

"I don't want to see you led down the primrose path, a path of carnal destruction. Hollywood will never tolerate that kind of sin and depravity."

She furrowed her brow in confusion. "Which Hollywood are you talking about?"

"The one we're en route to."

Moxie started counting on her fingers. "Fatty Arbuckle, William Desmond Taylor, Barbara La Marr, Jeanne Eagels. Any of those ring a bell? It's probably not because they shared a pew with you at high mass."

"Exactly. You should learn from their examples."

"So you think they were all anomalies? Everyone else in Los Angeles is God-fearing and temperate?"

"Look, you're too green to see how much sense I'm making."

"Is that the problem?" She took another mouthful of food from her fork.

"Yes. But I'm not going to let you fail." He seemed to have missed the sarcasm in her voice.

"Cotton, I realize that you see me as naïve. But I've been on my own long enough to know the score."

"Everyone *thinks* they know the score, doll. But only some really do."

"And you're one of the ones who does?"

He beamed. "Like the back of my hand."

❖

Violet, Wil, and Irene had decided to retreat to Violet and Wil's drawing room and order their dinner in, and after the meal Wil had changed into something navy blue and slinky, and was applying her makeup in the large mirror while the other two watched.

"I'm telling you," Wil asserted as she fussed with her mascara, "I *saw* her do it. I was there."

Irene looked stunned. "She actually managed to get a note out of a clarinet with her vagina?"

"Granted, it wasn't the best version I've ever heard, but it was discernibly 'Frère Jacques.'"

"The French are *amazing*," Irene declared.

"Wait until you hear how she plays the cello," Violet said.

Wil turned to address them both. "Europeans have a way of making you feel like you have a lazy twat. I mean, I can only do about six things proficiently with mine. Most Europeans are no doubt into double digits."

"Are you counting predicting the weather in your six?" Violet asked as she tossed a ball for Clitty to retrieve.

"Yes. And I'm also including that it can measure things up to sixteen inches long with reasonable accuracy." She turned back to the mirror and reviewed her appearance quickly. "Speaking of, I'm off, darlings."

"Where are you going?" Irene asked.

"Vi and I have a little bet that needs settling." She turned to Violet. "Give me about five minutes, doll. Then you should be in the clear."

"I do admire your confidence," Violet said with a smile.

"Judging by what I've seen," Wil said, "you'll need to work fast. He doesn't strike me as a marathon man, if you get my drift."

"Can't you try and go slowly?" Violet asked.

Wil rolled her eyes. "We've been over this before. What you do and what I do are like apples and oranges, darling."

"Fair enough. But can't you take some extra time to peel yours?"

"Sometimes I barely get it off the tree, sister," Wil said with a wink.

Violet stood. "Maybe it's how you're plucking your fruit. At times you need a light touch so you don't, you know, bruise the goods."

A wicked expression crossed Wil's face. "You can't get the juice without squeezing."

"Well, you don't squeeze apples. They're plenty juicy as is. That's why they make such tasty pie."

"You have a bigger sweet tooth than I have, darling. Wish me luck."

"All I have," Violet said as Wil stepped into the corridor and shut the door behind her.

"You know," Irene shook her head, "I never really know what the two of you are talking about."

Violet smiled. "This should help you. Whenever you're uncertain, we're talking about sex."

"So, most of the time."

"I'd say anywhere between seventy-five to ninety-eight percent of it, yes." She sat back down and resumed her game of fetch with Clitty.

"I can see why Moxie has so much fun with you. I don't mean *fun*," she amended quickly, stretching the last word out for several seconds. "Though maybe I do. But *I* don't want any fun, at least not the kind where I wake up somewhere else naked. I mean, what girl doesn't like to have a little fun? Good, wholesome, clothes-wearing fun. But I like men, and I want to keep it that way, if it's all the same to you."

Violet simply blinked at her. "Are you having some kind of spell? Speaking in tongues?"

"I'm okay."

"That's a relief." She took a sip of her drink.

"Do you know any famous people in Hollywood?"

"That depends on how you define famous."

"Um, people I might have heard of."

"Oh, then no."

"Well, who did you make your movie with?"

"Rex Kelly."

"Wow! Is he really as suave as he is in the movies?"

"No."

"Is he as sexy?"

"No."

"As tall?"

"Sure, he's tall."

Irene scowled. "What's wrong with him?"

"He's just not very exciting."

"Oh."

"But maybe that's because he's high all the time. Perhaps we should give him the benefit of the doubt. Let's assume he would be much more interesting if he weren't constantly in a state of self-sedation."

"Oh." Irene was even more dejected. "Did you meet anyone else when you were out there?"

"Sylvia King. One night at a dinner party."

"She's a doll. I saw her in *Daddy's Little Girl* and she was adorable."

"Did you see her in *Much Ado About Nothing*? I believe she played the role of nothing."

Irene's face fell. "Is something wrong with her too?"

"After I called her a cunt, I reconsidered and realized that it's an insult to cunts."

"An insult to—"

"And since I'm quite fond of the cunt in both feature and form, I'll have to think of another way to describe her that's not quite as flattering."

"But she always plays such a sweet young girl. I can't believe she's really that bad."

"She's an oozing pustule on the buttock of humanity."

Irene looked at Violet for a moment. "Wow."

"A walking and talking piece of feces."

"What about Mary Pickford? Did you meet her? Maybe attend some big party at Pickfair with her and Douglas Fairbanks?"

"Nope, sorry."

Irene seemed to be getting slightly frustrated. "So just the dope fiend and the turd?"

"Irene, you may be getting your hopes up too high. Sometimes famous people are just people who've been allowed to be more self-indulgent or hedonistic than the rest of us."

"And you and Wil seem pretty hedonistic already."

"Exactly. So imagine Wil with no limits at all."

At precisely that moment, Wil came back into the drawing room, looking decidedly irritated and dejected.

Violet glanced at her wristwatch. "You didn't make it to five minutes."

"Let's just say there's something unmanly and decidedly un-American about Ambassador Douchebag."

As disappointed as Violet was, she had to laugh. "I'll be the judge of that. Tell me how you approached him."

Wil flopped down on a chair and reached for her cigarette holder. "I knocked on his door, pushed my way in, and gave him my signature come-on line." She propped her right leg over the arm of the chair, either unaware or simply indifferent to the fact that her skirt was now splayed open.

"Oh, God, no," Violet said. "You didn't."

"It's never missed before."

Irene's eyebrows curved upward in curiosity. "What's your signature come-on line?"

Wil inhaled the smoke from her Chesterfield and exhaled it dramatically. "I like to fix the fella with a sultry look, narrow my eyes slightly, then say, 'I'll bet you like snatch.'"

Violet's face was in her hands, as she slowly shook it from side to side.

"What?" Wil asked.

"And what did he say?" Violet looked up at her, unable to cloak her incredulity. "After you broke the ice in such a demure, sophisticated way?"

"Well, darling, he said something terribly unkind about my snatch in particular, so after I kicked him the balls, I left."

Violet was momentarily unable to speak.

"You kicked someone in the balls?" Irene finally asked.

"Don't worry," Wil assured them. "I was prepared for this. We're just going to move on to plan B."

"Plan B?" Violet said. "Is that where you shove a stick of butter up his ass and hit him with a skillet?"

Wil grinned. "No, doll. That's plan C."

Violet stood and walked over to the table under the window, picking up the stationery there. "Irene, do you mind taking a letter back to Moxie tonight?"

"Not at all."

❖

It was well past the shank of the evening when Irene returned to her drawing room, a magazine folded under her arm.

Moxie sat reading a book as Irene flopped into a chair across from her. "So you *are* sober enough to remember which room is ours."

"I'm plenty sober, sister. I had a couple of drinks, but that was hours ago."

"Where have you been?" Moxie closed her book and set it in her lap.

"I had dinner with Wil and Violet in their room."

Moxie felt a pang of envy and tried not to let it show. "Oh, how'd that go?"

"They're a couple of real live wires. I can see why you have such a good time with them. Wil even tried to seduce some poor joe on a bet."

"Yes, I saw that disaster firsthand."

"You were there?" Irene seemed in awe.

"Yes. Cotton was right here with me."

"Holy Toledo. What did he think of all the hubbub?"

Moxie paused before answering, unsure of what Irene was asking. "Well, I had the steward bring him some ice. He's still trying to reduce the swelling."

Irene's mouth fell open but nothing immediately emerged. "You mean *he's* the sap she kneed in the goods?"

"No other. I assumed you knew that part."

Irene looked at the floor for a moment. "When Wil and Violet get to chinning, I only catch every third sentence or so. Their conversations are more like rounds from a Tommy gun."

"Very bawdy ones, yes. They require some getting used to, but believe me, it's well worth the effort."

"Oh, I almost forgot." Irene lowered her voice to a whisper. "Vi asked me to give you this." She pulled a sealed envelope from her magazine and handed it to Moxie.

"Thanks." She didn't bother to hide her eagerness as she ripped it open and began poring over the now-familiar script.

My darling Moxie,

    To say the Fates have again conspired to keep us apart does two things. One, it makes me sound very poetic, which certainly doesn't hurt in my endeavor to make you want to sleep with me. Two, it absolves your roommate and that rigidly puckered rectum that you call an agent of any and all blame.

Now, upon spending some time with Irene, I have found her to be quite likeable and realize that she is just an unwitting pawn in the rectum's grand plan—a bit like a diaper, to extend the metaphor. What your diaper of a roommate has agreed to do, while less than I had originally hoped, is to take you this letter. Sadly, I'm afraid this may be my only opportunity to communicate with you before we change trains in Chicago.

That being said, this missive is meant to pick up where we left off. To relieve some of your tension, so to speak. I want to tell you exactly how I want to touch you and how the taste of you has lingered both in my mind and on my lips like a fine wine. I need so much to drink in more of you. My tongue craves your wetness, my fingers ache to fill you, and I burn to once again feel your hips move hungrily against me, seeking release.

So fold this up and slip it somewhere discreet, excuse yourself to a private place where you won't be disturbed, and let me give you the climax you were cheated out of earlier.

"Holy shit," Moxie rasped. She flipped through the remaining two pages, her eye catching random words like *lick*, *stroke*, and *nipple*.

"What is it?" Irene asked.

"Just a...headache coming on." She folded the letter and slid it into her cleavage.

"Maybe you should lie down. We have another four hours or so before we get to Chicago."

"What about you? Are you going to sleep at all?" She tried to sound nonchalant.

"I don't think so." She again lowered her voice. "Don't tell Mr. McCann, but Vi gave me this movie magazine to read. She said there was something really spicy in here, but she wouldn't tell me what it was. I'm trying to find it."

"Ah, then maybe I *will* take that nap." Moxie closed the door to the bedroom before Irene could ramble any more.

CHAPTER TWELVE

"Y ou're not serious," Violet said.

Cotton stood in the train drawing room before Violet, Moxie, and Irene, holding his suitcase in one hand and an icepack to his groin with the other. "Completely." He dropped his bag, which landed with a loud thud. "This is the face of determination." He gestured toward his fixed jawline.

"And those are the bruised balls of arrogance." Violet pointed to his crotch.

"Cotton," Moxie said, "is this really necessary?"

"Since I can't trust anyone here, I simply visited the ticket counter and told them what I wanted. They were more than happy to give us accommodations beside each other so we can all share a drawing room. Moxie, you're still sharing a room with Irma—"

"Irene," they all corrected in unison.

"—and the other three rooms go to the rest of us," he continued without acknowledging them. "Choose whichever room you please, Miss London. Because either way, I'll be watching you like a hawk." He resolutely picked up his luggage, stalked into a bedroom, and shut the door.

Irene glanced into the double bedroom to her left. "I guess this one is ours." Taking her bag, she left Violet and Moxie alone in the drawing room.

"So," Violet said slowly. "Did you find some time to yourself?"

"I did. I…took a nap." A small smile tugged at Moxie's lips.

"Was it a satisfying nap?"

"Yes. All three of them were."

Violet exhaled loudly. "You must have been very weary."

"Oh, God, I was. I still am."

"I'm quite tired myself," Violet said softly.

Moxie ran her index finger sensuously over the back of Violet's hand. "We should do something about that."

"We should. Every time I see you I become completely exhausted."

"I've never wanted to rest so badly in my life."

The door to the drawing room opened loudly, and Wil strolled in with her bags. "Here I am, darlings."

"At last," Violet said. "I was worried you'd miss the train."

"I had that errand to run for plan B," Wil said, stacking her suitcases.

"And?" Violet asked.

"Complete success."

Moxie's eyebrows furrowed. "What's this about?"

Wil removed a mirror from her handbag and began to check her makeup. "Don't worry about it, sister. I had to pop out and find a stick of butter and a skillet."

Moxie now looked even more concerned. "That's a troubling admission."

"Relax," Violet said. "It's not what it sounds like. Wil's just trying to help us get more rest."

"So you're saying that I'm better off not knowing?"

Wil took a step closer to them. "Trust me, toots. If I didn't need to know, I wouldn't have told me."

Violet blinked. "What confidence that logic instills."

"So where are we?" Wil asked with a chuckle.

"Here," Violet replied. "The Right Honorable Helmut Von Douchebag arranged for all five of us to share a drawing room."

"That hinky little fart," Wil said, propping her hands on her hips. "So how are his oysters?"

Violet grinned. "Happily, I haven't seen them. But if his wobbly gait and the icepack he's still carrying mean anything, you may possibly have turned them to marmalade. What did he say to you to elicit such brutality?"

Wil's eyes narrowed. "I can't recall."

Violet turned to Moxie and cocked an eyebrow.

"From what I overheard, he told her he'd sooner put his member in a hot waffle iron and douse it with acid before subjecting it to her arid, syphilitic box."

Violet whistled a low tone. "Wow. Not much room for misinterpretation there."

"So you can see how those would be his final words while in possession of a functioning scrotum, can't you?" Wil asked. When neither of them answered, she shrugged. "It's very clear to me. I'm only sorry I didn't make him cough up blood." She looked at the four attached doors. "Which room is his, anyway?"

"That one," Moxie said, pointing.

"Then I'll be in here." Wil carried her bags into the room farthest from Cotton's. "See you two in the morning."

Violet leaned close to Moxie. "Wait an hour and then come to my room," she whispered.

"How about half an hour?"

"Fifteen minutes?"

Cotton emerged from his room, wearing a smoking jacket and carrying a book. "You can quit your murmuring," he said as he sat down. "I'll be sitting out here all night."

"What?" Moxie asked. "Why?"

"Because I'll not have my top act ruined before she gets to Hollywood."

Violet leaned on the wall and crossed her arms in defiance. "Yes, all the really big stars wait to get ruined *after* they get to Los Angeles."

Moxie's eyes brimmed with indignation. "That can't be nearly as enjoyable."

"It all depends on your preferred method of ruination." Violet gazed at Moxie and lingered on her breasts.

"You look very tired," Moxie said, the innuendo heavy in her voice.

"I am. I could rest for hours."

"Mmm, so could I."

Cotton coughed. "What are you two prattling about? Go to sleep if you're tired."

Violet continued to study Moxie in hunger. "Well, good night."

"You too," Moxie said, though neither made a move toward her room.

"Do you mind controlling your dog?" Cotton snapped.

Violet saw that Clitty was playfully tugging on Cotton's slipper, though it was still on his foot, and she couldn't suppress her smile. "C'mon, Clitty." She snapped her fingers and he trotted over to her side. "See you in the morning," she told Moxie softly, then walked into the remaining bedroom.

Moxie watched Violet as she shut the door, then shuffled over to the doorway of her room. "Good night, Cotton," she said as she turned her back to him. "You douchebag," she mumbled.

❖

In the morning, when Violet and Clitty ventured back into the drawing room, she felt refreshed, though still sexually frustrated, and took great pleasure in the sight of Cotton—rumpled, ungroomed, and miserable looking, propped in a chair with his eyelids barely open.

"Good morning," she called, smiling cruelly. "My goodness, but you look a mess. You really should try and get some sleep, Mr. McCann."

He looked at her through bleary eyes without turning his head. "Harpy."

"Though I doubt that sleep will make you any less of a dick," she said, sitting beside him and crossing her legs. "That, sadly, may be out of all our hands."

Seeming uncomfortable with her proximity, he stood and stretched. "I'm going to change. Try to stifle your deviant urges while I'm gone."

"If only I could control my base and vulgar feminine wiles." She batted her eyelashes several times in rapid succession, prompting his sneer.

Cotton hadn't been gone more than a few seconds when Wil entered, closing the door to her room behind her.

"You just missed your favorite scrotum," Violet said.

"He hasn't had breakfast yet, has he?"

"Doubtful. He sat outside our doors all night to keep Moxie and me apart."

Wil snorted. "That fat gink. Let's order breakfast for everyone, and we can launch plan B."

"Which is?"

Wil reached into her handbag and pulled out a glass bottle with a cork stopper. "This," she replied, shaking it.

"Calomel? Isn't that a laxative?"

"Some call it that." Wil stroked the glass lovingly. "I prefer the term *ass grenade*."

"Sounds dangerous."

"No, silly. What about the word *grenade* implies danger?" Wil slipped the bottle back into her bag.

"Could this kill him?"

Wil paused. "I don't think so. Now, it may make him *want* to die. Does that count?"

"You're sure this will just keep him out of our hair? I don't want to be charged as an accomplice to any kind of maiming or murder."

"I'll only give him one dose. And once he spends a day or so shedding his lower intestine like a snakeskin, Brigadier General Douchebag will be back to his day-to-day job of flushing out vaginas with irritating regularity."

Violet sighed. "Then I'd better order breakfast."

Wil's face lit up. "I'd like French toast."

❖

When Moxie and Irene came out of their bedroom, Moxie was flabbergasted to see Cotton, Wil, and Violet seated together around a table in the drawing room, eating breakfast together.

"Good morning?" Moxie said. "Do I know you people?"

"Hey," Violet said warmly. "We decided to order breakfast. We got you two omelettes and coffee. I hope that's okay."

"I love omelettes," Irene squealed, scurrying over and pulling up a chair.

Moxie approached more slowly as Violet poured Irene a cup of coffee. "So has everyone buried the hatchet?"

"Oh, God, no," Wil answered.

Cotton shook his head as he chewed a piece of toast. "No, I still want to repeatedly strike them."

"It's very mutual." Violet glared at Cotton dramatically over the brim of her coffee cup.

Moxie took a seat beside them. "Oh."

"Of course," Violet said, "that doesn't mean we can't all sit down and have a civil meal together." She put a covered plate in front of Moxie and removed the lid to reveal a steaming, cheesy three-egg omelette. "How did everyone sleep? That is, those of us who *chose* to sleep."

Wil spread more butter on her toast. "I, for one, am finding train travel quite agreeable."

Cotton, who looked bedraggled and exhausted, scoffed. "Perhaps the rocking simulates coitus."

Wil's left eyebrow rose defiantly. "No doubt even better than you might simulate it, darling. How purple are your testicles this morning?"

"You're a dirty whore." His eyes were narrow slits.

"Still smarting a bit then, huh?" Wil's amusement was obvious.

"I may have you arrested for assault," Cotton murmured through gritted teeth.

Wil seemed unfazed. "I can't wait to tell the police how you cried like a schoolgirl. I imagine you died a little inside. More syrup?"

He looked livid. "Fuck your syrup."

Wil was clearly not done with Cotton yet. "Hmm, not an altogether unpleasant way to get sticky, I suppose. At least the syrup wouldn't embarrass itself." She sipped her coffee and looked at him as though silently daring him to keep speaking to her.

"How's the food?" Violet asked, in a transparent attempt to break the tension.

Irene looked as though she was torn between continuing to eat and bursting into tears. "Um, good? Thanks?"

"Perhaps this wasn't the best idea," Moxie ventured.

"But it was Mr. McCann who wanted us to be together like a big family," Violet said. "This is what he wants. Isn't that so, Mr. McCann? Because if so, we can do *everything* together until we reach Pasadena."

Cotton's eye twitched as he turned to Violet. "What I wanted was to accompany my star client to Hollywood, unencumbered by lesbian predators"—his gaze shifted to Wil—"truculent harlots"—his eyes moved accusingly to Irene—"or quixotic sycophants. That is *not* what I've gotten."

Wil's expression remained unchanged. "Well, at least you got French toast, jug-butt. You're *welcome*."

"Quick, oddal sicky-pants?" Irene scowled. "I can't say I like the sound of that."

"*I* don't think you're a sicky-pants, kid," Violet said, the corner of her mouth curving upward. She patted Irene's hand.

"Thanks. Hey, by the way, Vi, I read that magazine you gave me last night cover to cover. But I never found the steamy part." She took another bite of breakfast.

Violet looked down at her plate guiltily. "Did you read that story about Clara Bow?"

"The one about her becoming a chanteuse?" Irene asked.

"Oh," Violet gasped. "Sorry, I must have misread that. I thought it said she was becoming a cannibal."

Moxie bit her lower lip as she tried not to laugh.

"Those two things aren't close at all," Irene muttered as she stabbed her eggs.

Cotton rolled his eyes. "This may be the longest three days of my life."

Wil sinisterly watched him chew. "It just may be, at that."

❖

"Go." Violet frowned at her cards.

"Thirty-one for two," Moxie said, setting down a card and moving her cribbage peg up the board.

"Three for one," Violet added, setting down her last card and advancing her peg as well.

Moxie tallied up her hand. "Fifteen two, fifteen four, fifteen six, seven, eight, nine, and one for his nob." She pointed to the jack of diamonds.

Violet smiled naughtily. "His nob? This game is absolutely filthy."

Moxie laughed. "That must be why you're so good at it."

Violet took the cards and started to shuffle. "Though arguably, nobs are not my specialty." She grimaced. "Speaking of nobs," she said, turning around to look at Cotton, who was lying on the settee in the fetal position. "Mr. McCann, is that continuing smell of decay and sewage coming from you? Or does this train route pass through a sulfur mine?"

"I don't feel well," he moaned.

"Thanks for sharing it with the rest of us," Violet said. "Dear Lord, I'm opening the windows. You're making my eyes burn."

Moxie had to admit that the stench emanating from Cotton was noxious and fetid. "I'll go get my perfume. Maybe that'll help."

"Wait," Violet said, sliding up a window pane. "Is there something else you can use? That may taint Twilight Moon for me forever. And I really like it."

Moxie thought for a moment. "I'll use Irene's."

"Perfect." Violet opened the remaining three drawing-room windows.

Moxie reappeared, spritzing the perfume liberally about the room.

Violet sat back down, and as the fragrances began to mingle in the air, a horrified look came over her face. "Oh, you're going to have to stop, Mox. Those two smells combined are vile." She struggled to swallow.

"God, you're right. Somehow adding the smell of flowers and powder has made things even worse."

"Perhaps you should head to the water closet, Mr. McCann," Violet suggested.

"I'm not leaving you two alone," he wailed into the upholstery, unmoving.

"I have to hand it to him," Violet said. "Few men would risk shitting their pants to ensure that no one anywhere ever had sex. That takes real tenacity."

"Cotton is nothing if not tenacious. That and, of course, rotten inside."

The door to the drawing room opened, and Wil and Irene entered.

"And that's when she put her hand on my thigh," Wil said. "And slid it *all* the way up."

"Barbara Stanwyck?" Irene gasped. "Really?"

Violet sighed. "Wil, are you still telling that story?"

"Of course, darling. Why wouldn't I?"

"Because you weren't sober when you met Barbara Stanwyck, and you got all that information secondhand."

Wil shut the door behind her. "Are you trying to say that Barbara Stanwyck wouldn't *want* to grope me while I'm drunk?" She stopped and sniffed the air. "What the fuck is that? It smells like a unicorn took a shit in here."

"Sadly, there was no magic or fairy dust involved." Violet pointed behind her with her thumb. "It's Shamus O'Anus back there."

"By all that's holy, man. Take that somewhere else." Wil put her hand over her nose. "That's not a natural smell. It's like a mixture of brimstone, gardenia, and despair."

"Hey," Irene called. "What's my perfume doing out here?"

Moxie handed the bottle back to her. "We thought it would help, but somehow it's taken something horrible and turned it into an abomination."

"Is he just going to lie there stinking?" Wil asked.

Violet's thumb lightly grazed her lips as she appeared to contemplate something. "Look, I'm going for a walk."

"I'll come with you," Moxie said quickly.

"Then so will I," Cotton warbled.

Violet put her hands up. "No, you stay here, Moxie. We can take turns breathing the clean air. If we both go, he'll just straggle along, releasing his mustard gas when we least expect it."

"But I thought we were having lunch soon in the dining car," Moxie said, disappointed that Violet didn't want her along.

"Start without me. I'll catch up with you before long."

Before Moxie could ask Violet where she was headed, she was already out the door, Clitty not far behind her.

Wil nudged Cotton with her knee before she retreated to the other side of the room. "You sickening bastard. Do you think as long as we don't hear it, we won't notice?"

"No," he croaked. "I just don't care."

❖

"Come on," Irene coaxed as she, Wil, and Moxie made their way to the dining car. "I'm *starving*."

"Can't we just wait another few minutes?" Moxie asked. "Violet's been gone almost an hour, and I'm sure she'll be back any time now."

"Then she can meet us there," Wil said. "I can't sit in that ass coffin any longer. I'm certain it's shortened my life. Luckily, we all know I don't care about things like that."

"I'm glad you said that so I didn't have to," Moxie replied.

When they arrived in the dining car, they sat at a table for four.

"And I can't tell you how happy I am that the angel of death agreed to stay behind." Wil perused the menu.

"We should take something back for him to eat," Moxie suggested. "I've never seen him so under the weather."

"I'm so hungry I want to order everything," Irene said. "Then I think about Mr. McCann and what's coming out of him. Maybe I'll just get some soup and crackers." Irene set the menu down and looked up. "Hey, isn't that Violet over there?"

Moxie spun around. "Where?"

"Right over there—" Irene started to point.

Wil knocked Irene's hand down. "The hunger must be making you hallucinate." She sounded irritated.

Moxie squinted as she continued to peer through the crowd. "Yeah, I don't—" Suddenly, she saw Violet, seated at a table for two with an attractive young blonde. They were laughing about something, but were far enough away that Moxie couldn't hear their conversation. "Who the hell is *that*?"

"Nice job, sicky-pants." Wil slapped Irene's arm. "Is there anything else you'd like to destroy? Maybe smother a kitten?"

Irene stared at her. "I didn't know," she whined.

Moxie adjusted her chair so she could watch Violet without the physical discomfort of turning completely around. Her chest tightened as Violet held a long wooden match to light the blonde's cigarette. The blonde steadied Violet's hand until the tobacco was aflame, then pulled it even closer to blow the match out. The gesture seemed decidedly intimate. "Wil, do you know who that woman is?" She didn't try to keep the anger from her voice.

"What woman?"

Moxie jerked her head back to glare at Wil, who was perusing her menu nonchalantly. "The one sitting with Violet, pawing her like a cougar with a pork chop."

"Hmm?" Wil asked innocently.

"Her." Moxie pointed. "There. The one with that I've-been-around-the-block look."

"Um." Wil stared at them across the car. "Her sister."

"She doesn't have any siblings."

"Her cousin?"

"She didn't mention she had a cousin traveling on the train," Moxie countered, tiring of this game.

"Yeah," Irene said, scowling. "That's weird."

Moxie felt her eyelid start to twitch. "You know, Wil, for an actress, you'd think you'd be a better liar."

"No one ever said I was a *good* actress." Wil's eyes were still glued to the bill of fare.

A waiter appeared, looking friendly and attentive. "Ladies, good afternoon. What may I bring you to drink?"

"Lemonade." Moxie couldn't match the man's pleasantness and didn't really care.

While Wil and Irene placed their orders, Moxie looked back over to Violet's table and saw that both ladies were gone. "Did you see them leave?" she blurted as the waiter walked away.

"Who?" Wil asked.

"Violet and that whore."

Wil merely blinked. "Well, maybe if you had been a little more accommodating, she wouldn't have to pay someone else for it." When Moxie only glared back, Wil acquiesced. "Just kidding. I doubt she's actually paying her for it."

Irene leaned closer to Wil. "You're not helping at *all*," she whispered out of the side of her mouth.

Wil looked moderately contrite. "Sorry, but I'm not very good at this. People don't invite me places because I'm sensitive or help them feel better. They invite me places because I tell great stories and have a tendency to drink too much and lift my skirt."

"Are you going to go look for her?" Irene asked Moxie.

Moxie considered the possibility. The train was large, so searching for Violet might prove arduous, not to mention frustrating. Ire was welling inside her. No, she refused to dash off to find Violet like her little dog. Moxie was better than that, and she deserved more. "I'm going to have lunch," she snapped. "And it's going to be the best fucking meal I've ever had."

"Mmm, yum," Wil said.

CHAPTER THIRTEEN

Wil, Irene, and Moxie started back to their drawing room with considerably less excitement than they left it. Most of the lunchtime conversation had revolved around Wil and Irene's attempt to engage in diversionary small talk, with little success.

Moxie shuffled down the passageway behind them, too distracted and troubled to even feign interest in whatever they were discussing now. No doubt Wil was recounting how some star had inserted some inanimate object—or God forbid, a live one—where it was never meant to go.

How had she let things end up this way? How did she not see this coming? Violet had seemed so enamored of her, so attentive. She had claimed that while in Hollywood she had been unable to think of anyone but Moxie, yet when faced with an opportunity to spend time together, Violet had consciously chosen to be with someone else.

"I'm such a dope," she whispered to herself.

Before she could curse herself further, someone reached out and pulled her by the wrist from the corridor and into a stateroom. By the time Moxie realized what was happening, she was pinned up against a closed compartment door, and Violet's face was alarmingly near hers.

"Did you miss me?" Violet kissed Moxie hungrily before she was able to form a reply.

Moxie didn't *want* to kiss her back, but somehow her lips didn't receive that directive from her pride, where it originated. Their mouths moved against each other and Violet nibbled Moxie's lower lip.

It was all Moxie could do to slide her arms behind her own body to trap them against the door. She warred with her desire not to let them roam Violet's body because, goddamn it, she was angry.

Violet moved her lips to Moxie's throat, her teeth gently grazing Moxie's exposed shoulder. "What's wrong?" she breathed, continuing her tour of Moxie's neck.

"Hmm?" Moxie was finding it difficult to maintain her steely resolve. Sure, she was irate and hurt. But in some perverse way, the power of those raw emotions seemed to blur with the intense carnal yearning that Violet evoked in her. Moxie had never imagined she could have enraged, bitter sex, but now she was starting to see things differently.

"Why aren't you participating?" Violet asked, her voice throaty with passion.

"I'm mad at you."

Violet's gaze bore into Moxie's, her gray eyes darkened with ardor. "Why?"

"I saw you with that woman," Moxie replied softly, "in the dining car. You two seemed very familiar."

Violet grinned ever so slightly. "I don't know her. She's just some actress who's doing me a favor."

"If you don't mind, I'd rather not hear about your anonymous favors. Call me old-fashioned."

"Not *sexual* favors." Violet's eyebrows arched. "I talked her into switching rooms with me. I told her that I had a slightly larger room that shared a drawing room with an agent whom I can't stand. She said she completely understood, that all agents are bastards, and that she wouldn't tell him where I was on the train."

"So you—"

"Missed lunch because I was hastily moving our belongings in here, while Mr. McCann was cloistered in the water closet. I wasn't having a tryst with someone else."

A wave of relief washed over Moxie, instantly replaced with romantic giddiness, a much better complement to her barely controlled lust. "You must be very…hungry." The desire in her voice sounded foreign to her.

Violet's eye's softened. "I'm fucking famished," she said, her mouth once again descending on Moxie's.

They no longer had any reason to wait or hold back. At last they were able to act on their insatiable craving.

Highly aroused, Moxie barely considered the fact that she didn't really know what she was doing. She mentally kicked any reservations into the back of her mind, to the left of her indulgence and just behind her lust. She brazenly pushed Violet backward onto the narrow bed, then locked the door. "Let's see what we can do about that."

In one moment, Moxie was on top of Violet, and in another, her tongue was in Violet's mouth. The sound of Violet's moan spurred on Moxie's confidence, and she let her right palm travel to Violet's breast, awed by the sudden stiffness of her nipple.

Violet covered Moxie's hand with her own, urging her to knead the tender flesh even harder. Quickly, Violet turned her attention to unbuttoning Moxie's dress. "I love how you touch me."

Moxie was overwhelmed by Violet's admission and gazed at her as she moved her fingers provocatively down to Violet's waist. "I've thought about this moment so much."

"Tell me what you've imagined."

"When I'm fantasizing about you? About us?"

Violet's look was smoldering. "Yes. Give me every detail."

"Well," Moxie said self-consciously, "more often than not, you... well, you sort of...take me."

"Take you?" Violet rolled Moxie onto her back so that she was straddling Moxie's thigh. "And what do I do to you?" She ground slowly against her as her hands caressed Moxie's hips.

Moxie felt breathless at the bold promise that Violet might do whatever she asked of her. "You make love to me with your incredible mouth," she whispered, brushing Violet's lips reverently with trembling fingers.

Violet suddenly appeared as though she wanted to devour Moxie whole, her eyes half-lidded with passion. "Really?"

"Like there's no tomorrow."

When Violet began unbuttoning Moxie's dress again, the incidental brush of her fingers made Moxie's skin tingle in anticipation. Their tongues hungrily fused as they stripped their clothing off and flung it aside until they were completely naked.

Violet pressed her mouth to a rosy nipple of Moxie's bare breasts, tracing it with her tongue. "And when I take you, am I gentle?" she asked, then increased the force to illustrate another option. "Or rough and urgent?"

Moxie arched her back. "Oh, you're urgent, and use your teeth. Oh, shit. Just like that."

Violet pulled away for a minute. "And what's my tongue doing? Is it staying up here?"

"No. Your tongue is…doing what it was doing in the baggage car."

Violet slid her hand down between Moxie's thighs. "So you want it down here?" she asked, beginning to stroke her with two fingers.

"Oh, my God, yes! There."

"So you want me to stop doing this?" Violet put her mouth back on Moxie's erect nipple, now licking it in perfect rhythm with the movement of her hand against Moxie's slick clitoris.

"No, wait. Don't stop. That's so…mmm."

Violet needed no further coaxing, and she followed Moxie's instructions as closely as possible. She was urgent, and she was *definitely* using her teeth.

Moxie's hips rocked in time with Violet's ministrations, and their pace quickened as Violet moved her lips over to Moxie's other, heretofore neglected, breast. It was clear that Moxie was close to orgasm, and though she contemplated putting it off, it had already been delayed far too long, days and weeks too long.

When Moxie's climax came, Violet savored every moment of it—Moxie's head thrown back, her suddenly rigid body, and her deep, guttural growl.

Moxie's chest heaved as her hands moved to her flushed face. "I don't think I've ever—what are you doing?"

Violet slowly descended farther down Moxie's body, pausing to kiss Moxie's stomach on her way south. "I can't stop thinking about how you taste, and how you thrust against my tongue when you're in my mouth."

"Shit," Moxie hissed.

"You're not the only one with fantasies, sugar." This time, Violet's movements were slow and deliberate. She kissed and licked Moxie everywhere, but lingered in the areas that made Moxie moan and, more strikingly, spew profanities.

Moxie's fingers threaded through Violet's hair, and she began to caress Violet's scalp, subtly directing her. Again, Violet followed the trajectory that Moxie set, and when she boldly slipped a finger into Moxie's vagina, she didn't slow her mouth's pace.

When Moxie's second orgasm hit, it seemed to last longer than the first, and Violet struggled to keep pressure directly on Moxie's clitoris to maximize it. Once it abated, Violet moved back up the bed, her eyes locking with Moxie's.

"That was incredible," Moxie gasped, kissing Violet deeply. "I want to make you feel this way."

"Mmm, I second that motion."

Moxie traced her fingertips lightly down Violet's jawline and neck, to her breasts. "Can I ask you something?"

"Anything."

"I'm a little embarrassed by this question."

Violet slid beside her on the bed and propped her head on her right fist. "It's all in the wrist, if you really want to know."

Moxie squinted her eyes and turned on her left side to face her directly. "Um, that's good information to have, I'm sure. But I was wondering what I...or rather, *if* I reciprocated that first night we were together."

"Reciprocated?"

"I mean, did I make you—"

"Sweetheart, what do you think happened that night?"

Moxie grimaced. "Well, I've imagined something very similar to what you and I just did."

Violet tried not to smile, but had a feeling she wasn't completely successful. "You don't remember any of it?"

"I think I remember you kissing me."

"Actually, you kissed me."

"So I initiated everything?" Moxie asked, looking self-conscious.

"Honey, that *was* everything."

"What?"

"Granted, without a doubt, that was the best kiss I've ever received."

"So we didn't—"

"You told me you liked me. Then you planted one on me—it made me see fucking stars—and you fell asleep."

"You mean I haven't been a lesbian all this time?"

Violet brought her index finger up to her mouth. "I don't know, you taste a little like a lesbian."

Moxie looked stunned, as though she had seen the dead rise and begin to spank each other. Violet felt a pang of guilt for being so glib.

"Why did you assume we had already been intimate?"

"The note you left me sounded very…and besides that, when I woke up my clothes were off."

Violet brushed Moxie's chin with her thumb. "I didn't want your dress to wrinkle."

"Oh. So you were just being nice?"

"Well, I was also dying to see you in your underwear." Violet ran her hands along Moxie's waist to the small of her back. "You didn't disappoint, by the way."

Moxie laughed. "Thanks. Did I do anything else that night that I should know about?"

"There was that bum on Fifty-second Street whom you tried to entice to suckle at your breast by baring a nipple and shouting 'free milk.'"

"What?"

"No, wait. That was Wil. Sorry."

"Thank God. So nothing else? I didn't lift up my skirt in Times Square for passersby?"

"No," Violet replied in amusement.

"Or offer to sing along with anyone who played a spirited ditty with a random body part?"

"Not that I recall. The only other noteworthy thing you did that night was get me to fall for you." Violet leaned closer. "And make me want you so badly."

"I did that?" Moxie's face was only inches from Violet's.

"Oh, yes," Violet whispered, still slowly massaging Moxie's waist and buttocks. "And I've ached for you ever since. I need you to touch me, love."

Moxie kissed her, tracing Violet's breasts, stomach, and the curve of her hip with her fingers. "Like this?"

"Mmm, that's a very nice start."

"Tell me what to do."

Violet brought Moxie's fingers to her lips, where she could nibble and lick them while Moxie watched, entranced. With great deliberation, Violet drew Moxie's wet digits down her naked body, lingering on her left breast before continuing down her abdomen. "Do you want to keep going?"

Moxie only nodded, seeming mesmerized.

Violet continued to gently direct Moxie's hand, guiding it between her legs and moving it sensually up and down. "Can you feel what you do to me?"

"God, yes."

Violet shifted onto her back, pulling Moxie with her so that Moxie now straddled her right thigh. "Touch me the way you touched yourself last night. I want to feel exactly what you felt."

Their mouths met, this time more insistently as Moxie began to stroke Violet in small, tight circles. As Moxie ground her pelvis against Violet, Moxie's slick wetness on Violet's skin was driving Violet crazy, and she began to rock her own hips in response.

Moxie briefly broke their hungry kiss as she continued her attention to Violet's clitoris. "How is it that when I'm touching *you*, I'm so close to coming?"

The question, coupled with the breathless way Moxie asked it, sent a surge of raw desire through Violet that brought her that much closer to climax. "Wait for me," she rasped.

"I'm not sure I can." Moxie continued riding Violet's thigh.

"I'm so close."

"Oh, baby, please."

Moxie's desperate plea put Violet over the edge, and as the waves of rapture flooded her, she felt Moxie tremble above her, succumbing to her own release. Moxie's body sank against Violet's as they both tried to catch their breath.

"Have I mentioned," Violet said, "what a pleasant surprise it is that you climax so easily?"

"You're not the only one who's surprised by that. If I'd known sex could be like this, I'd have been having it constantly."

Violet ran her fingers languidly through Moxie's hair as she held her close. "You should make a resolution to start doing that."

"Having constant sex?"

"With me," Violet added. "That's a very important element of the proposed resolution. One that you shouldn't overlook."

"Is that what you want, Vi?"

"Among other things."

Moxie shifted slightly and stared for a moment at Violet before speaking. "Other things like what?"

"You, Mox. I want you in my life, exclusively, and I selfishly want you to want the same."

"Oh, I do." She kissed Violet softly. "But what will we do about Cotton?"

"You know, he ultimately works for you. You could tell him to butt out or—"

"I'll fire him?"

"I was going to say you'd sic Wil on him." Violet chuckled. "But firing him might be more humane."

"You know, I underestimated Wil's vindictiveness."

"And you don't even know the half of it."

"I'm happy to leave it that way." She snuggled against Violet again. "You know, we should do something for that nice woman who agreed to switch rooms with you."

"Without whom none of this would have been possible."

"What was her name? Do you remember?"

"Um, I think it was Davis. Yes, Bette Davis."

❖

Cotton walked as slowly as he could from the water closet at the end of the train car back to the drawing room. He had never in his life been as ill as he had been for the last twenty-four hours. As though the horrible cramping and gas had not been bad enough, he had been cursed with a need to void his bowels almost every fifteen to twenty minutes, though *void* seemed like a vast understatement for something with the force of a fire hose. Worst of all, he was now reduced to limiting even simple movement, like bending or stretching, for fear that something ungodly would happen when he exerted himself.

He opened the door to the drawing room with deliberate caution and was surprised to see Wil, Irene, and some doe-eyed blonde playing cards.

"All hail, Caesar Bagodoucheus," Will said, not even looking up from her hand before she discarded. "How's the anus, chief?"

He was angry all over again. "Who is this? Where are Moxie and the dyke?"

The blonde scowled as she drew a card. "You weren't exaggerating. He's every bit as offensive as you described."

"Shocking, isn't it?" Wil asked.

"Rummy," Irene called, excitedly putting down all her cards.

Wil looked irritated. "You bitch."

"Hey. You said you'd stop calling me that if I kept playing."

"Sorry. You're right. I take that back."

The blonde finished adding the score and set her pencil down. "Irene, you're now ahead by fifty-five."

"Twat," Wil spat.

Irene pouted. "Hey!"

"What?" Wil asked innocently. "That's what you yell when someone leads by any number divisible by eleven. Don't you know the rules?"

"I didn't realize this was twat rummy," the blonde said.

Wil smiled. "Darling, that's the only kind of rummy I play."

"Who the hell *are* you?" Cotton repeated.

"To you, I'm Miss Davis," she answered, shuffling the cards, then dealing them. "Who the hell are you?"

"I'm sorry," Wil said. "Where are my manners?" She gestured to Cotton. "Bette, this is everything that's wrong with men."

Bette put her cigarette in her mouth as she began to sort the cards in her hand. "In that case, we've already met."

Irene laughed to the point of snorting.

"What the hell are you giggling at?" Cotton snapped. "And where are Moxie and Violet?"

"They traded rooms with Bette," Irene replied, adding her discard to the pile.

"What? But you were supposed to keep an eye on them!"

Irene didn't even look up. "Bette here is a contract player at Universal Studios. When we get to Hollywood, she's promised to introduce me to some important people."

He wasn't following her. "Huh?"

"I don't need you and your intimidation," Irene clarified. "So stuff it up your ass, pal."

Wil drew a card. "I don't know, 'Reeny. It's been a very busy orifice lately."

Bette exhaled smoke through her nose. "Do you mean him? Or are you actually talking about his rectum?"

Wil seemed to ponder the question. "As much as I can imagine referring to Cotton when I say it's been a very busy orifice, I meant his toxic—"

"Shut up!" They all stared at Cotton, though the disdain in their eyes was apparent. "I am sick of every one of you—your sarcasm and your base crassness."

Bette turned back to her cards. "Wil, you didn't mention what a blustering nance he was."

"Didn't I? It must have slipped my mind."

Cotton couldn't take any more of being spoken about as though he wasn't even in the room. "That's it! I'm done with all of you. Good luck trying to get your pathetic careers off the ground. You won't get any help from me." He looked directly at Bette. "Especially you, you bug-eyed bitch. You'll never get anywhere with that face."

He stormed into his room, slamming the door. As he lay on the bed, he felt no remorse for his outburst. Those women didn't know who they were dealing with.

CHAPTER FOURTEEN

One at a time, all five women descended the train steps, finally arriving at the final stop of Pasadena. Violet set Clitty down in the grass so he could frolic and tend to nature's impulses.

"My God," Moxie said. "It's beautiful here."

"You think that now," Bette answered with a throaty laugh, lighting her cigarette. "Wait until they start feasting on you like locusts."

Moxie's face fell. "Um—"

"And latch on to you until you're nothing but a dried husk," Bette continued.

"What a picturesque backdrop you've painted," Violet said.

"Good Lord." Wil extended her hand before her brow to block the bright sunlight. "Look at all those…what do you call those things that you vomit and pass out under?"

"Trees," Violet replied.

"Ah, yes. That's right."

"What have you been vomiting and passing out under since you've been in the city, Wil?" Moxie asked.

"Men." She adjusted her skirt.

"Wil, congratulations on keeping your legs together and your wits about you this entire trip," Violet said sincerely. "I realize it may have been difficult for you at times."

Bette smiled. "Especially with that agent."

Wil put her hands over Irene's ears. "Watch your language, madam. We try not to use the *A*-word."

"Especially since Moxie's *A*-word happens to *be* such an *A*-word," Violet added.

"Well, as horrid as that man and his emanations were, I did manage to have a lovely time," Bette said. "It was by far the best twat rummy I've ever played. But now I must be going." She hugged the others and bid them farewell.

"I can give you a lift, Bette," Violet said. "My driver is here."

"Thanks, Vi. But I have a ride waiting too. He's right over there." Bette pointed to a convertible coupe. "So you're all staying at the Garden of Allah?"

"As long as they'll have us," Wil said.

Bette removed her cigarette from her mouth as she chuckled. "Clearly you've never stayed there before. I'm not sure there's anyone they *wouldn't* have."

Violet put her hand on Wil's shoulder. "And in that way, the Garden of Allah is very much like Wil."

Wil's eyes narrowed. "Are you channeling Julian or something?"

"As a tribute to him," Violet explained, "I couldn't let a golden opportunity to call you a whore slip by untried."

Wil sighed. "It does make me miss him."

"Well," Bette said, "I know where to reach you all. Good luck."

"Where's Cotton?" Moxie asked, as they all waved good-bye to Bette.

"I'm not sure," Violet replied. "But there's our car. We should probably get in it before Mr. McCann appears and sees Clitty."

Moxie frowned. "Why?"

Violet gestured to the two porters carrying their bags which car was hers. "Clitty may have left a souvenir of sorts in Mr. McCann's shoe."

"A souvenir?" Irene asked. "Like what?"

"It's smaller than a breadbox," Wil hinted. "And it smells like shit."

"Oh."

"Hiya, Fitzy." As he waited dutifully holding the rear door open, Violet grabbed his chin and gave him a quick kiss on the lips. "Ladies, may I present Fitzhugh, driver to the stars and currently slumming it with me. Fitzy, this is Irene, Wil, and Moxie."

"It's a pleasure, ladies," he said as they all piled in. "Are you headed to the Garden, Vi?" He started the engine.

"Yes, thanks." Violet set Clitty on the seat beside her.

"Wait," Moxie said. "We can't leave without Cotton. How will he find us?"

"She's serious, isn't she?" Wil looked incredulous.

"It would seem so," Violet answered.

"We can't just leave him."

They all stared at each other in silence.

"The hell we can't." Irene banged her fist twice on the upholstered roof of the vehicle. "Let's go!"

"Well, I'm sure he'll be fine," Moxie mumbled softly.

"Of course he will. He's not a child, after all," Wil said. "Even if he *does* shit his pants like one."

When there were no further protestations, Fitzhugh pulled into the street, headed toward Los Angeles.

Violet caught Fitzhugh's gaze in the rearview mirror. "Did you manage to get hold of some contraband, Fitzy?"

"I couldn't look you in the eye if I hadn't, Vi. Check under the blanket."

Wil pulled the blanket to her left away to reveal a bucket filled with an iced bottle of champagne and several glasses. "Holy shit! We're not even there yet, and it's already like heaven." She started fiddling with the cork.

"So, Fitzy, have I missed anything beyond the standard daily moral decay?"

"Your agent has been trying to reach you about your next picture for Pinnacle. Did you have a good jaunt to New York?"

Violet couldn't suppress a grin. "It was the best fucking train trip ever."

Moxie blushed slightly.

The loud pop of the cork surprised everyone, and Wil made quick work of filling a glass for each passenger. "Ladies, let us all toast to our success out here. To bright lights and free booze."

"Wait, Wil," Violet said. "Isn't that what you just left in Manhattan?"

"Good point. Then to trees, movie contracts, and free booze."

"Hear, hear," Irene added.

They clinked their glasses together as the fragrant smell from the orange groves washed over them.

❖

"Wow." Irene couldn't contain her excitement and wonder at the passing view of Hollywood as they drove to Sunset Boulevard.

"See that little bungalow?" Violet pointed out the limo window.

"Yeah."

"That's where Charlie Chaplin molested his first underage girl."

Irene's face fell. "What? The little tramp?"

"Chaplin?" Wil asked. "Or the girl?"

Moxie elbowed Violet in the side. "Can you try a little harder not to disillusion her before we even get out of the car?"

"I guess you don't want to stop and read the commemorative plaque, then," she said, twisting the corner of her mouth wryly upward.

"Perhaps another time," Moxie whispered in amusement.

"Hey, while we're sightseeing," Wil said, "can we see where Clara Bow lost her dignity? That must be out here somewhere."

Irene seemed irritated by this turn in the conversation. "You guys are pretty glib about other people's careers. I bet you'd feel differently if it were yours."

"Perhaps," Violet replied. "But try and remember what I told you, Irene. People out here are just folks, like you and me. They aren't royalty."

"I'll try— Jumpin' cats! Is this where we're staying?"

The limo turned into the driveway in front of the big house at the Garden of Allah.

"It is," Violet said slowly.

Moxie was awestruck as well. The place was nothing if not impressive with its beautiful Spanish bungalows, shady trees, and exotic-looking vegetation. Once they came to a stop, Fitzhugh opened the door and they all poured out.

"By the way, Vi," Fitzhugh said. "Peter says he's having a little soirée tonight to welcome you all."

"Wonderful. What time?"

"Seven."

"Done. We'll see you there?"

Fitzhugh smiled warmly as he started to remove their bags from the car and set them in the driveway. "You will."

"Thanks for the ride, Fitzy." Violet blew him a kiss before walking into the front office, the others following. "Good day, Captain," Violet called to the plump man behind the counter. "I've brought you some new guests who need to check in."

"Captain?" Irene asked Moxie softly.

"Captain Napkin," she whispered. "I'll have to tell you that story later."

As Lyle turned to greet then, Moxie quickly realized that the garment around his neck was not a silky ascot, but a brassiere for a rather busty woman. "Miss London. Welcome home. And how many bungalows will you ladies require?" He snapped open the register with a flourish.

"I think just one," Wil said. "Nice necktie, Blinky."

"Thank you kindly." He straightened the cup closest to his chin. "I'll give you bungalow ten, so you can be near Miss London." Lyle handed Wil a fountain pen. "If you could just enter your information on line three, please, I'll have your bags taken there for you."

Violet motioned for Moxie to follow her back several feet from the counter. "I figure you can stay with me in eleven. There's plenty of room, provided you're comfortable with that arrangement."

Moxie's libido sprang to life, and she bit her lower lip and smiled flirtatiously. "Oh, I'm *very* comfortable with that."

Violet looked at her with unconcealed lust. "That's good to hear, because I have a surprise for you."

Moxie couldn't break eye contact with her. "You have a real penchant for surprises, don't you?"

"I do." Violet brushed a strand of Moxie's hair back behind her ear. "Know what else I have a penchant for?"

"Hmm, does it have to do with me?"

"Yes."

"Am I naked?"

"You are, yes."

"And is someone being pleasured?"

"You're really good at this game," Violet said.

"Well, I can do more than just fill out a mean crossword puzzle."

"Don't I know it."

Wil approached, her expression one of confusion. "Ladies, let's go."

"What's wrong?" Violet asked.

"I don't think that fella's drunk," Wil whispered discreetly.

"No, he's not."

"I was okay with the lingerie cravat when I just thought he was lit," Wil explained. "Stone-cold sober, it's kinda creepy."

"Fair enough." Violet faced Lyle. "Thanks so much, Captain. See you later."

Lyle nodded politely. "Good day to you all."

Moxie looked around curiously. "Where's Irene?"

"She's waiting outside," Wil said. "She thought he was subtly trying to entice her to rub her breasts on him."

Violet chuckled as they walked back out to the driveway. "If that's subtle, I'd love to see her idea of something overt."

"There you are, Reeny," Wil said to Irene, who was seated on their luggage. "Good news. None of us rubbed anything on him."

"As tempting as it was," Violet added.

"Is this what they're all like out here?" Irene asked as she jumped up.

Violet squinted into the sun as the bellboy came out to gather their bags. "That depends on who *they* are. But so far, he's the only one I've met since I've been here who wears women's undergarments on the *outside*."

"Feel better now?" Wil asked Irene as they followed the bellboy around the right side of the main house.

"Hey, Vi. Welcome back."

They all turned to see a young blonde seated by the pool about thirty yards away, waving at them.

"Hey, Ginger," Violet called back. "You went blond after all?"

Ginger laughed and ran her hand through her hair. "Turns out the studio had the same idea you did."

"You like it?"

"You know, I think I do. You're a pretty smart cookie, Vi. See you around."

Violet nodded. "See you."

"Who is *that*?" Moxie said in a hushed tone.

"Just a nice kid who lives over in six with her mother."

"A nice kid?" Moxie eyed the woman's curvy figure in a black bathing suit.

"Sure."

"And you recommended that she color her hair?"

"It was just a suggestion. But you wear it so much better, baby."

"What a brilliant observation."

Violet tapped her temple. "Well, I *am* a smart cookie."

"Among other things."

When they got to bungalow ten, both Irene and Wil seemed elated to be somewhere they could rest that wasn't moving and didn't share space with Cotton. They hastily disappeared inside, with Violet reminding them about meeting at Peter's for the evening.

Violet, Moxie, and Clitty continued to eleven, and though both of them were just as tired as Irene and Wil, the excitement of spending more time alone with each other trumped their fatigue.

"This is quaint," Moxie said, once the bellboy left.

"Thanks. I built it with my own two hands."

Moxie moved across the room, stepped into Violet's arms, and kissed her. "You do have extraordinary hands. I can attest to that."

Violet nibbled Moxie's earlobe. "That's sweet of you to say. You do much to keep them occupied."

"Christ, Vi. You make me want you so much."

Violet's hands slowly traveled down Moxie's shoulders to her breasts, then to her hips. "Show me."

"Oh, I will. But first, where is my surprise?"

"This feels a little like extortion."

"Considering that what you're currently feeling is actually my ass, are you saying my *ass* feels like extortion?"

"Not at all. Your ass feels more like sunshine."

"That's such—"

"Poetry?"

"Crap."

"You have a very discerning ear." Violet walked over to the kitchen. "Let's see if Fitzy came through. Ah, he did. What a good man." She returned to the room with a bottle of champagne and two glasses.

"This is your surprise?"

"If you recall, I promised you some champagne to celebrate your success."

"That's not what we had in the limo?"

Violet popped the cork dramatically. "Oh, no. That was to celebrate our arrival." She filled the glasses and handed one to Moxie.

"You sure do like to celebrate."

Violet took a sip, then set her glass down. "I like to consider my life a series of transitions between celebrations." She moved closer to Moxie and kissed her neck.

"Mmm, let's transition right now," Moxie groaned, putting her drink on the table.

Their mouths met urgently, and Moxie ran her fingers through Violet's dark tresses while Violet struggled to unbutton Moxie's dress without the luxury of looking at what she was doing. Moxie, wanting to move this frustrating undressing part along, began to remove her own clothes.

"You're very helpful," Violet said between kisses.

"It's pure selfishness," Moxie murmured, pulling her dress over her head and tugging down her underpants.

Within minutes they were both naked and hungrily exploring each other, though still standing in the living room. Violet pulled away long enough to nudge Moxie over to the sofa. "Lie down."

Moxie did as she was told, and she felt like she might explode from the desire coursing through her. She raised her eyebrow when Violet picked up the champagne bottle before moving toward her. "What's that for?"

"I was just thinking what it might taste like to drink you in." She tilted the bottle above Moxie's stomach, but stopped before any liquid spilled out. "Are you game?"

"It'll be cold."

Violet smiled wickedly. "And bubbly. And very, very tasty."

Moxie thought for a second. "Do it."

The effervescent liquid landed on her breasts and abdomen, and Violet wasted no time in moving her tongue along Moxie's erect nipples, at the same time drinking in the small puddles she encountered along the way.

"Mmm, it tingles." Moxie groaned as she raked her fingers through Violet's hair.

Violet moved up to kiss Moxie, and Moxie savored the taste of the champagne that Violet had just drunk from her skin. "I need more," Violet said, her eyes darkened with desire.

"Oh, yes."

Before Moxie knew what had happened, chilled champagne was running into her belly button and between her thighs, where Violet met the fizzy tsunami with her tongue. It was a sensation unlike any other Moxie had ever experienced—cold, but infused with a pronounced heat. Wherever the liquid met her genitals felt electric, and she was thankful Violet fervently licked the bubbly away before it segued from erotic to uncomfortable.

"God," Moxie gasped. "Mmm, faster."

Violet accelerated the movement of her tongue along Moxie's labia, and for Moxie, a different kind of fire rapidly replaced the heat that the alcohol sparked. She rocked her hips to try to increase the pressure from Violet's mouth, and slid her hands to her own breasts and began to massage them as her orgasm slowly built.

When pleasure and release finally racked her body, she cried out and her vision became only kaleidoscopic color. She closed her eyes and tried to slow her breathing as Violet moved above her and kissed her.

"So would you recommend the champagne?" Violet asked before tasting Moxie's mouth again.

"It depends."

"On?"

Moxie ran her hands up Violet's back. "On whether or not I get a rash. Though even if I did, after how amazing that was, I might find it hard to be mad at you."

"I have an idea," Violet said. "Let's go to bed."

"You think you can control yourself now to make it all the way to the next room without ravaging me?"

"Perhaps, if we hurry." Violet stood and pulled Moxie to her feet.

"Wait. Bring the bottle."

Violet smiled broadly. "Yeah?" She grabbed the champagne bottle by the neck.

"Turnabout is fair play."

"What if I want to play dirty?" Violet asked.

"We'll talk about that after I make you come."

❖

By the time Moxie and Violet reached bungalow sixteen, they were worn out. Not only had Moxie never really enjoyed sex until she'd had Violet as her partner, but she hadn't realized just how often you could have it. She'd have been more content at that moment to sleep, but Violet seemed excited to see her friend Mr. Easton. And since he was supposedly throwing a party in their honor, it would have been rude not to attend.

Moxie put her hand up to knock, and Violet pushed it away.

"That'll get you nowhere with Peter."

"Knocking?"

Violet picked up Clitty, then opened the door and stood off to the side so Moxie had a clear view of the carousing. She was astounded at all the people. Over forty were stuffed into a rather small room. A man in the corner played the clarinet quite well. All had a drink in their hands, and a server was milling through the crowd holding a platter filled with hors d'oeuvres.

"Here we are." Wil appeared from around the corner with Irene. "Good timing. Hot dog! Food *and* gin."

"Violet!" a tall, plump man with an arresting handlebar mustache called from the corner. "We've missed you. How have you been?"

"Hitting on all sixes." Violet crossed the busy room and gave him a quick kiss and hug. "Peter, may I present my traveling party. This is Irene Cavendish—dancer, Wil Skoog—actress, and Moxie Valette—singer extraordinaire. Ladies, this is Peter Easton, writer of marginal screenplays."

"Charmed." Peter took Moxie's hand and kissed her knuckles. "So you are the renowned Moxie."

Moxie felt slightly uncomfortable with Peter's attention. "That's me."

"I've heard quite a bit about you," he said, releasing her. "I'm interested to hear you sing so I can hear the choir of seraphim that Violet described."

Moxie looked at Violet accusingly. "Did you embellish slightly?"

"Not at all." Violet shook her head in amusement. "I just said that you made me see God, nothing more."

"Well, if you want to summon any deities," Peter began, "you're more than welcome to do a number here. I'm sure we'd all love to get a little religion."

Moxie cleared her throat. "Maybe a little later, but I'd love a drink, if you're got one."

He laughed loudly. "If I've *got* one?" He walked over to his bar, pieced together with liquor crates and plywood, but visibly stocked to the hilt. "What would you like, doll? I can do it all."

"Peter prides himself on the fact that he knows every cocktail in existence," Violet explained. "He insists he can't be stumped."

"Is that so?" Wil asked.

He smiled. "Test me."

Wil crossed her arms defiantly. "How about a Ward Eight?"

"I'm a New Englander, for Christ's sake. Rye whiskey, lemon juice, and grenadine."

It was apparent that Wil was taking this challenge to heart. "French seventy-five?"

"Gin, Cointreau, champagne, and lemon juice."

"A Charlie Chaplin." She moved her hands to her hips.

His mustache angled upward. "Sloe gin, apricot brandy, and lime juice."

Wil's eyes narrowed. "A pompous bastard."

Peter's smugness visibly left him. "Um, how do you make that?"

"Put a lemon twist in your ass and shake." Wil raised her eyebrow defiantly.

Violet laughed. "You know, Wil, I would have thought that you, of all people, would be able to appreciate Peter's talent."

"Just because he knows them doesn't mean he can mix them."

"What's your poison?" Peter appeared as though he wanted to start over with her.

One corner of Wil's mouth curved up. "Just to properly test your mixing skills, mind you, how about a Floradora?"

Peter's eyes glimmered with humor as he grabbed a bottle of gin and began the concoction. "I love a woman who's a challenge."

Violet sighed. "Not the first word that typically comes to mind when describing Wil."

Wil propped her elbow on the bar. "Don't listen to her, Pete. She's recently sleep-deprived, if you follow me."

Peter glanced at Violet and Moxie with brazen amusement. "Oh, I think I do. Floradoras for all of you, ladies?"

"Please," Irene said.

"Excellent." He stirred up a pitcher. "Have you ladies met Harpo?" Peter nodded to his left as he continued to add ingredients.

Irene froze. "As in—?"

"How are you?" Moxie asked the actor as she shook his hand. "I'm Moxie."

"Nice to meet you." His voice was much deeper than Moxie would have guessed it to be, since he never spoke in his films. "You staying at the Garden?"

"I am, yes. With Violet. Do you live here as well?"

Harpo nodded and pointed with his thumb. "I'm in eighteen."

Irene still sputtered unintelligibly, and Moxie took pity on her. "This is my friend Irene."

"Huhhhh," Irene rasped, the syllable lasting a ridiculously long time.

Harpo tilted his head slightly and put up his hand to wave. "Hiya."

Peter mercifully shoved a glass in Irene's hand. "It seems like this isn't your first drink tonight, tomato. But enjoy it anyway."

"My God," Wil said after tasting her drink.

"You like it?" Peter handed the remaining two to Moxie and Violet.

"It beats a punch in the quim." Wil took another sip.

"From Wil, that's a rousing endorsement," Violet said.

Harpo shifted uncomfortably and pointed to Wil. "Are you with her?" he asked Irene.

"Nnnurrr," Irene burbled.

"See ya around," Harpo said, disappearing into the crowd.

Irene's wide eyes grew even larger. "Whhaayyy."

Moxie took a few steps toward Violet and brushed her back to get her attention. "I don't think your stars-are-simple-folk chat had the effect on Irene that you may have hoped."

Violet looked at their catatonic friend. "Hmm. Is she salivating?"

"Not yet. Is there something we can do for her?"

"She just needs to relax. Maybe if we introduce her to a schlub she'll feel more at ease."

"A schlub?"

"Sure, let me ask Peter." Violet whispered something in Peter's ear that made him look at Irene, then snort. He nodded, then receded into the crowd. "He's going to take care of it."

"He's not going to set her up with some sap, is he?"

"Hopefully not," Violet said, "but clearly she needs someone a little more her speed."

"If she wants to be able to speak at all, she does."

Peter returned, pushing a short, nebbishy fellow in front of him. "Ladies, this is Wallace. Wallace, this is Moxie, Violet, and Irene."

Wallace blinked three times and bowed.

"Wally, darling," Wil said, approaching him with her hand extended. "I'm Wil Skoog."

"Hello," he stuttered, neglecting to take her hand.

Wil frowned. "Say, you're not in the later stages of syphilis, are you? You seem a little squirrelly."

"Huh?"

Peter laughed. "How about you kids take a seat over here and get acquainted?" He snapped his fingers impatiently at the couple seated on his love seat. "Come on, folks. People need to sit." They quickly leapt up, and Peter directed Irene and Wallace to take their place. "That's just fine. Wallace, what are you drinking?"

"Uh—"

"I'll get you a refill." Peter dashed back to the bar.

Moxie shook her head and took a sip of her Floradora. "He's not much of a matchmaker, but he makes a hell of a drink."

Violet shrugged. "It beats a punch in the quim."

CHAPTER FIFTEEN

Violet sat quietly in the back of a darkened room on a Pinnacle soundstage, watching Moxie audition for Henry Childs. As Moxie's fingers caressed the microphone, Violet felt phantom digits somehow stroking her in the same manner. Was it because, just last night, she had felt Moxie's sensuous touch? Or was *anyone* who was watching Moxie experiencing the same sensations? Could Henry possibly be imagining Moxie touching him so provocatively?

From where Violet was sitting, she couldn't see the director's face. She momentarily warred within herself between *wanting* Henry to find Moxie desirable and jealously wanting to keep Moxie to herself. She chastised herself as the song ended and tried to focus on what was best for Moxie and her career.

Henry stood and approached Moxie, clapping enthusiastically. "That was great." He turned to the back of the room and put his hand across his brow to search the darkness for Violet. "You weren't kidding, Vi. This doll is dynamite."

"When have I ever steered you wrong?" Violet stood, and Clitty hopped up to follow her.

Suddenly Cotton burst through the door, looking rumpled, sweaty, and out of breath, his wrinkled jacket slung over his arm. When he fixed his gaze on Moxie, he sighed heavily and approached her. "Moxie, thank God I've finally found you."

Moxie's expression was decidedly less pleased. "Oh, hello."

"Where did you go?" He sounded desperate. "I looked for you on the train and you were gone. Did you know someone shit in my shoe?"

Moxie was visibly in distress. Violet quickly closed the distance between them, hoping to intervene before McCann said anything untoward that might negate the power of Moxie's performance. Up close, his appearance was even more troubling, his shirt sporting colossal armpit stains and what appeared to be the remnants of some type of fricassee across his expansive chest.

"Can I help you?" Henry was clearly nonplussed by this man, who could still plausibly be labeled a lunatic.

"Who the hell are *you*?" Cotton barked.

Henry scowled. "Since this is a closed set, perhaps you should explain who *you* are, Mac."

"Uncle." Violet put her hand on the small of Cotton's back. "How did you get in here? Where is your nurse?"

"What the hell are you talking about?" Cotton tried to recoil from her touch.

"I'm sorry, Henry," Violet said softly, trying to lead Cotton out of the room. "This is my Uncle Douch…ay."

"Uncle who?" Henry repeated slowly.

Moxie was obviously avoiding eye contact with them as she struggled not to laugh.

Violet continued to direct Cotton toward the door by his shoulders. "Uncle DuChé," she repeated, more confidently this time. "Our family is French. Uncle, you've interrupted Moxie's audition with director Henry Childs." She emphasized Henry's name as much as she could, in the hope that Cotton would recognize the name.

Cotton's brow creased. "Hen—"

"—ry Childs, yes." Violet nodded slowly.

Cotton slicked his hair back, apparently unaware of how little he actually helped his appearance. "Oh, allow me to—"

"Wait in the hall?" Violet shoved Cotton toward the door more forcefully now. Clitty trailed her closely. "But of course, *mon oncle. Certainement*. We'll just leave you two to chat." She smiled at Henry and Moxie.

Once the door shut behind them, Cotton's acquiescence immediately dissolved. "Stop pushing me, you shrew!"

Violet grabbed his upper arm and pulled him farther from the door. "Look here, you oozing ulcer of a man. What do you think you're going to accomplish for Moxie, bursting in on her Hollywood audition,

looking like an overtaxed sweat gland, and smelling curiously of—"
She paused and sniffed the air near him. "Shit and Belgian cheese? Do
you somehow think that's helping?"

His face fell. "But I'm her agent."

Violet was surprised by a momentary twinge of sympathy. "I
know. What happened to you? You look like you were raped by an
angry plate of veal piccata."

"Well, you bitches *left* me at the train station," he said through
clenched teeth. "I had feces in my shoe, my luggage was gone, and I
had no idea where any of you were staying. I only knew that Moxie had
an appointment for this morning, somewhere on this studio lot." He
sighed. "This vast, expansive, labyrinthine lot."

Violet tapped her index finger lightly on her pursed lips while
she considered his plight. She felt ninety-eight percent certain that Wil
was responsible for the disappearance of Cotton's bags, but she felt no
need to voice this hunch. "So where have you been staying the last two
days?"

"A dingy place on Hollywood Boulevard called Los Reyes de
Armas."

"And this?" Violet pointed to the large golden stain on his shirt.

"Was deposited on me by a drunken waiter a day and a half ago.
But I have nothing to change into."

"As much as this pains me, *mon oncle*," she said, arching an
eyebrow in wonder, "I'm going to help you."

"What?"

"C'mon." Violet gingerly tugged his elbow. They walked outside
where Fitzhugh sat in the limo, reading the newspaper. "Hey, Fitzy. I
have a little favor to ask. D'ya mind?"

Fitzhugh got out of the driver's seat, folding the paper and tossing
it back through the open car window. He looked Cotton up and down
and whistled solemnly. "Is he the favor?"

She nodded. "He's lost his luggage, so would you take him over to
see Emma in wardrobe? She should be able to fit him with something
so he can get this suit to the cleaners. Just tell her it's for me."

"But what about the audition?" Cotton asked, seeming somewhat
ambivalent.

"Trust me. You're doing the best possible thing for Moxie right
now. Now, go meet Emma and let her help you. And don't be a dick to

her, please. We'll come by your hotel tonight at seven to pick you up and take you to dinner. Hopefully we'll have good news to celebrate."

Cotton seemed to finally have no fight left in him, and he nodded tiredly and got into the backseat.

Fitzhugh shut the door and looked at Violet suspiciously.

"You're invited to dinner too, Fitzy."

"Do you need me to come back and collect you?"

She shook her head and smiled. "If you could just help my filthy friend here, that's more than enough. When he's all gussied up, drop him back at Los Reyes de Armas on Hollywood Boulevard and then come by the Garden for drinks."

He winked at her. "Consider it done, Vi."

"Thanks." As Violet watched the limo slowly pull away, she contemplated Cotton's weary form as it sagged against the back window. She supposed he wasn't *completely* horrid.

"Hiya, tomato." Moxie was standing behind her, a broad grin on her face.

"My goodness, a sexy stranger, come to tempt me. You're beautiful enough to be an actress. Are you one?"

Moxie's chin dropped, but her smile remained radiant. "I am, yes."

Violet swept her into a fast embrace and spun her excitedly. "That's wonderful."

"I don't have any lines," Moxie quickly said. "I'm playing the nightclub singer."

"So you do a number?"

"Actually, I do *two*." Moxie's voice was thrumming with elation.

Violet was very proud of Moxie and fought to suppress the desire to kiss her there in plain sight, on the steps of the soundstage. "What's the picture?"

"*Love Comes Sailing*."

"And who's in it?"

"Gloria Swanson."

"Hmm, you might want to keep your distance from her." Violet gestured with her head that they should start walking.

"And why is that? Worried I might fall for her charms?"

"Not as much as I'm worried about all the powerful people she knows. Rumor has it that until recently she was Joe Kennedy's mistress, and in exchange he was managing her career."

"The financial mogul?"

"The very one. When do you start filming?"

"I'm supposed to be back Tuesday morning for wardrobe fittings. Hey, where are we going?" Moxie asked. "And where's Fitzhugh?"

"I sent him off on an errand to help our poor Uncle DuChé properly groom himself. We're now headed to T. Z. Walter's office. I have an appointment to see him about my next picture."

"Hmm, and then?"

Violet's voice was suddenly soft and raspy. "Then we take a cab back to the Garden, where I can spend a few hours making love to you."

Moxie's forward motion stopped the instant Violet finished the sentence, and she exhaled loudly. "Mmm."

"Does that mean yes?"

"It means that I find it mildly infuriating that when I'm with you, you make sure that I can *never* have on dry underpants."

Violet couldn't hide her amusement. "Is it wrong if I take some perverse pride in that gift?" They started walking again.

"It depends."

"On?"

"Whether or not I get to make you come in my mouth."

This time, Violet halted and momentarily stood still, her breath briefly caught in her chest. When she looked at Moxie, she saw a nefarious expression, framed by perfect dimples. "I'm almost certain that can be arranged," she said with some difficulty. "Even though I know you're just trying to make me wet before I have to go talk to the head of the studio."

Moxie began her trek again. "Be that as it may, doll, that doesn't mean it's *not* my plan for the evening."

Violet hurriedly caught up to her. "You know, when we first met, I had no idea what a lusty little sex monkey you really are."

"Me either," Moxie said, her eyes sparkling. "It's a nice surprise, isn't it?"

"Every day is like Christmas morning."

❖

"So, Violet, I suppose you want to know about the new movie."
T. Z. Walter sat casually on the edge of his massive desk while Violet
scratched Clitty between the ears before setting him on the floor to
explore.

"Shall I try and guess?"

He seemed indulgent. "Sure. Go ahead."

"Is it a romantic comedy?"

"Nope."

"A dramatic war picture where my fiancé's plane goes down and I
have to courageously press on?"

"Closer, but no."

"Ooh, a period piece where I get to wear a bustle?"

"No, sorry." He picked up a script from his desk and handed it to
her.

Violet glanced at the title. "*September Moon?*" Interested, she
started flipping through the manuscript.

He stood and began to pace, his hands behind his back. "It's a
drama, but it's about a love triangle."

"I'm the dark, bad girl, aren't I?"

He chuckled. "Well, yes."

"Have you already cast the leading man and the sweet, good
girl?"

T. Z. cleared his throat nervously. "The male lead will be Frank
Thatcher."

"Okay, and the other actress?" Violet repeated skeptically. He
clearly looked like he didn't want to tell her. "Christ, T. Z. It's Sylvia,
isn't it?"

"Yes."

"Are you punishing me? I thought you were pleased with my work
in *Manhattan Rhapsody*."

"I was, Violet. Very much so." He rubbed the back of his head. "I
was afraid you would see this as a bad thing."

"This *isn't* a bad thing?"

He grinned awkwardly. "Not at all."

"So casting me in a film with the one person in Hollywood who
openly despises me is actually a boon?"

T. Z. sighed. "Look, Vi, Sylvia King is the biggest star at this studio."

"Perhaps if you'd stop telling her that, she'd behave a little less like anal discharge."

He plodded on, undeterred. "And *because* you did so marvelously in *Manhattan Rhapsody*, I want you in a high-profile vehicle. Putting you in a Sylvia King movie shifts you straight into A pictures."

Violet scratched her cheek as she closed the script on her lap. "How long will I need to be conciliatory? This won't be the start of a long series of films called *The Homewrecker*, where I repeatedly steal Sylvia's man, will it?"

He laughed nervously again. "I'll promise you right now, that it won't be."

"But can you promise me that I won't have to make *other* pictures with her?"

"You know I can't, Violet."

She exhaled loudly and looked out the window. Surely there must be a way to make this ordeal better—more enjoyable. "Do I get to *really* dirty him up?"

"Who?"

"Sylvia's love interest." Violet skimmed through the script again. "Her husband, it says here. Do I thoroughly taint and debauch him? Desecrate their wedding vows, perhaps in their own bed?"

"Would that make this role more appealing to you?"

She smiled malevolently and nodded. "I want to be the nettle that burrows into the flabby flesh of her ass, T. Z. I assume Sylvia gets the guy in the end?"

"Well, yes—"

"What if, instead, I go insane and kill her?"

T. Z.'s jaw slackened. "What?"

"We could turn it into a modern-day morality play. This is what happens when people commit adultery. They get thrown from a cliff, onto the jagged rocks below."

"But Sylvia's character is the one who *doesn't* commit adultery."

"That's what gives it the surprise ending. Or maybe she kills her husband and then gets the death penalty."

"You really have a dark side, Vi."

"Tell me that some small part of you wouldn't relish making that change."

His mouth opened, but after a moment of silence, he closed it again. "I can't say that."

❖

Peter jiggled the chilled cocktail shaker, making the melting ice rattle, before he poured himself another drink. "Ladies, does anyone need a refill?"

Violet shook her head no, and Wil nodded vigorously. Moxie mused over how that very moment epitomized both women perfectly. She took a sip of her Dr. Pepper and sighed. This was *not* how she and Violet had planned to spend their day.

"Mox, I'm sure Irene is just fine." Violet patted Moxie's thigh comfortingly.

"I hope so," Moxie replied, almost absently. "I mean, she's not a bumpkin by any stretch of the imagination, but she's never stayed out all night before."

Wil inhaled the smoke through her cigarette holder before taking a sip of her martini. "That's perhaps the real tragedy here. Is she still a virgin?" She said the last word as though it meant something despicable.

"I don't know," Moxie said. "She has a beau back in New York, but he's horrible, really. Spending time with Tom is a bit like having someone read Leviticus to you in Latin."

Violet squinted. "Inexplicable, yet you still feel dirty?"

"No," Moxie replied. "That was obviously a bad metaphor. I meant he was terribly boring."

"Well, then," Peter said, "perhaps she's finally met a man who was able to show her a good time. Maybe that's all this is."

"I can't believe she didn't take me with her," Wil muttered. "I am *nothing* if not fun."

"Say, Wil," Violet said. "Didn't you mention that Irene was talking about seeing that fellow from the party the other night? What was his name?"

"Wallace?" Peter nearly choked on his libation. "She went out with Wallace?"

Moxie narrowed her eyes. "Why? What's wrong with him? You were the one who put them together, after all."

"He wasn't meant for her to *date*," Peter explained. "He was just someone for her to talk to until she—"

"Regained her senses?" Wil suggested.

"Exactly," Peter said. "The man is a complete clod."

Moxie was concerned again, but in a new way. "What do you know of Wallace, Peter?"

The question seemed to catch him off guard. "I believe he's a Protestant."

Violet rolled her eyes. "Well, *that's* a relief. How about some information that might actually be helpful, Peter? His last name? A profession? Where he lives?"

Peter closed his eyes, seeming to plumb the depths of his memory, but he opened them again and shook his head in resignation. "Sorry."

"When did you meet him?" Moxie asked.

"The night you all arrived," he replied weakly.

Violet's irritation was becoming more apparent. "How did he end up in your bungalow, Peter?"

"Someone brought him," he said confidently.

"Who?" Moxie asked.

"That tall fellow with the mustache who was drinking gimlets."

Moxie tried to calm herself and covered her mouth with her clenched fist. "You don't know *his* name either?"

"But I *do* remember what he was drinking," Peter said smugly.

Violet stood and set her drink down. "Well done, Sherlock. Now if only you could remember his hat size, we could blow this case wide open."

"I didn't know I was supposed to gather everyone's personal information before they could come in," Peter replied tersely.

After a moment of awkward silence, Wil spoke. "The good news is Irene can easily outrun that lug." When everyone turned toward her in incredulity, she appeared to nearly have a moment of self-awareness. "What? That's *not* a good thing?"

At that moment, Irene entered, animated and elated. "Hey, everyone. The party's here tonight?"

"Irene, where have you been?" Moxie's relief mingled with her chagrin.

Irene's face lit up. "I was with a certain fella." She sat beside Moxie on the sofa and coyly bit her lower lip.

"You see?" Peter said, reclining back into the chair. "She was having the time of her life."

"I was." Irene seemed giddy.

"With Wallace?" Wil asked in disbelief.

Irene scowled momentarily. "Who? Oh, that mook I met at Peter's party?" She began to laugh into her hand.

"Then who?" Violet finally asked.

"Well," Irene said, "Bette called and asked me to meet her at Universal yesterday so I could try out as a chorus girl in a new picture."

"Where was I when she called?" Wil was clearly disappointed.

Irene looked annoyed at the question. "Passed out by the pool. There was no waking you. Believe me, I tried. So I had to leave you behind."

"Mmm, I'd be completely sunburned if I hadn't been fully clothed," Wil replied, as though she'd found her silver lining.

"And underneath that busboy," Violet added. "At any rate, Irene, how did it go?"

Irene cleared her throat. "The audition, not so hot. The director said something about the size of my can, so I took a page from Wil's handbook and socked him right in the sack."

"Attagirl," Wil said, lifting her glass with a wink.

Violet's expression did much to dampen their celebration. "Wait, you punched a director in the balls?"

"I sure did," Irene said proudly. "As hard as I could."

"Empowering, isn't it, Reeny?" Wil asked.

Peter stood and began to refill the shaker with gin and ice. "I had no idea that the potency of testicles was an endowment so easily transferred to others."

Irene inhaled deeply. "At first, I didn't feel empowered at all. I got all angry and hysterical, and I ran out of there, bawling."

"No pun intended," Wil added, waggling her empty glass at Peter from across the room.

"But then a guy stopped me right outside," Irene said. "He asked me to dinner and told me that he liked my spunk."

Peter walked back and poured a fresh cocktail for Wil, handing Irene a full glass as well. "Are you sure he wasn't offering you some of *his* spunk?"

"Peter, please tell me that line has never worked for you," Violet said.

"I'm jotting it down now," he said, picking up a pencil. "I'll let you know tomorrow."

The corner of Violet's mouth rose slightly. "Remember to find out how much bail is before you call, darling."

Peter chuckled. "I always do."

Moxie hushed them both. "So, Irene, you went out to dinner with this fella?"

She nodded wildly. "And how. We went to this swanky place called the Polo Lounge and had the fanciest dinner I've ever eaten."

"The Polo Lounge inside the Beverly Hills Hotel?" Peter's eyebrows were raised.

"Um, yeah. That's the one."

Moxie was a little surprised. "Not to pry, Irene. But is that where you were all last night and today?"

Wil sat forward in interest. "If I wasn't so proud of you, my little protégée, I'd be jealous as hell." She slapped Irene on the thigh playfully. "So, Goodtime Reeny, what's his name?"

Irene looked as though she were about to explode. "Howard Hughes."

Violet looked at Moxie with wide eyes. "As in, *Hell's Angels*, Howard Hughes?"

"That's the one," Irene practically shouted.

"Isn't he with United Artists?" Peter asked. "What's he doing on a lot at Universal?"

"Did you see any ID before you touched his cock?" Wil asked.

Irene's face fell. "What are you all saying?"

Violet approached her slowly. "Just that in a town like this one, sometimes people are not always what, or who, they present themselves to be."

Irene scoffed and stood back up, setting down her untouched drink. "You're all screwy. I need to get ready for my date."

"You're going out with him again tonight?" Moxie asked.

"You bet I am."

"Why don't you bring him with all of us?" Moxie offered. "We're going to dinner to celebrate."

Irene's mouth formed an O shape. "What are we celebrating?"

"I got the part in the picture," Moxie said happily.

Irene squealed as she hugged her. "That's great."

"Now tell her the bad news," Wil said.

Moxie pulled back slightly. "Oh, Cotton's coming along."

Irene immediately looked less jubilant. "Oh. That's too bad. I'll catch up with all of you tomorrow."

Violet pointed casually to Irene. "If I told you that he reeked in a completely different way, would that make you reconsider?"

Irene's expression softened. "You could tell me he smelled like lilacs and was made of kittens, and I wouldn't reconsider. Besides, he's probably figured out by now that I took his luggage."

"*You* took Cotton's luggage?" Moxie coughed.

Wil snorted indignantly. "See? I told you it wasn't me. I don't know why you never believe me." She casually poured the contents of Irene's martini into her own glass.

Violet crossed her arms. "I think it's partially because you frequently get so blotto you can't remember what you've done and said."

"Well, yes," Wil replied meekly. "But that's not the same as *lying*. If I remember doing it, for Christ's sake, I admit it."

"Honorable," Violet said.

"You're goddamn right it is." Wil belched.

CHAPTER SIXTEEN

Violet sat on the set, brushing Clitty's coat as he sat dutifully in her lap, enduring it. "What is this back here? Is this crusty caviar? Who *have* you been socializing with?" As though in response, he stretched his body as the wire brush came into contact with an area that clearly felt pleasurable.

Moxie appeared and sat in the chair next to Violet, unable to suppress a smile. "Do you promise to devote that kind of attention to my clitty later?"

Violet nodded slowly as she stared at Moxie hungrily. "Though I'm hoping that yours isn't smeared with fish roe like this one is."

"I do what I can to prevent that."

"A good rule to live by, really. Fish was never meant to go some places. You look like you got some good news."

"I did. Mr. Walter said that he saw a rough cut of *Love Comes Sailing* and that I lit up the screen."

"I'd say that's a good thing." Violet continued Clitty's grooming.

"He's offered me a speaking part in a new picture."

"And by speaking part he means?"

Moxie's excitement seemed unabated. "I'm in only one scene, but I have a whole page of dialogue."

"Who are you playing?"

"The nightclub singer." She coughed self-consciously.

Violet ran her tongue over her teeth quickly. "Ah. But this time you're the *talking* nightclub singer," she said, trying to sound upbeat. "And are you singing in it too?"

"Yep."

"Congratulations, sweetheart."

Moxie relaxed into the chair. "Thanks, I'm already planning tonight's celebration."

Violet arched her eyebrows. "That sounds promising. Will nudity be involved?"

"Count on it."

"Do I need to RSVP?"

"Not to be presumptuous, but I was assuming you'd attend. I'll be hard-pressed to find someone to stroke repeatedly to climax this late in the day."

Violet stopped her brushing to focus on recovering the breath that suddenly evaporated from her lungs. "I'd hate to leave you in a bind, love. You can definitely count me in."

"I love your dependability, Vi. It's such an admirable trait. So, how's it going here?"

Violet sighed. "Once again, we're all waiting for Sylvia."

"She's quite the prima donna, isn't she?"

"Mox, as always, you've found a very tactful and delicate way to phrase it."

"Because if *you* were to describe her, you would say—"

"That she's a rancid, viscous wad of phlegm so horrifically vile that no bath can cleanse her and no amount of purity can erase her malodorous taint."

Moxie pulled her sunglasses out of her handbag and put them on, relaxing back in the chair. "I'm glad to hear that you two have made up."

"Yes. So how is Goodtime Reeny doing?"

Moxie winced. "I think she felt slightly less foolish before she went to her audition at Warner Brothers this morning and met a completely different Howard Hughes there."

"I had no idea he was so ubiquitous these days. It shows a shockingly unacceptable lack of imagination amongst our resident degenerates."

"And then she stopped at the pharmacy for a malt and met Louis B. Mayer there."

Violet rolled her eyes. "Oh, no."

"Apparently, he was bald and fat, but that was where the similarity ended."

"Well, why *wouldn't* the head of MGM be hanging out at a soda fountain, introducing himself to all the patrons? Did he ask to see her naked so he could cast his next picture?"

"Irene gets it now," Moxie assured her. "She sees how this town works. But I think she's feeling a little gullible and depressed."

Violet set both the brush and Clitty down on the ground. "Unfortunately Wil isn't faring too much better. Since her agent dropped her, she hasn't gotten a single audition. Well, one that she was conscious for."

"She just needs a new agent."

"If only it was that simple. Do you think Cotton would agree to represent her?"

Moxie laughed loudly, unintentionally snorting.

"And for the same reasons, neither will mine," Violet said.

"What she really needs is an agent who will never meet her."

"Or someone eccentric enough to appreciate her hedonistic and somewhat abrasive idiosyncrasies."

"Or just too high to care."

"Good thinking," Violet said with a grin. "We don't want to leave out the dope fiends."

"I'm sure they make exceptional agents."

"They can't all be surly asses, like yours is."

"And praise the Lord for that," Moxie said. "I wonder if anyone staying at the Garden can help Wil."

"You know, Peter would be more than happy to do a little entertaining for a good cause, or for a few good causes."

"A few?"

"Sure. We can celebrate your new role, cheer up sicky-pants, and see if we can find Wil a thoroughly indiscriminate agent." Violet was counting on her fingers.

Moxie sat back in her chair again, letting the sun warm her. "I love that you delude yourself into thinking that Peter's parties require a reason."

"It makes the debauchery feel more noble."

❖

Sylvia King sat in her dressing room while her hair stylist continued to work on her curls. "Jesus Christ, are you done yet, Arthur?"

"I hope so," he said, teasing her curls with a comb. "But so far today, I've thought I was done three times already."

"If you'd concentrated on making me look beautiful instead of bloated, you *would* have been done." Sylvia glanced into the mirror and rolled her eyes. "All right, let's just end this torture. I suppose that's good enough." She stood and posed for a moment in the mirror. "But come with me to the set so you can touch me up between takes."

Arthur clutched his comb tight to his chest and nodded at her. "Yes, Miss King." As she marched outside to the set, he submissively fell in line behind her.

Sylvia didn't understand how this had happened to her. In all the films she had made for Pinnacle, she had never been given a picture this horrible or a role this unattractive. She was rightfully considered America's darling, so why T. Z. had thought she was right to play a meek woman whose husband has an affair behind her back and ends up being killed by him to be with his mistress completely escaped her.

Even worse, the mistress was being played by Violet London, that brash, filthy-mouthed whore who seemed more interested in being disrespectful than really sitting down and learning from a pro how Hollywood worked. The notion that a man would choose her over Sylvia was, in a word, ludicrous. Though no matter how much she argued that point with T. Z., he didn't seem interested in what she had to say.

A production assistant whose name escaped her approached nervously. "Sylvia, it's about time. The director has been cursing you for the last half hour."

"Tell him that I've been cursing him for the last two weeks."

He stared at her. "Are you ready to shoot the scene?" His voice was devoid of emotion.

"Of course. As soon as I look over the script."

The little man seemed agitated. "You mean you don't know your lines?"

Sylvia glared back. "If you people didn't keep changing them every day, I'd know them by now, wouldn't I?"

He sighed and walked away, heading over to speak with the director, Leo Graham, a man known as much for his directness and intensity as for the pictures he made. Sylvia felt fairly certain that

T. Z. had purposely assigned Leo to this picture to try to control her. She reached for her script and grinned to herself at how disappointed they would both be.

"Sylvia!"

She looked up to see Leo angrily striding toward her. She vowed that she would not allow him to intimidate her.

"What's this I hear about you still not being ready to shoot the scene?"

"As I told your little minion," she said in irritation, "I can't learn the script when you keep changing it daily."

"Violet has no problem with the updates," he said, his eyes narrowing.

"Please, no one would notice if she was getting it wrong. It's not like the eye is exactly drawn to her. I would imagine that the audience won't even realize she's in this film."

A muscle in his cheek began to spasm violently, and Sylvia was drawn into its freakish dance. "Look here," he rasped, his voice lowered. "Don't think you're so goddamn special that I won't have you replaced on this picture, because I damn well will if you continue to give me cause."

She blinked once at him. "Your breath smells."

"Don't…fuck…with me, Sylvia," he said malevolently. "You're not running this set. I am."

"Ha," she blurted. "You wouldn't want me to go to T. Z. about this, Leo."

"You think he's not aware of the problem you've become? If you decide to press this issue, you'll be relegated to making the shittiest B movies ever wiped onto a piece of paper."

"What?" Was he actually threatening her?

"You heard me. Don't think we won't make an example of you. Your job is to listen to the studio, not the other way around. Now, you have five minutes to get your lines down for this scene, or I'm suspending you from the production and replacing you with someone who takes her job a little more seriously. You can explain to T. Z. why you were fired."

She was unable to speak, and Leo turned and walked back to the camera crane.

"Wow," Arthur whispered as he adjusted Sylvia's hair.

"Shut up," she snapped, opening the script, then glanced across to the other side of the set. Violet was seated next to an attractive blond woman. They were laughing together, and when they stopped, the blonde kissed her index finger and pressed it to Violet's lips intimately. Sylvia gasped as Violet kissed the woman's finger and the two shared a rather sultry look. "Arthur!"

"Hmm?" He continued to comb.

"Who is that woman over there?"

Arthur squinted. "Where?"

"Over there with Violet London—the blonde."

"Oh. You know, I've seen her on-set before, but I've never spoken to her. She may be a contract player."

"Well, leave my goddamn hair alone and go find out who she is."

"What? Why?"

"Just do it. And don't let on that I want to know. Be sneaky."

He looked confused. "All right."

Sylvia forced herself to look over her lines as Arthur slipped through the crew and began to chat with Violet and her admirer. He returned just as Leo was calling everyone to places.

"Well?" Sylvia asked.

"I was right," Arthur said conspiratorially. "She *is* an actress for the studio."

"What's her name?"

"Genny Finklestein."

"Good Lord." Sylvia rose and straightened her skirt. She looked up and saw both women looking at her, smiling and waving. So much for not letting on who was asking. "Well, someone should tell her that she'll need to change that." She smiled to herself at the power of this newfound knowledge.

❖

"Absolutely not," Cotton spat.

Moxie crossed her arms defiantly. "Why not?"

"Because the studio will never approve, that's why." He nodded his thanks to Peter, who appeared and handed him a drink before disappearing back into the crowd gathered in his bungalow. "A woman cannot accompany another woman to a film premiere."

Violet raised an eyebrow. "I would think it would cause a real buzz. Isn't that what you're always talking about?"

Cotton appeared irritated by this line of logic. "Buzz is having people talk about your dress, or how beautiful they think you are, not trying to imagine which one of you is the man."

Violet huffed, indignant. "No doubt if I took *you* to the premiere as my escort, Mr. McCann, they might wonder the same thing."

"No," he replied, ignoring the barb. "And I'm sure T. Z. Walter would agree. Moxie's Hollywood career is just getting started. I won't have her labeled a lesbian. Her public needs to see her as young, glamorous, available, and profoundly heterosexual."

Wil poked her head over Cotton's shoulder. "Did someone call me?"

Cotton scowled. "No, I would have said gin-soaked, abusive, foul-mouthed, and sexually indiscriminate if I had been referring to you."

Moxie turned to Violet. "He's starting to fit right in, isn't he?"

"It brings a tear to my eye," Violet said.

Wil scowled. "It makes my ass twitch."

"It does what?" Cotton asked.

"Relax," Violet assured him. "That just means that Wil has now moved you into a category heretofore only occupied by mimes, panhandlers, and carnies."

Wil inhaled deeply through her cigarette holder before expelling the smoke dramatically. "Don't forget Apache dancers, darling. I can't stand those fuckers."

"With any luck, Mr. McCann, Wil might soon elevate you to the equivalent of, oh, say, a pimp or a pederast." Violet took a sip of her drink.

"Or an *agent*," Wil said, her tone rife with denunciation.

"I'm all atwitter in anticipation."

"Cotton," Moxie began, "what if Violet and I were sisters?"

Wil's face contorted as though she had just smelled something rancid. "Just how small a town are you from, sister?"

"No, I mean if we *told* people we were sisters. Then we could socialize together and no one would care, like Lillian and Dorothy Gish."

"You realize that if we want to go to the premiere together badly enough, we'll somehow make it happen, don't you?" Violet said casually. "I would think that if you've learned anything about us by now, Mr. McCann, it's that we are not easily dissuaded."

Cotton stroked his pencil-thin mustache with his thumb and forefinger while he considered her point. "Look, if you each take a date, a male date, then I suppose there's no reason why you can't go together. But you'll need to make some kind of an effort to appear to be attracted to whichever man you bring. Walk on his arm. Pose for pictures with him." He paused and looked directly at Moxie. "Moxie, if you wish, I will be your escort for the evening."

Moxie looked at him blankly. "I thought I was supposed to seem attracted to my date."

Violet laughed. "She's got you there, *mon oncle*."

Cotton appeared only mildly hurt. "Then let me see what I can do. I'm sure I can get you both very prominent, masculine bachelors."

"That sounds horrible," Violet said.

"Speak for yourself," Wil replied, shoving Violet behind her. "I want one. Can I give you a list of what I'm looking for in a man while you're at it?"

Cotton looked stunned. "Wealthy and breathing?"

"Oh, good." Wil breathed in relief and patted his shoulder. "You've already got it. Don't forget me, darling."

"Believe me, I've tried."

"Men who don't know me just *love* me," Wil added.

"And speaking of men who don't know you, did you talk to Mr. Dickover yet?" Violet asked.

"I started to, but I just couldn't get past how funny his name is."

"Wil, Mr. Dickover is interested in being your new agent. This is hardly the time to be so juvenile."

"Did you know he goes by *Ace*?" Wil asked the group, clearly amused.

"Ace Dickover?" Cotton asked.

Moxie turned to Violet, biting her lower lip to keep from laughing. "You want Wil to sign a contract with *Ace Dickover*?"

Violet seemed to acquiesce. "Do you think it's a sign?"

"A sign?" Wil asked. "It's a fucking billboard, darling."

Irene approached the group, looking more cheerful than she had for several days. "Hey, kids," she said with a wave. "Can anybody vouch for that fella over there in the corner?"

Moxie peered through the crowd and saw a gangly, fair-haired man with a mustache and Vandyke beard, propped leisurely against the wall. "I don't think I know him."

"Me either," Violet said. "Hey, Peter. C'mere."

After handing out freshly mixed drinks to the two women in front of him, Peter made his way over from his bar. "Yes?"

"Do you know that guy over there?" Violet tried to gesture nonchalantly with her head.

"Who, Joe?"

"The blond fella in the pinstripe suit," Irene explained.

Peter smiled. "Yes, that's Joe Kilkenney. He's a screenwriter. Not doing too badly either."

"How's that?" Irene asked.

"He just adapted one of his own novels for MGM. So he's no slouch."

Moxie spoke softly to Irene. "Why do you ask?"

"He's a tall drink of water—the eel's hips," Irene replied loudly. "I just wanted to make sure he was on the up-and-up, you know? That he wasn't just some drugstore cowboy."

"What do you think of him now?" Violet asked.

Irene smiled. "Well, now I can go back and answer his question."

Moxie eyed her carefully. "What question?"

"He asked me my name. I told him I'd get back to him."

Violet's hand moved to her mouth, perhaps to hide her amusement. "Hopefully he doesn't think you didn't know the answer and had to go find out."

"You should have said Ace Dickover." Wil snorted.

Irene laughed too. "Wil, what a horrible joke."

"That's what I thought. Wait until you meet him," Wil added.

CHAPTER SEVENTEEN

"Wil, are you decent?" Violet walked into Wil and Irene's bungalow trying to make as much noise as possible, in case she unwittingly interrupted anything embarrassing. She had already learned that lesson the hard way.

"You know the answer to that question," came a depressed murmur from Violet's left.

"Wil?" Violet asked again, perplexed that the voice apparently had come from an empty couch.

"I'm down here."

Violet approached the phantom voice hesitantly, relieved to see that Wil was lying behind the couch on the floor, wearing only her stockings, brassiere, and slip. "Dare I ask?"

"I was hoping *you* could tell *me*." Wil ran her hand over her face.

Violet extended her arm and pulled Wil unceremoniously to her feet. "I need you to pull yourself together."

"What time is it?" Wil rasped, opening her mouth several times and grimacing, as though trying to identify some familiar taste.

"Noon."

"Good Lord, it's early." She rubbed her eyes miserably.

"For Bela Lugosi perhaps. For us humans, it's the shank of the day."

Wil's brow furrowed. "Did you and I have sex last night?"

"Not last night, or ever."

"Because my mouth tastes suspiciously like snatch." Wil stuck her tongue out as though contemplating the flavor further.

Violet sighed in irritation. "If you like, I'll try and help you piece together your last twenty-four hours, but that will need to wait."

"For what?"

"I have an audition for you," Violet replied, her eagerness returning.

"Really?" Wil looked shocked.

"Really. It seems Miss Sylvia King got herself fired from my picture today for mouthing off to the director while everyone and their brother was watching."

"Ooh, what did she say to him?"

"Something about demanding that he grab his ankles and jump up her ass, though I think she called it her puckered brown grotto, or some such nonsense."

Wil's eyebrows rose, but she said nothing.

"Anyway, as we were less than a week into filming, they want to immediately recast her part—try and cut their losses. I told them I knew the perfect undiscovered ingénue."

"And who would that be?"

Violet looked at her incredulously. "You, you silly bitch."

"Me, an ingénue?" Wil held her arms out to her side and turned her palms upward. "Have you not been paying attention?"

"That's why they call it *acting*," Violet explained. "So now, you have a choice. You can either continue to sleep through your life in this bungalow, trying to reconcile the shadowy taste of one stranger's genitalia as it blends into the next, or you can get in the shower, clean yourself up, and start doing what you came here to do."

"Hmm, but what if I actually came here for the genitalia?"

Violet glared. "Get in the damn shower."

Wil tried to keep a straight face, though quickly gave up. "Thanks, Vi."

"Uh-huh."

"It will only take me a few minutes to get ready."

"Good. Fitzy's outside waiting to take us to the studio. We can go over the scene in the car."

❖

Louella Parsons sat in a booth at the Hollywood Brown Derby, doodling on her notepad and staring at the second hand on her watch.

It seemed as though she had been sitting there forever when the waiter came back for what was easily the tenth time. "Would you like to go ahead and order now, Miss Parsons?"

She sighed. "I suppose so. Bring me the club sandwich, will you?"

The waiter took the menu, nodded, and disappeared into the kitchen.

Louella was muttering to herself in irritation when she looked back to the front door and saw Sylvia King striding confidently in. She seemed to possess no sense of urgency as she sauntered over to Louella and sat across from her.

"Do you have any idea how long you've kept me waiting, Sylvia?" She made no attempt to hide her annoyance as she drummed her fingers on the table.

As Sylvia's face split into a sinister grin, Louella was instantly unsettled by the sudden transformation of America's darling into this arcane nucleus of villainy.

"Trust me, Louella, this scoop will be worth it."

❖

Moxie dug through her handbag looking for the bungalow key, squinting to see in the moonlight. From behind her, Violet's hands provocatively roamed her waist, abdomen, and breasts.

"You're not helping my concentration," Moxie said softly, closing her eyes as Violet's mouth descended on her exposed shoulder.

"You did little for mine all evening, love. I couldn't stop staring at your curvy deliciousness."

Moxie chuckled, then with surprising dexterity, she found the key and put it in the lock before turning around in Violet's arms, putting her hands around Violet's neck, and kissing her back. "I didn't really enjoy watching you on the arm of that preening ass all evening," she murmured against Violet's mouth.

The brush of Violet's tongue instantly aroused Moxie, and their kiss deepened as Violet pinned her to the door.

"I want you," Violet groaned. Her palm caressed Moxie's left breast as it moved slowly down to turn the doorknob. As the door swung inward, both of them rode it without their mouths breaking contact.

Violet turned her head slightly when something in her peripheral vision triggered an alarm. Not only were their lights on, but inside sat Wil, Irene, Irene's date Joe, Fitzhugh, and Peter. "Oh, fuck."

"Mmm, yes," Moxie replied eagerly.

"No," Violet whispered, gesturing toward their company with her head.

"Hmm?" Moxie turned, her back still against the door, and tried to feign delight. "Oh, hello, everyone. Look at all of you…here in our bungalow. How—"

"Ill-timed," Violet said.

"Yes." Moxie stepped all the way inside.

Irene seemed oblivious to the comment. "How was the premiere? Were there just gobs of stars there?"

Moxie took a seat beside Irene on the sofa. "I suppose so."

"And where are your virile escorts?" Wil lit a cigarette.

Violet shut the door and sighed. "Judging by how they were eyeing each other, I'm guessing they're somewhere ejaculating."

Wil smiled. "It's never a party until someone does."

Violet crossed her arms. "Would it be impolite to ask how you all got in here?"

"We bribed Captain Napkin," Wil replied. "He let us in, in exchange for a small token."

Moxie grimaced. "Do I want to know what?"

"Probably, since it was a pair of your underpants," Wil said casually.

"What?" Moxie was unable to verbalize anything else.

"Relax," Wil said. "It's nothing perverted. They're for him to wear on his head. I made sure to pick a pair I thought would flatter him."

"You're such a good friend," Violet said.

"If only that were true," Wil replied.

Fitzhugh cleared his throat. "Unfortunately, there's a reason we're here, Vi."

Violet's eyebrow arched. "A reason beyond rifling through our underwear?"

"Sadly, yes," Peter said.

"What is it?" Moxie asked. "What's wrong?"

Fitzhugh handed over a copy of the *Los Angeles Examiner*, folded over to a particular page. "You need to read Louella Parson's column from this morning."

Violet took the newspaper, sat on the arm of the sofa, and began to read aloud. "What glamorous, dark-haired, newcomer of *Manhattan Rhapsody* has been seen indulging her depraved Sapphic fancies with an up-and-coming Jewish contract actress for Pinnacle?"

A hush fell over the group before Wil finally turned to Moxie. "You're Jewish?"

"No," Moxie replied, her chest tightening. "But I know just who might think I am."

Violet gritted her teeth. "Sylvia King, that disease-ridden, worm-eaten bag of spume."

"I'm sure she's just angry about Wil replacing her in *September Moon*," Moxie said, her mind still reeling.

"Just as angry as I am that she is a vengeful, poisonous succubus," Violet said.

Moxie took the newspaper from Violet's hand. "I wonder if Cotton has seen this yet."

Violet exhaled loudly. "The fact that I'm still alive implies that he hasn't."

Peter leaned forward, stroking his mustache. "Vi, you'd better call your agent and figure out a way to deny this before it ruins you."

"I'm not going to deny it, Peter."

He seemed incredulous. "What? An item like this could end you in this town."

Violet stood and began to pace. "But it's true. It's not as though it's libelous."

"But Vi," Irene said, "you're not going to let Sylvia King destroy your career, are you?"

Violet looked at the floor for a moment, as though she was considering the question. "I hope not. But the last thing I'm going to do is pretend that I'm something that I'm not, career be damned."

"What are you saying?" Moxie asked.

"What I've said my whole life—that I'm not some moral degenerate or sideshow attraction to be trotted out to the masses so strangers can either be titillated or denounce what I do in my own bedroom."

"Or baggage car," Wil added.

Violet continued without missing a beat. "Acting is my livelihood, not my lifestyle, and who I choose to share my time or my bed with should be immaterial to how well people think I do my job."

Joe finally spoke, the cadence of his voice soft and metered. "Well, yes. It *should* be immaterial, but it isn't. When people hear you're a lesbian, that will be all they need to decide that you're wanton and depraved."

"They'll run you out of town on a rail, Vi," Peter said.

"Then so be it," Violet declared glibly. "But this is who I am and how I live my life, and I refuse to apologize for it. I intend to report to the set first thing Monday morning, just like any other workday. It's possible that this will just blow over, unnoticed."

Irene's brow furrowed. "But what about Moxie?"

Violet's expression took on a grave, pensive quality. "She's unidentified and in the clear, for now." She turned to address Moxie directly. "If you don't want to be seen publicly with me, I'll understand."

Moxie was stunned. "What?"

"I can only speak for myself," Violet explained. "I'm not going to tell you what you should do. Your career is just starting to take off, and you don't want to put yourself in a position to regret anything later on. Now if you all don't mind, I'm going to bed. You're welcome to stay as long as you please, but I think I'm quite tired. Good night."

After Violet disappeared into the bedroom Wil sat dejectedly in an armchair. "Well, shit."

"What are you going to do, Mox?" Irene asked.

"I'm not sure." Moxie shook her head slowly. "I guess I need to talk to Cotton."

"I think we all know what he'll tell you," Wil said.

Moxie dragged her hand through her hair. "Yeah, I know. Listen, I need to make sure Violet's okay. I'll be right back."

As Moxie vanished into the back bedroom too, Irene was overcome with concern for them both. "This is terrible," she said softly, trying not to be overheard by Moxie or Violet. "Isn't there anything we can do?"

Joe put his arm around Irene protectively. "Not now that the column has already come out. It's reprinted in papers all over the country."

"Sadly, I think Vi's right," Fitzhugh said. "All we can do is try to make sure that the press doesn't find out about Moxie and try to ruin her too."

Peter sipped his martini. "Yes, we can certainly do that. But that's not *all* we can do."

"No?" Joe asked.

Peter shook his head as he grinned nefariously.

"Peter, darling," Wil said, her voice sounding hopeful. "Your menacing look is making me thoroughly wet."

CHAPTER EIGHTEEN

Violet wasn't surprised when she received word to report to T. Z. Walter's house the following day. She prepared herself for what she considered the worst-case scenario, being released from her contract with Pinnacle immediately.

As T. Z.'s humorless butler showed Violet and Clitty into the drawing room, a calm washed over her, a resignation about the coming of the inevitable, perhaps. She plopped down in a plush armchair as she glanced around at the rest of his furnishings.

"Ah, Violet. I'm glad you came straightaway," T. Z. said, sweeping into the room surrounded by plumes of smoke from his pipe.

"Call it morbid curiosity," Violet said, her chin on her fist.

"Do you know what I want to talk to you about?" He sat on a velvet settee across from her.

"I just might. Is it black and white and sometimes masquerades as real journalism?"

T. Z. drew thoughtfully on his pipe. "The whole town's abuzz."

"I wish I were."

"We can respond one of two ways to this rumor, Vi. We can either ignore it and hope it goes away—"

"A personal favorite of mine."

"Or we can put you out front and center, with a virile young man on your arm."

Violet scowled. "I definitely prefer the first one."

"Vi, we have to head this rumor off as soon as possible."

"Head it off, or off its head?"

"Both," he said with a nod. "The studio or, rather, I have spent a lot of money on you—a bundle. You could say I have a vested interest in your career and its success. Would you say that's fair?"

"Yes."

"In a couple of weeks, Pinnacle is having a large, formal studio party. You, as a Pinnacle star will, of course, attend."

Violet was becoming very skeptical. "Okay."

"You're going to bring, as your escort, Hollywood's most eligible bachelor. Hell, you can even pick him. You name him, and I'll get him for you."

"I don't know, T. Z. I'm not sure how comfortable I am with this."

He puffed out tobacco smoke several times in quick succession before responding. "Look, Vi, I'm not asking you if you're a dyke. If you are, I don't want to know. I'm happier that way. But no one else can know either. While you're representing this studio, you need to conduct yourself as a well-bred socialite—no pussy, drugs, nudity, or pregnancy out of wedlock. And when you do those things anyway, make sure no one finds out about it."

"That last bit seems to be the tricky part."

"It always is, doll. Look, I get that this is inconvenient for you, and besides the fact that I think you're a hell of an actress, I genuinely like you. I don't want you to have to do anything you don't want to. I mean, no one's asking you to suck this guy off."

"That's a relief," Violet said. "Otherwise I might need to renegotiate my contract."

"And you don't need to say anything to the press. Just walk right by them if you want. But you owe it to this studio, and yourself, to try and distance yourself from this scandal. You've got a picture just released and another one in production."

Violet looked at him warily. "So you still want me to finish it?"

T. Z. stood and began to pace. "Of course I do. I've seen the dailies and you're great in it. Incidentally, so's that redhead you brought in to replace Sylvia. She has real talent. She could be bigger than Sylvia King ever was."

"I think so too," Violet replied slowly.

"So it would be a shame if this film ended up not getting finished because we couldn't count on you to help dispel this rumor. If you want this movie completed and seen, if you want your friend to have a career as an actress, you'll need to do what I'm asking."

❖

Cotton sat on the sofa in Moxie's bungalow with a decidedly smug look on his face. "Didn't I tell you this would happen?"

Moxie bit her lower lip. "Cotton, can we please get past your superior self-righteousness?"

He sighed. "Fine. But it should be duly noted that I ultimately was right about this. The only good news is that the press doesn't know that you and Violet are involved."

"Yet."

His eyebrows arched dramatically. "Yet? Are you insane? You need to break off this dangerous tryst right now, before it's made public."

Moxie shook her head. "I won't do that."

"Why the hell not?"

"Because I'm happier than I've ever been in my life, Cotton."

"Of course you are. You've never been this successful before. Is this out of some perverse form of guilt? Are you just trying not to seem ungrateful to her?"

"No, that's not it at all. I *want* to be with Violet, in every way. This isn't about what she can or can't give me."

"So are you deluded enough to think that you can be romantically involved with this woman and still work in this town?"

She smiled. "One man's delusion is another man's optimism."

Cotton leaned forward, his hands on his knees. "All right, look. I've told you how I feel."

"Many times."

"Obviously, I haven't had any success in keeping you two apart."

Moxie considered this point. "Let's say you had limited success, because for a time, your intervention was *intensely* aggravating."

"Regardless, let's focus on what can be done to protect and further your career."

"Okay. That sounds suspiciously reasonable."

"I'm told there is a Pinnacle Studio party in the works."

Moxie nodded. "There is, in a couple weeks. Mr. Walter is making Violet go with an escort."

"Excellent." Cotton's face brightened. "You shall do the same."

Moxie's only response was to sigh deeply.

"And we're going to take it a step further."

"Which is?"

"We're going to announce your engagement at the party."

"What? That's just *one* step forward? The U.S. infantry doesn't march this fast!"

Cotton put up his hands in a calming manner. "Which is exactly the point. It makes it clear to everyone that you've obviously been dating this man for quite some time and are therefore not spending your time dallying with Violet London."

"You're completely insane."

"Not at all, Moxie. It's called a lavender marriage, and it's helped more than a few troubled celebrities in your particular dilemma."

"A lavender marriage? And where will we get my fiancé, Cotton? From the Montgomery Ward catalog?"

"What makes a lavender marriage work is finding someone who will benefit as much from the union as you will," he said, his voice filled with innuendo.

"I'm still not following you," she admitted in irritation.

"An actor who's rumored to be queer. You two get married and tongues no longer wag about either of you."

Moxie cringed at the sudden realization. "You already have someone in mind, don't you?"

"I do. In fact, he was your date to Friday night's premiere."

She buried her face in her hands. "Tell me you haven't discussed this with him yet."

"I have, and he and his agent seemed *very* interested."

"Cotton, this is crazy. I can't marry someone I barely know when I love someone else." She paused and contemplated her word choice. She *did* love Violet. She made a mental note to tell her so.

"It's just a formality, I assure you. You can both carry on whatever relationships you please, provided you're discreet and you keep up the ruse. After a year or so, feel free to divorce. In this town, it might seem even stranger if you didn't. By then, the rumors will have died and the seeds of your fame will have taken root."

"I just don't know."

Cotton grabbed her hands and held them. "Moxie, I know you're probably tired of hearing this, but you need to consider your future. You have a chance to become a major star, bigger than you ever dreamed. If you walk away from this opportunity and your secret gets revealed, even that little gin joint in Nebraska won't hire you back. You really need to decide if you want to be a success."

"You know I do."

"Then stop acting like it doesn't matter to you and do what needs to be done."

❖

Moxie stood at the corner of the room at the Pinnacle party, dressed to the nines, with her faux beau on her arm, yet feeling completely hollow. She had spied Wil earlier from across the room, and true to form, she had been surrounded by doting men tripping over themselves to light her cigarette, while she no doubt told ribald stories and showed a chosen few her genitalia.

When Moxie finally glimpsed Violet through the crowd, her breath caught in her chest. The gown that the studio had put her in was a striking cobalt blue with hanging fringe and a sexy side slit. She was chatting amiably with someone near the buffet, her date on one arm and Clitty in the other.

She knew she shouldn't go talk with Violet out in the open, but she was feeling bold, and the sight of Violet in such a provocative evening dress made her feel even more so.

She turned to her soon-to-be fiancé. "Excuse me, Cary. I'll be right back."

He flashed her a perfect smile. "Certainly."

As she approached Violet, their eyes met briefly, and desire surged through her from the way Violet's eyes raked hungrily over her body.

"No tuxedo for Clitty?" Moxie asked.

"I tried, but I found it difficult to walk with the bowtie on." Violet feigned realization. "Oh, you mean him," she said, pointing to the terrier.

"That joke just never gets old," Moxie said, laughing. "You look beautiful, by the way." Moxie struggled not to look at Violet like she wanted to devour her.

Violet's date excused himself, leaving the two of them standing alone. "Thanks. You look stunning yourself, doll," Violet replied softly.

"This party feels so strange to me."

"Is it because no one has launched anything from their anus?"

"No. And I'll have you know I had a nightmare about Smokey Bender and a flying squirrel."

Violet winced. "Ouch."

"It feels strange because we're both here but we're not together."

"You realize if T. Z. sees us chatting, he'll skin us both alive."

Moxie eyed Violet appreciatively. "I know, but I just wanted to tell you how striking that dress is."

"I was hoping you'd like it."

Two middle-aged women approached the buffet, surveying the elaborate spread and the melting ice sculpture carved in the shape of a swan.

"Goodness," the shorter of them said. "This all looks marvelous."

The plump, tall one grabbed two plates and handed her friend one. "Here, Frieda."

"I can't wait to try this shrimp," Frieda said excitedly, building a mountain of crustaceans on her plate. "So, Claire, did you see that story about Sylvia King?"

"See it?" Claire squealed. "I've committed it to memory. It just goes to show you that no one is ever as innocent as they seem."

Violet and Moxie exchanged curious, concerned looks as they continued to eavesdrop.

"And how," Frieda replied, stuffing her mouth with several shellfish and chewing with her mouth open. "Who knew that America's darling was spending all her time in opium dens to dull the pain of rampant syphilis?"

Violet began to cough violently, prompting Moxie to slap her repeatedly on the back.

Claire continued to accost the hors d'oeuvres unabated. "I heard that T. Z. already released her from her contract."

"How could he *not*?" Frieda asked. "The woman's an embarrassment."

Once Violet caught her breath, she wiped a tear away and whispered to Moxie, "This has all the markings of a Wil Skoog confidence game."

"I was thinking the same thing."

"It has her gin-soaked fingerprints all over it. She's over there, so excuse me while I accuse her. I'll be right back."

"Was that Violet London?" Frieda asked her friend. If she had been attempting to whisper or be discreet in any way, she failed miserably.

"I think so." Claire looked at Moxie. "You know, young lady, you should be more careful about who you're seen with."

"What do you mean?" Moxie asked.

Claire walked closer to her and lowered her voice slightly. "I'm sure you weren't aware. You seem like a lovely young person. But that woman who was just chatting with you was Violet London."

Moxie's blood pressure began to rise. "So?"

"Well, I'm not one to talk out of turn," Claire began.

"Clearly," Moxie said.

"But she's notorious."

"Is that so?" Moxie didn't care even slightly how irritated she sounded.

Frieda nodded excitedly, looking as though she might burst from the excitement of saying something illicit. "It's true. She's a lesbian." She whispered the last word as though it were a synonym for the scourge of humanity.

Moxie pretended to be shocked, bringing her open hand to her mouth and gasping audibly. "Good Lord, no! She never told me. But maybe she simply couldn't speak because she had my clitoris in her mouth."

Both women stared at Moxie.

"Dear Lord," Claire wheezed. She struggled to swallow the canapé that was now fluttering about in her mouth.

"*You* are a sick, sick girl," Frieda added, glaring.

Moxie crossed her arms and smiled insincerely. "That's funny, because it seems to me that you two are the sick ones, feeding off gossip and salacious lies. Why not focus on your own pathetic love lives, instead of rudely inserting yourself like a dry dildo into the relationships of strangers and then having the gall to disapprove of whatever it is that you *think* you've found?"

Violet returned with Wil in tow, though both of them were clearly startled by the altercation they were interrupting.

Frieda set her plate down angrily. "I refuse to let a perverted whore address me that way."

Moxie stood her ground calmly. "Which is fine, you judgmental, sanctimonious bitch, because instead *I'll* address you. And while I'm at it, I'll berate you for your hypocrisy and mock you for your small-minded bigotry." She let her eyes travel down Frieda's frame with visible distaste. "Not to mention that hideous dress." With that, she took Violet's face in her hands and kissed her deeply for several seconds.

"Thank God," Wil said. "I was starting to think this was the most boring fucking party I've ever been to."

Violet pulled back, glancing at the two horrified strangers looking on. "Um, having second thoughts about announcing your engagement tonight, sweetheart?"

"What makes you say that?"

"Your tongue in my mouth," Violet replied matter-of-factly.

Moxie grinned. "I can never get anything past you." She faced Wil somberly. "I'm sorry if I've ruined anything for you tonight."

Wil seemed amused. "Darling, do you know how ironic it is for you to apologize to me about your behavior?"

"Yes," Moxie said. "It felt strange coming out of my mouth."

"Which is odd," Wil countered. "Usually for me, things feel strangest on their way *into* my mouth. Ladies," Wil said, extending her hand to Frieda and Claire, "nice to meet you. I'm Greta Garbo. I assume you've already met my friends Norma Shearer and Jean Harlow."

"You're all disgusting," Claire spat.

"We'll find out who you are," Frieda said. "Don't you worry."

Wil's smile disappeared. "Ah, then more to the point, fuck off, pigs."

"It was *lovely* to meet you both." Violet's sarcasm was pronounced.

"Like having a tooth drilled," Moxie added.

Wil waved to them as both Claire and Frieda rushed out of the room. "Now have a wonderful evening. Don't forget to fuck off."

Violet's expression became somber. "Mox, you do realize the choice you've just made?"

"I do, yes."

"Odds are there's no going back."

Moxie beamed. "I certainly hope not."

EPILOGUE

Los Angeles
December 31, 1931

Julian and Gary got out of the cab and looked around for anything that might provide a clue that they were near their destination. All Julian saw at the address he was given was what appeared to be a run-down warehouse. He squinted at the scrap of paper in his hand, the moonlight providing only minimal illumination. "This is supposed to be it," he said, more to convince himself than anything.

"Good," Gary replied. "Because our cab just left us here to die, otherwise."

"And I thought Manhattan was frightening," Julian murmured as he crossed the street to face a large black steel door. Taking a deep breath, he knocked.

An eye-level panel slid open. "Yeah?" came a gruff voice from inside.

Julian glanced back down to the paper. "Um…Urethra Dejeuner sent me," he read.

The massive door unlocked with a clang and swung open. Inside the vestibule, it looked even more like a warehouse, except for a neon sign over a door that led off to the right and read Genny's Place. Julian straightened his tie as he and Gary headed inside.

He was stunned when he saw the inside of the club itself, with lots of mission-style dark wood, steel, and stained glass. The light fixtures appeared to be beautiful obsidian works of art, and the bar was long and S-shaped, with people shoulder to shoulder around it.

"Wow," Gary said above the sound of jazz that the pianist played in the corner.

Julian continued to weave through the crowd. "It's packed."

"Julian!"

He turned to see Violet coming toward him through the celebrating throng. "Vi!"

When she reached them, she hugged them both and gave them each a kiss. "I was worried you two wouldn't make it before midnight."

"Vi, this place is beautiful," Gary said. "When I heard you owned a club, I pictured a little hole in the wall under a bridge somewhere."

"Guarded by a troll?" she asked with a grin.

Gary chuckled. "Perhaps."

"That's a very New York City perspective, I'm afraid. We don't have trolls in LA."

Julian looked around at the festive, very queer clientele. "Though clearly you have your share of fairies."

"It's that damned silent partner of mine, Peter Pan. He keeps bringing them," Violet said. "Come on into the back room, fellas, to Wil's table."

Julian was stunned that there was even more to the club. "I naturally assumed Wil had a standing table here."

Violet slowly led them through the wall of people. "Only because we don't yet have a safe place reserved for her to pass out."

Gary laughed. "That would save so much time and effort."

The back room Violet had referred to was another space nearly as big as the front room, though it had a palpably different feel. Out front, the atmosphere was lively, like a beating heart. But back here, it was darker, bluer, and somehow more intimate. Onstage Moxie, looking glamorous, was singing a sultry version of the Gershwin ballad "'S Wonderful."

Violet paused appreciatively before she snapped out of it and directed Julian and Gary to a large round table up front, near the wall. "Gentlemen, allow me to do the introductions for the new faces, and for those of us who may have been too drunk the last time we were together to remember who we all are." Already sitting at the table were Wil, Irene, Lady Dulce La Boeuf, and three unfamiliar men. "Julian and Gary, this is Peter Easton, screenwriter, and Charles Fitzhugh, chauffeur extraordinaire. And this gentleman is Irene's fiancé Joe Kilkenney, a screenwriter much like Peter, only better. I believe you know everyone else." She grabbed a chair for herself.

Wil rose and rounded the table to kiss Julian and Gary. "How was your trip, darlings?"

"The train was nice, but it rained for days," Gary replied as he took a seat. "It was long, tiring, and wet."

Wil returned to her chair and settled in. "Hmm, the last time I described an evening in those terms, I had spent thirty-six hours straight with a streetcar conductor, an Alsatian, and a freakishly phallic zucchini. It was fabulous."

Julian sighed contentedly as a gangly young man arrived to take his drink order. "I've missed having someone of such questionable virtue to openly mock, Wil." He nodded to the waiter. "I'll have a gin rickey, please."

Wil slid a Chesterfield into her cigarette holder. "And I've missed the way you frequently make me laugh so hard that I pee a little. Did you get checked into the Garden?"

Gary nodded, his brow furrowed. "We did, but the fella at the front desk—he didn't seem quite right."

"Was he wearing women's undergarments?" Irene asked.

"And wearing them completely incorrectly?" Lady Dulce clarified.

"No," Julian replied. "He seemed completely normal, until he turned around to get us the bungalow key and we noticed a live flower sticking out of his pants, like it was growing from his ass crack."

"A bird of paradise," Gary added helpfully.

"Well, those are very pretty," Violet said weakly. "And the stems are quite firm."

Irene nodded. "And they don't have thorns."

Julian winced. "So Vi, Genny's Place? Who exactly is Genny?"

"It's a bit of an inside joke," Violet explained. "Though for you, Gary, and Peter, it would be an *outside* joke, if you follow me."

Julian scowled. "I'm afraid I don't."

Wil leaned forward on the table. "As in, 'I wish I could scratch my gennies, but people are looking.'"

"How classy," Peter said, taking a sip of his martini.

"Good breeding pervades everything I do, Peter," Violet said.

"That kind of thing can't be learned," Julian added. "Look at Wil, for example."

"So, Lady Dulce, how long have you been in California?" Gary asked.

"About a month."

"The West Coast seems to agree with you," Julian said.

Lady Dulce beamed. "I have to say that working here is definitely a step up from the shit factory I was singing in back East. Though, for the record, you two bastards missed my set."

"No doubt you were terrific," Gary said in appeasement.

"You bet your ass I was," Lady Dulce replied. "Just ask Ramon Novarro. He was sitting down front, and he loved every minute of it."

Peter's upper lip curled. "Well, we don't need to know exactly *how* you know he loved it."

"Speak for yourself, darling." Wil exhaled the smoke from her cigarette before turning to Lady Dulce. "Did you make him come in his pants?"

Lady Dulce winked. "I sure as hell tried."

"T. Z. is loaning me out to MGM studios next month to make a picture with him," Wil said. "I'll try too, and we'll see who gets closer."

Lady Dulce's eyes narrowed at the challenge. "Deal."

"Wil, explain to me why you haven't been fired yet." Julian lit a match for his Lucky Strike.

Wil laughed. "Believe me, darling, I'm just as shocked as you are. Who knew that *September Moon* would be such a hit? I mean, the character I played was so fucking sweet and pure. I found her utterly tedious, but somehow the public loved her."

"Remarkable," Julian said.

"Why don't you tell Gary and Julian how you ended Sylvia King's career, Wil?" Violet said, propping her chin on her fist.

"Oh, they don't want to hear that boring old chestnut," Wil mumbled.

"Sylvia King, the dope fiend?" Gary asked excitedly.

"That's the one," Violet said. "Go ahead, Wil, Peter."

"It was easy, really," Peter explained with less visible compunction than Wil showed. "It seems that when you are a wretched cunt to everyone, it's very easy to find people who take great glee in getting revenge." He polished off his drink. "In fact, Rex Kelly took it upon himself to make up the part about Sylvia having syphilis. He got a little carried away, apparently."

Wil pointed at Violet. "You know we—"

"Did it all for me. Yes, so you say," Violet remarked. "I'd like to say it's the thought that counts, but the thought was actually rather dark and vicious."

"You're welcome," Peter said sarcastically.

Violet sighed. "Next time, just get me a card."

"Would anyone like another drink?" the waiter asked.

Peter nodded. "I would."

"No, thanks," Wil said.

Julian was stunned. "Did you just *refuse* a refill?"

"I did, yes. I have to be at the studio tomorrow for some costume fittings, and Cotton will kill me if I'm late."

"Your new agent is *Cotton*?" Julian sputtered.

"Yeah," Irene said, clearly amused. "Ain't that a shocker?"

"How did that happen?" Gary asked.

"Well," Wil said, "Cotton's main client was Moxie, and when she decided to stop acting, he realized he needed something I could give him."

"An ulcer?" Violet suggested.

"Suicidal thoughts?" Peter said.

"Gonorrhea?" Julian offered.

Everyone paused for a moment, before Wil responded. "That round goes to Julian."

"Thanks," Julian replied, his mustache curving upward slightly. "I'd like to thank all the little people, whose constant drinking, carousing, and exceedingly poor judgment have provided endless inspiration."

Violet chuckled and shook her head slowly, not realizing until that moment just how much she loved her friends. She rose and straightened her dress. "I'll be right back, everyone. Make sure you order at least two bottles of champagne. We'll need to toast at midnight."

She walked up the steps and stood in the wings to watch Moxie finish her last number. She loved the way Moxie's fingers slid provocatively up the length of the microphone as she sang. Who was she kidding? She loved the way anything of Moxie's moved against any object of choice.

As the song ended, the applause commenced and Moxie took her bows. As she exited the stage, she smiled seductively when she saw Violet waiting for her. "How'd I do?"

Violet was speechless. "You were—"

"All right?" Moxie suggested.

"I was going to say mouthwateringly delicious."

The corners of Moxie's mouth rose slightly, and her hands went around Violet's waist. "You're sweet."

"Sweet wasn't exactly what I was going for," Violet said breathily.

Moxie gently pushed Violet so that her back was pressed against the wall, then kissed her hungrily. "Don't underestimate the power of being sweet, Vi," she said softly, as she shifted to nibble Violet's neck. "Odds are good that it will get me into bed."

Violet's pulse was racing from the feel of Moxie's mouth as it made its way to her earlobe. "Mmm, they do say that whatever you do on New Year's Eve, you'll be doing all year long."

"Well, I don't know who *they* are," Moxie whispered before snaking her tongue into Violet's ear, "but I'd hate to disappoint them."

"God bless them."

"Speaking of them," Moxie said, "did I see Gary and Julian arrive?" Her hands began to caress the small of Violet's back.

"You did. The gang's all here."

"It's going to be a hell of a night."

"Yes. The perfect end to a hell of a year," Violet said, trailing kisses along Moxie's jawline. "Any regrets?"

Moxie pulled back to look into Violet's gray eyes. "Are you kidding? Do you know what this is?"

"What?"

"I'm the water," she said as her lips gently brushed the base of Violet's throat. "And you're the absinthe." Her mouth slowly made its way up to Violet's neck. "This is the louche."

Violet smiled and reverently ran her fingers along Moxie's collarbone. "That it is."

Aperitif—Or the Appendix of Cocktails

Extensive research went into the creation of *The Seduction of Moxie*, and as such, it was necessary to mix many a classic cocktail. I spent countless hours in this endeavor and will never recount some of the resulting evenings because, frankly, their details now escape me.

I decided to include some of the drinks in this book as a sort of companion piece. A few old favorites have been transcribed, but also some unique creations—*Seduction of Moxie* originals—will hopefully inspire you to indulge in some debauchery of your own.

The Moxie

This subtle yet sweet concoction packs a wallop. Bar games involving the cherry stem are optional, though enthusiastically encouraged.

In a champagne flute, add the following:
1 tablespoon fresh lemon juice
½ tablespoon cherry brandy
1 maraschino cherry

Top with your favorite bubbly. I tend to like this drink on the sweeter side, so I usually use a Demi-Sec or Doux. But feel free to experiment until you get a blend you like.

The Violet London

Crème de Violette is a bit tricky to find in your neighborhood liquor establishment, but you may be able to find a few online stores that carry it.

In a cocktail shaker, add the following:
1 ounce gin
1 ounce vodka
4 ounces lemon-lime soda
¾ tablespoon Crème de Violette
ice

Give the ingredients a good shake and strain into a martini glass. Add a lemon twist or slice to garnish.

The Lady Dulce

While I didn't intend to create a drink for the fabulous Lady Dulce La Boeuf, this concoction came about one experimental Sunday morning and I thought, "Yes, this would most certainly hit the spot after a night in the buffet flats." Just be sure you're not driving out to brunch (or anywhere, really) after having one of these.

To a mug of regular coffee, add the following:
1 tablespoon Kahlúa
1 tablespoon Frangelico
1 tablespoon Café Bohême

The Pompous Bastard

In a cocktail shaker, add the following:
2 ounces gin
½ tablespoon Galliano
½ tablespoon Cointreau

1 tablespoon fresh lemon juice
ice

Give the ingredients a good shake and strain into a martini glass.
Add a lemon twist to garnish.

The Classic Gin Rickey

Finding a bartender who could properly craft Julian's drink of choice was a bit challenging, but after giving the briefest of instructions, I was able to find a few establishments that produced a truly magnificent beverage. Let's bring about a resurgence of this classic.

In an ice-filled highball glass, add the following:
2½ ounces gin
2 tablespoons fresh lime juice
5 ounces club soda

Give the ingredients a brief stir and add a lime wedge for garnish.
It's also delicious if you add a little simple syrup.

The Bronx

One of Miss Skoog's favorites, if she had to prioritize her liquid diet.

In a cocktail shaker ⅔ full of ice, add the following:
2 ounces gin
2 tablespoons fresh orange juice
2 teaspoons dry vermouth
2 teaspoons sweet vermouth

Give the ingredients a good shake and strain into a chilled cocktail glass.

The Floradora

In an ice-filled highball glass, add the following:
1 ½ ounces gin
½ ounce fresh lime juice
½ ounce framboise liqueur

Top with ginger ale and garnish with a lime wedge.

The Sidecar

In a cocktail shaker ⅔ full of ice, add the following:
1 ounce brandy
1 ounce Cointreau (or triple sec)
1 ounce fresh lemon juice

Shake vigorously and pour into a cocktail glass rimmed with sugar.

About the Author

Colette Moody is an avid fan of history and politics. When she isn't doing research or crafting scenes for her next romp of a novel, she can be found doing one or more of the following: watching classic films; sequestering herself in the kitchen eagerly trying to prove that everything does taste better with bacon; meticulously recreating cocktails from the 1930s and '40s; or planning her next trip to Disneyland. By day, her alter ego toils at what she fondly refers to as her "crap job." She lives in Virginia with her very naughty dog and her only slightly less naughty partner of ten years.

The Seduction of Moxie is Colette Moody's second novel. Her first, also for Bold Strokes Books, was the rollicking pirate tale *The Sublime and Spirited Voyage of Original Sin.*

Books Available From Bold Strokes Books

The Seduction of Moxie by Colette Moody. When 1930s Broadway actress Violet London meets speakeasy singer Moxie Valette, she is instantly attracted and her Hollywood trip takes an unexpected turn. (978-1-60282-114-9)

Goldenseal by Gill McKnight. When Amy Fortune returns to her childhood home, she discovers something sinister in the air— but is former lover Leone Garoul stalking her or protecting her? (978-1-60282-115-6)

Romantic Interludes 2: Secrets edited by Radclyffe and Stacia Seaman. An anthology of sensual lesbian love stories: passion, surprises, and secret desires. (978-1-60282-116-3)

Femme Noir by Clara Nipper. Nora Delaney meets her match in Max Abbott, a sex-crazed dame who may or may not have the information Nora needs to solve a murder—but can she contain her lust for Max long enough to find out? (978-1-60282-117-0)

The Reluctant Daughter by Lesléa Newman. Heartwarming, heartbreaking, and ultimately triumphant—the story every daughter recognizes of the lifelong struggle for our mothers to really see us. (978-1-60282-118-7)

Erosistible by Gill McKnight. When Win Martin arrives at a luxurious Greek hotel for a much-anticipated week of sun and sex with her new girlfriend, she is stunned to find her ex-girlfriend, Benny, is the proprietor. Aeros Ebook. (978-1-60282-134-7)

Looking Glass Lives by Felice Picano. Cousins Roger and Alistair become lifelong friends and discover their sexuality amidst the backdrop of twentieth-century gay culture. (978-1-60282-089-0)

Breaking the Ice by Kim Baldwin. Nothing is easy about life above the Arctic Circle—except, perhaps, falling in love. At least that's what pilot Bryson Faulkner hopes when she meets Karla Edwards. (978-1-60282-087-6)

It Should Be a Crime by Carsen Taite. Two women fulfill their mutual desire with a night of passion, neither expecting more until law professor Morgan Bradley and student Parker Casey meet again…in the classroom. (978-1-60282-086-9)

Rough Trade edited by Todd Gregory. Top male erotica writers pen their own hot, sexy versions of the term "rough trade," producing some of the hottest, nastiest, and most dangerous fiction ever published. (978-1-60282-092-0)

The High Priest and the Idol by Jane Fletcher. Jemeryl and Tevi's relationship is put to the test when the Guardian sends Jemeryl on a mission that puts her not only in harm's way, but back into the sights of a previous lover. (978-1-60282-085-2)

Point of Ignition by Erin Dutton. Amid a blaze that threatens to consume them both, firefighter Kate Chambers and property owner Alexi Clark redefine love and trust. (978-1-60282-084-5)

Secrets in the Stone by Radclyffe. Reclusive sculptor Rooke Tyler suddenly finds herself the object of two very different women's affections, and choosing between them will change her life forever. (978-1-60282-083-8)

Dark Garden by Jennifer Fulton. Vienna Blake and Mason Cavender are sworn enemies—who can't resist each other. Something has to give. (978-1-60282-036-4)

Late in the Season by Felice Picano. Set on Fire Island, this is the story of an unlikely pair of friends—a gay composer in his late thirties and an eighteen-year-old schoolgirl. (978-1-60282-082-1)

Punishment with Kisses by Diane Anderson-Minshall. Will Megan find the answers she seeks about her sister Ashley's murder or will her growing relationship with one of Ash's exes blind her to the real truth? (978-1-60282-081-4)

September Canvas by Gun Brooke. When Deanna Moore meets TV personality Faythe she is reluctantly attracted to her, but will Faythe side with the people spreading rumors about Deanna? (978-1-60282-080-7)

No Leavin' Love by Larkin Rose. Beautiful, successful Mercedes Miller thinks she can resume her affair with ranch foreman Sydney Campbell, but the rules have changed. (978-1-60282-079-1)

Between the Lines by Bobbi Marolt. When romance writer Gail Prescott meets actress Tannen Albright, she develops feelings that she usually only experiences through her characters. (978-1-60282-078-4)

Blue Skies by Ali Vali. Commander Berkley Levine leads an elite group of pilots on missions ordered by her ex-lover Captain Aidan Sullivan and everything is on the line—including love. (978-1-60282-077-7)

The Lure by Felice Picano. When Noel Cummings is recruited by the police to go undercover to find a killer, his life will never be the same. (978-1-60282-076-0)

Death of a Dying Man by J.M. Redmann. Mickey Knight, Private Eye and partner of Dr. Cordelia James, doesn't need a drop-dead gorgeous assistant—not until nature steps in. (978-1-60282-075-3)

Justice for All by Radclyffe. Dell Mitchell goes undercover to expose a human traffic ring and ends up in the middle of an even deadlier conspiracy. (978-1-60282-074-6)

Sanctuary by I. Beacham. Cate Canton faces one major obstacle to her goal of crushing her business rival, Dita Newton—her uncontrollable attraction to Dita. (978-1-60282-055-5)

The Sublime and Spirited Voyage of Original Sin by Colette Moody. Pirate Gayle Malvern finds the presence of an abducted seamstress, Celia Pierce, a welcome distraction until the captive comes to mean more to her than is wise. (978-1-60282-054-8)

Suspect Passions by VK Powell. Can two women, a city attorney and a beat cop, put aside their differences long enough to see that they're perfect for each other? (978-1-60282-053-1)

Just Business by Julie Cannon. Two women who come together—each for her own selfish needs—discover that love can never be as simple as a business transaction. (978-1-60282-052-4)